Blue
Magic

MICQUEAL HARRIS

Dedication

"She believed she could so she did."

—R.S. Grey, Scoring Wilder

I can't put into words what this book means to me. I dedicate this book to my readers. Be encouraged. I am a walking testimony that anything is possible. Your current situation does not have to define your future. No matter what you're going through, there is always a way out.

Secondly, I have to dedicate this book to Pops aka Lowell Massey. He had so much faith in my dreams and I am forever grateful for his love and support. I will continue to raise your granddaughter in memory of you. She will forever be your Juicy Yam. We love you, Pops and miss you daily. Thank you for teaching me my worth as a woman. Until we meet again!

Thank You

First and foremost, I want to thank God for giving me this vision and strength to complete this project. It wasn't easy, but he forced me to P.U.S.H (Pray Until Something Happens). I had an idea to write this book my sophomore year in college, but I never completed it. I started it over four times before I was able to stick with it and finally produce a finished product.

To my mother, thank you for supporting my dreams no matter the slip-ups I may have had. Thank you for being the best grandparent to my daughter.

To my father, I appreciate all your kind words throughout this process. No matter what, I know you will always have my back.

My best friend Treasure, my dear friend Amber, Grandmother Ellen, My Sandz, and many others, I appreciate your words of encouragement throughout this process. I am sorry if I forgot to personally name you. I love y'all so much.

To you, the reader, THANK YOU for giving me a chance to make my dreams come true. If it weren't for you picking up this book, none of this would be possible. I am forever grateful for your faith in me.

Enjoy!

Prologue

June 7, 2007

Beep! Beep! Beep!

The sensors located outside of our home were suddenly going off. The motion detectors must've alerted my mother before anyone could even reach our front steps. Queen made her way to my room fast with only seconds left to try to prepare me for what was about to happen; she shook me as if I wasn't already awake. I slowly squinted at the bold red numbers on the clock; it was four in the morning. "Baby, get up, get up!" she said, her voice a little louder than a whisper.

"What's wrong, Mama?" I asked.

"Here, take this," she said as she handed me a key and a piece of paper. She kept glancing at me, then back at my bedroom door, as if she was expecting someone to come through the door. This didn't seem like the usual jail and murders news she explained when it happened to people in our family. I never slept without the television on, so the lighting from one of my shows allowed me to see her clammy, pale skin. Queen's features were stoic, but I could feel her panic. "Pay attention, you hear me? Pay attention! Guard this with your life. They aren't here for you, so they won't physically search you. Tuck it! TUCK IT NOW!" And those were the last words of advice given to me.

Clink! Clank! Clang!

The sounds of metal banging against metal resounded throughout the house. What would have been an explosion on a regular wooden door seemed like a simple, unpleasant knock against our reinforced steel door. Two weeks prior, my mother cautiously paid twenty thousand for the door after robbers invaded her friend's home. This decision gave us a little extra time in preparing for the inevitable. She snatched the house key from the dresser and made her way to open the door before any outsiders could kick it in. My mother must have been nervous because she just couldn't get the key to turn the right way. With a racing heart and shaking hands, the door finally flew open.

"Get down! Get the fuck down! Now! Down, now!" They knocked my mother over and kept their guns pointed directly at her head. Not knowing what to do, I crouched down at the foot of the stairs. My stomach threatened to release, and I was seconds from shitting all over myself. "Don't move! Don't fucking move!" the masked men yelled repeatedly.

I lifted my hands in the air and stuttered, "O-o-o-okay." It wasn't until I saw the back of their jackets that I knew who these men posing as black ninjas were: FBI, DEA, and ATF. I'm sure everyone on the block and miles away could hear the commotion. *What are the neighbors thinking?* I wondered. *Are they scared too?*

My entire life I've had a front row seat to my mother's crime and didn't even know it. A single tear dropped from the corner of my left eye. My mother and I locked eyes as they dragged her in the kitchen to question her. She randomly whispered, "Magic." I could only imagine the intense chills going up her spine, seeing as though the day she always dreaded had come to fruition, and without a moment's notice. These men were all throughout the house, and their sole purpose was to take my mother away from me, or so I thought. Sitting at the bottom of the staircase, I was frightened beyond words. And although these were the same steps that I intentionally walked up and down only a thousand times, they abruptly became the scariest place ever. Covered in fear, I wanted to piss my pants just to see if this was all a dream. Releasing my bladder was the only movement that I was willing to risk.

Whenever the men looked as if they were about to cross my path, my mother would attempt to mouth words to me, but one officer put an end to that. "No more fucking talking, or I will shoot the both of you!"

This felt like something straight out of the movies. The scene was missing only a few important things, such as the director's chair, Morris Chestnut in SWAT gear, rehearsed scripts, funny bloopers, and the ability to act out someone else's life. With a few officers' weapons already pointed at both my mother's and my head, the other officers rushed through our home with tactical gear, going from room to room. "All clear! There's no one else in the house. Send in the dogs to search," an officer spoke over the radio.

With the red beam pointed at my head, I kept my eyes completely shut and listened to my heartbeat pound in my ears. In a panic I managed to whisper, "Please . . . Please don't shoot."

"That all depends on if you listen to my directions. Now get on the fucking ground!" He must've heard me. They were ready to take me out, so I knew there was nowhere to run.

Oddly, my mother had prepared me for this day. I just didn't know when. All the preparation in the world couldn't have changed my thoughts or emotions. This was a living nightmare. They searched our home for what seemed like hours. I now lay face down on the ground looking through the doorway of the kitchen. My mother was in clear view, and my eyes were locked in on her. I hoped she could read my thoughts. *Why aren't you saying anything to me? I need you to tell me everything's going to be okay.* Her head hung low and silent tears streamed down her face.

"Ma! Don't cry, it's going to be okay," I tried reassuring her, even through my confusion. "I love you, Ma; they can't hold you down forever . . ."

Damn . . .

1
Welcome to My World

In 1990, Detroit was at the peak of its latest takeover, the drug industry. The Motor City was well on its way to topping the charts at number one for the most murders and other crimes in the United States. Detroit's high crime rate was easily met due to its history's most notorious gangs: YBI, Best Friends, and the Chamberlin brothers, just to name a few. Nelson Mandela, who was one of the world's inspirational figures and Civil Rights Activist, was a free man and America was at war. On this exact day, *The God Father Part III* was being released, and my father Ace was trying to make it to the premiere.

♪ *The ol' bitch down the street must've turned me in*

'cause the Feds was at the door ten deep ♪

My father rapped along with Ice Cube's "AmeriKKKa's Most Wanted" in his 190 Benz as my pregnant mother tried to contact him because she felt that I was ready to make my entrance into the world. However, my father was too far in his zone to give in to any distractions outside of the echoes from Ice Cube. He was cruising through the city to make a few drops before heading back home. No one was expecting me to come for at least another month, so he carelessly cruised without any anticipation of my arrival. And even if my father noticed his phone ringing, he would've effortlessly felt no sense of urgency, due to the aftermath of so many failed attempts.

* * * * *

My seventeen-year-old mom was over to Granny Vicky's house in full-blown labor. Sitting without any moans or cries, my mother bobbed her head to the beat playing through the speakers. Contractions struck her belly every five minutes, but because the hasty pains felt more like gas, she was able to fight through it.

Vicky sat on the pink velour sofa sipping her favorite drink, Remy Martin XO. Buzzing like a bee, she told my mother, "You better not have that baby tonight, girl. This is the Lord's birthday!"

The nerve of her to indulge in drinking the devil's juice and talk about God all in the same breath. It was the holiday, and my family was celebrating like any other family would for Christmas. Gift exchanges, seasonal decorations, food, drinks, and laughter filled each room of the house. We displayed our love for the holiday in the same traditional expressions as the next-door neighbor, but my family didn't quite fit on the ordinary family list.

Vicky, who was tall with a slim yet chic figure, was also a well-known drug affiliate throughout the city. Vicky always had a way of stating biblical facts and being the prayer spokesperson for the family, yet continued to lead all those behind her in the wrong direction. She had a very persuasive gift, and her ability to alter her conversation style would always win anyone over. Even Vicky's suggestion for my mother to prolong her delivery somehow took effect. I decided to enter this cold world on December 26, 1990 at 4:15 a.m.

I was very tiny. Preemies were still pretty shocking to most back then. "How could a baby so small live?" My pops was amazed at how little I was. After making his last drops, he decided to go home to shower and ended up falling asleep; he missed the entire delivery process. Once he made it to the hospital, the doctor came to speak with both of my parents. "It's not by magic that this child is alive; God really wanted her to see the world!"

Suddenly something clicked in my father's head. "Magic! That's exactly what it is—Magic!" In my father's aha moment, he decided that Magic would be my name, and there was nothing that my mother could do about it. My mother didn't like the new declaration, but at the time my father could have preferred Tweety and she would have done it. "Look, baby. It's like magic that she's alive at only four pounds and one ounce. We have to name her that!" he pleaded for the name.

"Whatever! You just make sure you explain the shit to her when she's older," she shot back at him. Clearly, she was still mad about him missing the birth and couldn't care less about any name selection.

I like to think they named me Magic, perhaps because they already knew that I would be slicker than the rest of these 'hos. I was born to a pair of true hustlers. My father was Ace and my mother was Queen. They weren't two of a kind but the perfect pair. My father was nineteen when he met young, fifteen-year-old Queen. They were addicted to the same thing, the art of the hustle. My father started off as a lookout for YBI (Young Boys Incorporated), and my grandmother Elle taught my mother the game. Queen started off as a stamp girl who would eventually have the bag years later.

Since both of my parents made a career of being drug dealers, I grew up privileged. Some people would frown at the thought of the word 'privileged' being used in the same sentence as 'drug dealer,' but some would also smile. I lived a life most of my peers who were raised by successful parents only dreamed of. My privileges came without limits. I was accustomed to the best of everything, and of course, I enjoyed the over-the-top birthday parties, spontaneous vacations, and the best education. I'm not referring to your neighborhood drug dealers. My parents were at the top of the food chain. My parents were straight bosses!

My life wasn't going to be easy with a father like Ace and a mother like Queen. Both of my parents were just teenagers when they had me, but would later become some of the most well-known people in the city of Detroit. Ace and Queen were true products of their environment.

First, let me tell you a little about my father, Ace. Light-skinned with curly hair, he was one of the most ruthless drug dealers in Detroit. In addition to local land, he had territory all over the United States. He was THAT NIGGA, you know? He was the one that everyone knew about and his name rang from the Westside of Detroit to Memphis, and even to the city of Angels. He had a flock of bad bitches that surrounded him in every city that he resided in, and he practically coined the phrase: *Poppa was a Rolling Stone.* I wasn't his firstborn; he had a son who was two years older than me named Ace Jr. We would have to wait years to get to know one another because our mothers just couldn't get along. Typical!

Despite Ace's lifestyle, what he had with Queen was

something special. They didn't have your normal admirable relationship. My father adored my mother's hustle. And my mother didn't look at my father as just a man getting money, she saw him as a man whom she could get money with. Money came before everything. If it didn't make money, it didn't make sense. They mastered the game together, often-comparing notes. Through all the love they had for each other, hustling came before the love. Money was the only thing that mattered. Their motto was "Let's get this money, and everything else will fall into place." My father had undeniably, never met a girl like Queen. Instantly, he fell head first for her young ass on sight.

At the age of eleven, Ace was a lookout for the infamous YBI and progressed into selling drugs. Growing up around a drug-infested area like Dexter and Davison, there weren't too many job opportunities. Ball or get balled on. The role models in that area didn't work a nine to five; it was overpopulated with dope fiends and crack heads. Dealing became my parents' only source of income.

I loved hearing tales of when I was a baby and how my parents bossed together. My father was riding in foreign whips before any nigga thought about it. When Ace came through, he really came through! Pushing his mint green 190E Mercedes Benz, he was the coldest. If Ace was on the scene, everyone knew how and when. His four-seater had his name, "Ace" inscribed in a shade of yellow on the black leather seats; and of course, even through the tinted windows you could only see Queen seated there beside him. The rims stayed shining and sitting high. His speakers were so loud that if you were on Linwood you could hear him coming from Dexter. The leader of his own crew forever reppin' COA (Criminals of America);

they had the city on lock. He created a legacy that generations after his reign would make false claims to.

The COA crew had a call you could hear from everywhere. I guess you could say they were the "D" boys. "Ahh-De-Ahh," was the call, and when you heard it, you immediately knew that they were family.

Queen was only thirteen when Elle, her mother, turned her on to the game. While getting robbed one day at home, one of the thieves decided before exiting that they would attempt to rape Queen's young and innocent body. My great uncle, Demetrius Holloway's main man walked in and shot the two men directly in the head. The attempted rapist immediately fell lifeless and naked from the waist down beside Queen. She had witnessed this with her own two eyes, and from that moment on, she was in. She was in so deep and spiraling down a slippery slope, she would never reach the top again. It wasn't a walk in the park, but when Maserati Rick, Big James, The Best Friends, and Demetrius Holloway taught you the game, you were destined to be great.

Queen was something different, "a bad mutha" as my father would reference her. She stood five foot two and thick as a Snicker: big tits, small waist, and a fat ass. With her skin the color of pecans, a set of pearly whites and a smile that would light up a room in its darkest hour. Queen was strapped with a body of a true goddess. Most men felt intimidated by her and wouldn't dare step to her incorrectly. Aside from being drop dead gorgeous, Queen was a straight go-getter; there was no stopping her.

When she solidified her position in the streets, Queen demanded and commanded her respect. She could out hustle any nigga. She started from the very bottom and quickly worked her way to the highest of highs. On a bad day, her take was fifty racks or better. You mention her name and nothing but good things were said about her. She grew up on the east side of Detroit, and far above her being Ace's baby momma, she rightfully earned her respect. In her early years she witnessed things that caused her to grow up real fast and real quick.

The apple didn't fall too far from the tree, and with a mother like Elle, she was destined to have some type of hustle. Elle had a way to stretch the bag and make a few extra bucks on each brick of cocaine or a pound of marijuana. By seventeen, Queen was the breadwinner, not Elle. Aside from what Elle taught her, she had a way of finessing anyone who crossed her path. They would throw a few stacks on top just so she could shop. But Queen was no dummy, she knew what to do with her money—stack it! By seventeen she had her own house, car, money, and jewelry and was taking trips when and wherever she wanted.

Like most hustlers, she spent money frivolously, a couple hundred here and couple thousand there. Yes, they were both living the life that people dreamed of having, including me. She kept me focused and in the right things so I wouldn't end up like her. She was a master at putting on a smile to make me believe life was always good. I was never aware that we faced hard times too. No matter what, I never went without, and I only possessed the cream of the crop.

I knew my mother didn't work a regular job similar to my peers' parents, but knowing my mother's job title never really mattered to me. By age six, I had already traveled the world; you name it and I'd been there and back.

If I didn't know anything else, I knew that I was birthed to a true Ace and Queen. From paying my way to private schools, to giving me the best of the best of everything, they gave me all that their deck of cards offered. No matter how hard they tried to keep our family from danger, it would always seem to find us. Their most significant goal in life was to keep the people they cared about safe. They were my protectors. My mother, being more active in my life, was naturally my first line of defense. She would literally kill for me, and I made sure to never test it.

Life started out great! I loved our first home that stood three-stories high on the Westside of Detroit; we were right in the heart of Ace's hood (Dexter and Davison). Broad street was where my first memorable times were created. When Queen originally bought the house it wasn't too spectacular, but she had mad talent when it came to interior designing. I always felt that her talent should've been her career path. Once she hooked the house up, it looked like it could've been a whole new house. When first walking into our home, there was a huge living room with an amazing open front window and a fireplace where Queen would lay out pallets for her special guests. The house was huge! Absolutely stunning! The best part was the chandelier that hung from the dining room ceiling where we ate. The chandelier was made out of real diamonds and was breathtaking. Everyone that walked in the house would always take their time and admire it. Queen had a way of making people notice all of the details in her work. It was like art, and she had a true gift.

Each room had a different theme: my room was Barbie Pink. I had a built-in bunk bed set that came with a bookshelf, a desk, and a jungle gym side. It was like a room out of a magazine. The few friends of mine that did come to visit never wanted to go home. I had the best of everything. I even had a separate room, the Purple Room.

The Purple Room was my very own play quest; any toy that I could think of was in that room. Surprisingly, I wasn't into toys much because I loved to read. I devoted myself to learning how to add up numbers and work computers.

My mom had her own living area upstairs, but it was more of a separate house. I loved her bed because it was so big. She always had the best of everything as well. The headboard was made of all mirrors and went from wall-to-wall. The bedpost was so high to the ceiling that it almost looked endless. Sheer drapes fell effortlessly around the bed, which created a sense of heaven laying in between the sheets. Her five-thousand-count sheets were so soft that you could instantly fall asleep if you dared to lie beneath them. Everything about my mother's room was magical.

My favorite time of year of course, was Christmas, seeing as though my birthday was the day after. We loved to show off our tree through the front window. We had the biggest, brightest tree you could find for miles and miles. My mom paid a thousand dollars just to get our tree dipped and decorated. The tree was 100% real, and the lady who made them owned a flower shop not too far from our home. I'm sure the lady made a decent living around Christmas time alone. The trees were so extravagant, and I knew people felt compelled to order them annually. They always had the most elaborate bows, the most beautiful ornaments, and unforgettable colors that changed with the year. My mom always made everything so special for me since there was no one else there with us. She never did bless me with a sister or brother, so it was always just the two of us; oh, and the crazy men she decided to bring around from time to time. You would've thought that I should have learned from her selection of unworthy men. However, in life it's not always easy to completely stay away from the things that you've vowed to never do.

Not all of the created memories were so pleasant though. You can seemingly have every material thing in the world, but the void from the very thing that your heart desires can cause an unexplainable uproar. Peace is all I ever wanted. Growing up in the way that I did was a very hard thing to come by. Seeing that my parents lived such a fast life, most days ended in drama and more drama. Mo money Mo problems, right?

Somehow my mother was notified that while my dad was away in Memphis, he wasn't just there for business. He had been cheating on her. My mother yearned for the white picket fence life. But a woman can only put up with so much, and my father was more than a bit much. He would be the only man that she would let see her cry, but she wanted out of the relationship. This was one of the low moments in my mom's life that I wasn't aware of; nevertheless, she wore her poker face well. I wouldn't have known of any problems. When I looked in her eyes that day, the only thing that she could do was shed a tear. There was nothing she wanted more than to have us three as a family. Ace often traveled out of town to sell drugs, and the distance complicated things. So early on I don't remember much, but I do remember a lot of arguments about his out of town shenanigans, as my mother would call them.

After being away in Memphis for a few weeks, my father was finally approaching our doorstep without any clue of what would come next. The door hadn't closed well before Queen was all up in his face. The five-foot-tall Queen was furious. "Nigga, you fuckin' one of those back woods bitches down there!" she yelled.

Ace ignored her and walked straight to me. "Hi, Daddy's little lady," he happily proclaimed while picking me up.

I squeezed his neck so tight. "I love you, Daddy." I missed him so much while he was gone.

My mother mushed the back of his head. "Hello? Nigga, I know you hear me?" She mushed him again. "You wanna play stupid, huh? I bet you will hear this! I'm about to get me somebody since you think that you can just do what the fuck you want!"

Ace placed me down gently and my feet met the floor again. He was so calm that I never saw his hand rise and apparently neither did my mother.

WHACK!

He smacked her so hard that she stumbled back and fell. *Why is he doing this?* My little mind was on overload. Queen jumped up off the floor throwing wild punches. He smacked her again. This turned into a knockout drag down fight. With no regard for little old me, who was now sitting in the corner holding my knees to my chest and begging for them to stop. I was silently crying with so many questions, but I dared not ask them. The image that I had of my father was forever changed that day. Only four years old and this could have been the end to the sweetest girl that I would ever be.

At that very moment, a piece of my heart had been taken from me, and the beginning stage of me becoming a very heartless girl venturing off into this mean cold world. No one would ever understand the pain I felt watching my mother go through this. I vowed to myself that I would never be that woman; I would never allow myself to be abused by any man.

A girl's father is her first impression of what a man

truly is. And if he does wrong by her mother, then he has silently given his daughter permission to accept what she sees over what she may be told. Yet, at that point in my life, I wouldn't have the slightest clue of the long-term effects just being a witness would have on my future thoughts and dealings with men. And as much as we try not to be a complete replica of our parents, we tend to naturally fall right into their reflections. Interestingly enough, I inherited shadows that I would be fighting for most of my life.

All of the things that ever mattered in my life changed in a blink of an eye. I was young, but the image of my parents fighting never went away. I would have nightmares of Ace hitting Queen, watching her fall, and the rhythm of my heart beating too fast to catch up to. That day was the last time that I would see both my mother and father together as a couple. The separation would always force my mother into trying to ban me from seeing my father, and for a while I really couldn't blame her. I never understood why he would allow himself to get so angry that it resulted in him hitting her. My grandmother Elle would always sneak me to see him, despite my mother's wishes. Queen grew angry every time she found out that I saw my father, even if it was for a few seconds. Her anger turned her into a loose cannon. Oftentimes, her episodes ended in fistfights with Elle. Queen would be so enraged.

"Didn't I tell you she couldn't see him? He isn't worthy of being in her life. You can't just take her to see a man who couldn't care less if she existed or not." I would hear her yell to Elle.

"That's not true, Queen, and you know it. He loves that little girl. Y'all just going through some things, but do not mix Magic in it. She deserves to be around her father,"

Elle replied, practically screaming at Queen.

"You got me fucked up! I pay for all this shit around here!" my mother spat with disrespect. "Maybe if you stop fucking up all your money gambling, you could do what you want and when you want. But I said that I didn't want her over there, and I meant that."

Slap!

Elle's hand struck right across Queen's face. "I don't know who the hell you think you're talking to. You may pay my bills, but I had you and I'll kill you before I allow you to disrespect me," Elle screamed. I could see Elle's handprint on Queen's face. Tears of hurt started to fall from my eyes. This was the second time I had to witness the woman that I cherished most being hit, and this time it was even more hurtful. The two women whom I idolized were right in front of me fighting like they were two bitches on the street without any record of knowing one another.

Queen was quick to hit her back without any thought. *How could you hit the woman who gave you life?* She even called her foul names like she was a bum on the corner. This was a sight that I never wanted to witness. A sight they shouldn't have continued once they saw my presence. All the sweet images of these two women started to vanish right in front of me. All of my confusion and pain started to bottle up inside of me, forcing me to give in to the 'fuck it' attitude. From all of the unasked questions and assumed answers that I had begun to gather from every single person whose job was to shield my sight, I quickly sensed that I would always have to push through any and all obstacles.

2
Crash and Burn

Most of my childhood memories are dark. The things I witnessed, no child should ever have to go through. After the big fight between Queen and Elle, I didn't get to see much of my father, especially with his travel schedule.

Since Ace wasn't as active in my life, Queen felt the need to be hard on me. The simplest shit would send her over the edge. It almost seemed as if she was waiting on me to fuck up. I get it! Queen had a fear that I would turn out like her or Elle. She kept me far away from the street life as much as possible, but beating me and calling me out my name didn't exactly get the job done.

Very young, I vowed that I wouldn't be like my mother. I watched horrible things happen to her, and I never wanted them to happen to me. I knew that I would do things differently. I dreamed of going to college, becoming a doctor, living life wealthy, happy, and carefree. I never would've guessed that the road to this beautiful life would either never exist, or be so damn hard to get to that I would give up before ever reaching an inch of what I set out to accomplish.

One day, my aunt Autumn was watching me at home. Autumn was my mother's little sister, and she lived with us most of the time since Elle was always on the go. She was real fast, as my grandmother would say. Autumn kept a boyfriend around. I can vividly remember because they were all really nice looking. One of her boyfriends was my boyfriend mentally. They always played it off laughing, but I really thought Scooby was in a relationship with me. I didn't know one thing about being in a relationship at all, but I just thought it sounded cool to say.

Scooby had caramel skin and wore braids that lay right past his shoulders. He always had them freshly braided like he had a live-in braider. I was convinced that my assumption was true because once his braids started to frizz, that damn live-in braider was there to adjust them. Scooby didn't have the regular "black people kind of hair," he had that Mexican mix stuff. He was my first crush. I think I blushed a million times whenever he was around.

Before I went to bed I saw her creeping upstairs in my mom room. I knew she was upstairs with whoever her boyfriend was at the time, and I was sure that I wouldn't be seeing her for the rest of the night. She was busy getting her groove on, and in Queen's bed. Only if Queen knew what was taking place, she would've flipped all the way out. *Autumn has her own bed, so why can't she bounce around in that?* Apparently, Autumn was trying to impress her company being upstairs and all. She was so caught up in the moment that she wasn't bothering to answer the phone that kept ringing. Autumn was only fifteen; she shouldn't have been doing anything besides watching me. I was about to come really close to death, and Autumn was focused on her boy-toy.

* * * * *

BANG! BANG! BANG!

What was that? I wondered. Hearing those loud noises, I opened my eyes and popped up. If I'd gotten up a second sooner, the gunshot would've traveled right through my head. Three holes were in the wall that was only a few inches above where my head was positioned. Quickly I tried to adjust my eyes to the light. If nothing else was clear, I could indisputably see a naked body standing in front of me. "What's happening?" I managed to ask Autumn in a very croaky tone. I attempted to lie back down because my brain wasn't processing what was taking place.

"Baby, get up. Get up!" Once I attempted to grab at my covers, Autumn stopped me. "Slip on some shoes, we are leaving right now. Let me run upstairs to slip on my clothes. Come with me."

I swung my feet out of the bed. "Auntie Autumn, I don't want to get out of bed. I'm tired. Can I lay down for a few more minutes?" I protested.

"Listen, there's some crazy shit happening right now, and we need to leave immediately!" she yelled with frustration.

By the time we made it upstairs, Autumn's latest boyfriend had already made his exit. I guess he wasn't a real nigga because he didn't even make sure we were straight before leaving. Autumn could barely put her clothes on without shaking. I could have died on her watch. I'm sure the thought of that was starting to consume her. It was going to take her some time to get over the event.

"Oh my God! I left Queen hanging on the phone!"

Autumn jumped from her trance and attempted to call her, but she didn't get an answer.

"Queen, we are safe. I called Scooby to come get us since he lives around the corner. We'll be at his house until you can come." Autumn was the one leaving a voicemail this time around. "Damn, she was just on the phone," Autumn said. "I hope they didn't get to her. Please Lord, keep my sister safe." We left the house as soon as Scooby pulled up and no sooner than we got in, he pulled off in record time.

We were safe. For now.

* * * * *

Scooby pulled up to my daddy's house, and he was already parked out front. So Autumn and I got into one of Ace's vintage old schools. He asked Autumn a bunch of questions: "What did they look like? Where were you? Did you talk to Queen?" He didn't give her a chance to answer one question before asking her another one. In an attempt to give my father some information, I told him the only thing that I knew.

"Autumn was upstairs with her friend." My father clenched his jaw in anger and probably made a mental note to tell my mother not to ever let Autumn watch me again. Autumn glanced in my direction and gave me the look of death.

Once we were all settled in, there was still no word from Queen. Ace figured he would go looking for her once we were somewhere safe. We were just minutes away from the house. Unsure of what to do or think, I looked out the window to calm me. At first glance, I noticed something yellow with flickering lights surrounding it. *My father loves yellow*, I thought. But as my vision sharpened, I realized the original speck of yellow was in fact my mother's car. Her car looked as if someone balled it up like a piece of paper and threw it off to the side. There was an imprint of the car in the low wall within the freeway. Police were everywhere, and the ambulance team was working hard on what looked to be a lifeless body.

We were heading in the opposite direction of where my mother was. Unable to fight back the tears and the pain thumping throughout my stomach, I screamed as loud as I could. "NOOOO, MOMMY! WAKE UP! I need you to wake up. Please. Pleassee!" I yelled, hoping she could hear me and follow my commands. I could barely get anything else out, but I had to try. "Stop the car, Daddy. Please! Just stop right here!"

Ace looked around to see what I was talking about. His eyes grew so big I could tell he was just as scared as I was, but he attempted to be strong for me. "Baby girl, mommy is going to be okay. I'm going to go back to get her. You need to go to Granny's house until I get this all handled. I don't want you to see her like this. Okay?"

He had this all wrong. My mother was laid out in the middle of the street, and he didn't think I would want to be near her. "No, Daddy, you have to take me to her now! She will be better if I'm there." I looked up at him with my big bright eyes, and there was no way he could say no to that. He exited the 96 freeway and turned around.

We came up on the Greenfield exit to get back on the freeway heading east where Queen was. When we arrived, Queen was still lying out on the ground. The paramedics were working hard on her body to get a steady heart rate. Finally I heard the guy say, "We have a pulse! Now let's get her to Sinai-Grace!"

I guess I wasn't the only one listening, because before they could lift Queen onto the stretcher and get her into the truck, Ace was yelling to the guy, "Oh, no the hell you're not! Take her to Beaumont Hospital. She will be much safer there!"

"Sorry, that's out of our district. She could die just trying to get her there," one of the paramedics responded.

Ace went in his pocket, pulling out nothing but hundreds. "I know money talks, so what they pay you? Twenty a hour?" Not really waiting for a response, he continued. "I don't give a fuck what's in your district, you're taking Queen to Beaumont Hospital. And that's *final!*" Ace started separating twenty freshly pulled hundred-dollar bills from the rest of the stack. "And if she dies, that's your life, sir. Do you understand?"

Although shocked by the strange request and large amount of money, the driver was no fool, so he quickly assured Ace of his acceptance. "No problem, sir. Sh-sh-she will b-b-b-be in good hands," he stuttered.

Before the paramedics could motion for me to leave my mother's side, I demanded to ride with her.

"No, Magic. You can't ride with them. Daddy will have to take you."

I was already in the truck with my mother holding her hand, and there was no way that I could be removed. My dad just followed while I sat with Queen. As we rode to the hospital, I refused to let her hand go. Her ring was still perfectly positioned on her finger. From the way the car had crashed, I thought she would be mushed with it, but my queen was still perfect!

Moments later, we had arrived at the hospital of Ace's choice. I knew that when things got rough, my mom would always call out to Jesus; so I figured I would try.

"Jesus, please help …"

Over the next few days, all sorts of people were in and out of her hospital room. There were so many flowers delivered to Queen that you would've thought it was a funeral service for at least ten people. I just wanted all of these people to leave and stop telling me, "You're in my prayers!" All that I could think was that one of these people was the reason for this mess in the first place. Hell! Any one of them could have been on the other side of that trigger. What's crazy is, Queen would never fully find out who made the threat or who actually fired the shots. And perhaps, it may have been best that way.

"Magic, Magic!" Queen groaned. Finally, Queen was awake, but before opening her eyes her first thoughts were of me. She hadn't spoken in days, so her throat and everything else was dry. She needed water to give her saliva glands some motivation.

Super excited, I could barely contain myself. I leaned over and gave her a big hug. "Yes, Mommy. I'm here!" *Thank you, God!* I prayed out loud.

I was so relieved to hear her voice and feel her warm touch on her body. She hadn't been awake five minutes but Queen was already to escape this place. "Oh thank you, God! Now let's get out of here. Y'all know how much I hate these crackers being in my damn business," Queen said, and she was indeed back to her feisty self and was ready to start back running things.

"You're still at the hospital, Mommy. We have been here for almost two weeks. Everyone kept trying to get me to leave you, but I couldn't."

"You're so sweet, baby girl. I heard you praying for mommy. I'll never leave you," she promised. But little did she know, she was making a promise that she wouldn't be able to keep. She thought that she was untouchable. Clearly, that wasn't the case after bullets were just flying through our home. "Where is Autumn? Wasn't she watching you?"

"She's been coming back and forth. Daddy is here though!" I yelled with excitement. I hadn't seen the two of them in the same room in a while. It would be so nice if they saw each other and fell in love again. But could life ever be so simple?

The look of confusion and anger coated her face. She was bitter and heartbroken by this man, and didn't care to see him. He was the very last person she wanted to see right now. "Your dad is here? Why is he still here?" She must've noticed him coming and going these last couple of days, but didn't have enough strength to share her sentiments.

Before I could answer the question, Ace came rushing through the door. He entered with a Kool-Aid smile, one that showed all of his teeth at once. He always had a way of brightening up the room. He had to have known she would be completely alert today because he had ten dozen roses in hand and a big ass bear with GET WELL SOON written all over it.

This was exactly the kind of stunts Ace loved to pull. He always tried to go over the top. And of course, it wouldn't be wise to believe anything that came out of his mouth, because he only told complete lies or altered truths. He meant well though, and I had the ability to see that. My father wasn't always a man of his word, and this was one of the many things that would ruin my thoughts of men in the near future. The one man who was supposed to give me fatherly talks on what to accept from a boyfriend never did. The one man who was supposed to show me that his word was his bond, showed me exactly how to keep making promises and breaking them.

It took my mom a few more weeks to fully recover. Within those weeks, Ace had already figured out who shot up our home and dealt with them the way he always did. Although Queen would never get confirmation, she was right to suspect that one of Ace's 'hos had gotten jealous and was acting out. Queen was assured that everything was taken care of and that's all that mattered to her. Luckily, Queen didn't have to continue to worry about my safety and neither did Ace.

I was sitting in the room next to Queen when Ace stood over her bed.

"You ready to tell me what happened?" Daddy asked. Queen rolled her eyes.

"All I know is that I was riding through the city on my way home and my phone started ringing. I wasn't going to answer but the called more than twice. I thought that whoever it was it had better be fucking important.

'Hello?'

'Hey Queennn! I'm on my way to kill you and your whole family, bitch!'

Click.

"Did you catch a voice?" Ace asked Queen.

She nodded. "Naw. I was just trying to call Autumn so she could get Magic and leave the house. But she wouldn't pick up. I kept calling and calling but she just wouldn't pick up the phone. So I started speeding and praying that Magic didn't get hurt."

"So how did Autumn know she needed to leave then?"

"She finally answered the fucking phone, breathing all heavy. I told her to get my baby out of there right now, then I heard three shots."

"That's when you panicked and had the accident," Daddy assumed.

"That's when one of your stupid bitches caused me to have the accident. Find out which one of them is responsible and handle your business. Don't make me have to do it."

"Chill man everything has been handled." Ace assured her.

* * * * *

Queen's car was totaled, but when we returned home, Ace had already had another one waiting for her, but Queen wasn't the type to be impressed by that though. She made her own money, so whatever a man did for her was always extra. She walked right past the car like it wasn't even there, and her attitude was what I loved most about Queen. She showed me how to be independent and to never let a man do more for me than what I can do for myself. No matter how much she preached about having her own, I would watch her more closely. She may not have been taken care of by a man, but she for sure seemed to always be taking care of one. She kept a man who needed her more than she needed him. And maybe she learned that from Elle, who married a man ten years younger than her.

Elle married while her significant other was in jail, just to take care of him his entire ten-year bid. To make matters worse, he was my uncle on my dad's side; which meant he was my granddad and my uncle. I was raised by a generation of dysfunctional people. My grandmother had no business marrying my uncle. However, he would later come home and take over the city; he was known best as "Beanie with the coke."

I couldn't blame Queen for all of her mistakes, because she didn't quite have a good example. This resulted in her making some very poor decisions when it came to men. These reasons alone would soon send me down a path of many failed attempts at love.

3
The Beginning

Prior to being able to fully embody the simple freedoms of peace and happiness, one must experience rock bottom, and in all of its levels. Before I was ten, I watched the people around me go from good to bad in an instant. It was as if bad shit was destined to happen.

On September 11, 1998, around seven in the morning, Queen got a call. The call had better have been important. Everyone knew Queen wasn't into doing anything before nine in the morning. Queen wasn't an early bird. She barely woke to get me ready for school. She made sure that I had my alarm set, and when it went off, I had to be up with it. This was one of the ways that she showed me how to be independent. I had to learn these things at an early age, and I had to keep up. Even though some days I felt more like a slave than a child, it was a blessing that I was taught so many things early on in life. I knew how to cook full meals, wash and sort clothes, and many other household chores to keep my overall life in order. I am forever grateful for those lessons.

On this day, Queen woke me up before her alarm could

sound. "Magic, wake up, we have to make a stop before school." I didn't notice her red eyes because I was still in sleep mode. I didn't feel like moving. My legs felt heavy and the light from outside was just beginning to come through my window.

"You're taking me school?" I questioned with excitement. I loved riding in her car; the fresh scent of Jolly Wholly air freshener always made me wish that I could stay in the car much longer than the allotted time slot. Queen was the queen of clean.

Her car was always perfectly polished, and the scent inside of car could instantly put my mind at ease. I was pumped that my mother was taking me to school. Hopefully we would get there early enough for everyone to see the car. I would be in the passenger seat of the yellow Benz, and I couldn't wait to ride! I hopped out of bed and rushed to brush my teeth.

"Yes, baby. I'm taking you, but I need you to move quickly. We have something we have to do, okay?"

"Yes, Mommy! I'll be ready in two seconds." Once I finished brushing my teeth and washing my face we were out the door.

Queen was silent during the ride, but she kept glancing at me and then looking forward. I didn't know where we were headed until we walked in Sinai Grace Hospital. Queen kneeled down to meet me face to face. "Magic, your daddy's been shot and stabbed and he's in surgery." This wasn't the best method of delivering bad news about my father because I completely flipped out inside that damn hospital. I felt like a crazy person because I couldn't control myself. They had to strap me down to the chair! I so desperately needed to see my daddy one more time. I needed to tell him I loved him one more time. I was just with him last week. I was going back over to his house in a few days; I was only waiting for the weekend to come. How could this stuff be happening to my family? First Queen was in a car crash, now this. I was always wondering what would happen next.

When I was finally able to regroup, I joined my family, who was sitting all around the waiting room. We were anticipating the doctor coming through the doors at any second with great news to share with us. Hours passed and it looked as if none of my family members was working that day; they must've called off. I guess no one really had a job. It was unknown to me at the time, but everyone in the room was a product of the streets: Vicky, Elle, all of my uncles, my aunts, and Queen. They didn't have to go to a nine to five, so it was nothing for them to sit there all day because they had no one to report to and no real schedule to stick with.

Vicky sat in the middle of the floor praying for her firstborn; her precious boy. She did the best job that she could with raising him. With the upbringing that she had, she tried her best to give him all of his heart's desires and of course, keep him safe. As a parent, keeping your child safe is the most important thing to you. Parents have an unexplainable connection with their children, and when their children aren't safe, there is no such thing as peace of mind.

She sat and prayed for God to release his angels so that they could cover her son.

Seeing the doctor burst through the door caused Vicky to snap from her racing thoughts. The tension was thick. I held my breath, waiting for the right words to come out of the doctor's mouth. He looked like he was fresh out of battle. His forehead glistened with sweat; his lips were chapped, and he spoke as if he'd ran ten miles to get to where we were.

"Good news! We were able to stabilize him. He has lost a lot of blood and will need further surgery, but for now he's in stable condition. He's a very lucky man. Thank God whoever did this didn't sever his arteries."

"Thank you, JESUS!" Vicky clasped her hands together. Eager to see him and get this nightmare over, she asked the doctor, "Can we see him?"

There were more than twenty people in the waiting area, so the doctor was slightly concerned. "No more than five at a time. He's just waking up, so he may be a little woozy; he'll need to get his rest soon. All in all, he should heal fine and feel just like new." All of this news was music to our ears. I could feel the weight lifted as we all let out a breath of air.

"God is so good. What room please?" Vicky asked.

"Room 262!" the doctor responded.

Wow, what a coincidence, I thought. The code that my father would've used to indicate an emergency, was the same number written on the outside of his room. We all took a moment to be thankful and praise God for the blessing we all received. We would get one more day to tell him we loved him and many more to follow.

Vicky, Binky, Queen, Ace Jr., and I were the first five people to see him. For the entire wait, Ace Jr. was silent and sat by himself. I guess he was feeling how I was feeling; he wasn't sure if he'd ever get to see his father alive again. It wasn't until he laid eyes on his father that he would feel a release. He ran to Ace and hugged him, trying his best not to hurt him; all he could do was cry. Watching my brother break down caused all of us to cry. Our tears were filled with both joy and sadness. Yes, we were blessed to see him again, however, the thought that someone out there actually wanted to take his life was unsettling.

"I'm good, y'all. Everything is good. I'm about to move away from here though. I don't need anybody having access to me like that." He was all business and wasted no time informing us on his moving plans. All that I could think of was being able to see him every weekend. And just like that, I was sad all over again.

And of course, Queen was all business too. "I'm just glad you're alive. Did you get to see who it was? Do you know why anyone would do this to you?"

"Man, I don't know. It's probably a million niggas in this city who want to see me dead!" His words were sharp but slightly hinted with fear. "All I know is that they knew exactly where to find me and how to get in. I was upstairs sleep, so I didn't hear them come in. They knocked on the door and Shauna's sister had to have let them in. I guess she thought it was somebody we were expecting, so she opened the side door without looking. They had her taped up by the time that I made it downstairs. The house sat on a corner, so they had to come through the alley. Once inside, they had masks on and guns in hand. I'm not sure what all took place yet, but I woke up to them running up the stairs. I shook ol girl trying to get her up. I didn't have time to make sure she got up. I tried to reach for my gun but they came in shooting. They were there just for me. They didn't do anything to Shauna. They moved in close and started to stab me. Shauna reached for the gun, and she just started shooting. She kept missing, but she did cause them to leave and not continue with the attack. I don't know how many times I was stabbed or shot, but Shauna managed to get me to the main floor to call for help. That's when we noticed her sister taped up and the kids locked in the room. I started to feel lightheaded, and then I woke up here," he explained all in one breath. Ace was just happy to be alive and to be able to hold his kids one more time. He looked in my direction, smiled at me, and I knew everything would be fine.

During the next few months, a mini war was taking place in the city. Queen and I were instructed to lay low. Ace was finally fully recovered, and he made his move to Ohio. He wasn't too far, but just far enough to separate him from the war going on. Ace Jr. moved with him and did one school year there.

Things were finally back to a normal routine, and I started to live my life as a normal kid. I even joined the best organization around. My momma wanted to get me into things she never was able to do as child, and I was glad that she did. I would meet my lifelong friends on a football field.

I lived for my squad. I loved to cheer! My talent amazed the coaches, and I was a natural. I cheered for the one and only, West Side Cubs. We were citywide champs! And as you can see, I still get excited! Cheering helped me meet some of the best people that I could ever meet. I met Tiara, Lanae, Treasure, and Bianca. We were all on different cheer squads because of our ages. My first friend in life was Tiara and she was gorgeous: big green eyes and sandy brown hair. Then there was my big sister Lanae, who was four years older than us. Treasure became my best friend and still is to this day. Bianca was introduced to the crew a little after all of our relationships were established. She was the only one that I wished I never met. We were dubbed the mean girls.

4
The Monster

Once Queen and Ace split, I wasn't aware of her personal life when it came to men. If she was dating, she was doing a good job hiding it. But once I turned six, the man that would come into my life as a male friend of my mom, would bring love and hate in the same package. He did many things that benefited my life. He took care of me as his own. He even gave me sisters and brothers that I never thought that I would have. However, his mistreatment of my mother caused me to fear men and would forever damage my thoughts of men. Although I wasn't the person being abused, the woman who had conceived me was. And seeing all of this would have such a long lasting effect on me.

I was so fearful of a man hitting me, that if a guy raised his voice too loud, I would lose it. Determined not to be hit, I would do the hitting. Many failed relationships would come due to my defenses toward men. I was guarded, and it was hard to get me to trust. I always thought a man was cheating, so I tried to beat him to the punch. The constant drive to compete caused more hurt and pain.

Some called him Birdman. I called him Monster. He was the first guy that my mother introduced to me. He stood about six foot one with brown skin, and well-toned legs. His waves were like an ocean that could make you real life seasick. He wasn't the flashy type, but he was loaded. He reminded me of Frank Lucas. The loudest man in the room is the one caught first, and he kept a real low profile. Birdman had fear in the streets. He was very well respected and sometimes he was the most wanted. The way he talked in his smooth tone would have any woman in a daze. They called him the Birdman because he pushed so much weight across the states. He was a true ladies' man, but nothing in the world was more important to him than his family. He had a load of mouths to feed. He fed his own family, of course, and then he made sure blocks of families were eating daily. And that was one of the things that I respected most about him. He was never boastful and never cared to mention all of the people he helped with food, bills, and other necessities. The hood loved and praised him as if he was a god, but I couldn't blame them because he wore the title well. While showing love often, he also instilled much fear.

He was known for taking off his brand new tennis shoes and leaving them on the corner for anyone that wanted them. He never talked about what he did or what he was going to do for that matter. He just did it and kept doing it.

After being introduced to Queen through Ace, Birdman started to push heavy weight. Queen had her own connects and so did he. I wasn't too much aware of the dynamics, but they were both getting some real money. You couldn't do nothing but respect Queen, because she was one of the very few women in the game who held down her own. It was evident that they often would run into each other. Queen preferred to handle her business in loud places and was very strict about not talking in cars or on the phone. Whenever Queen would come up off an exit, she would make sure to watch for who took the exit with her. She made sure to teach me all of that.

This is what I later learned about Queen and Birdman when they first hooked up. Queen was in the strip club when Birdman walked in. She conducted business in this one, particularly because she owned it. The smoke-filled club was not as crowded as usual. Queen would be there two or three nights out of the week. She was part-owner of the Juicy Gentleman's Club. No one knew this, and she liked it that way. The staff knew who she was and respected her. And as long as she was making money, she didn't care who else knew. The staff was ordered to make sure that anyone that came near her be searched thoroughly.

Birdman was in the booth across from her, enjoying a dance from one of the hottest strippers in the city, but his eyes were glued to something else. Out of all of the times he had run into Queen, he never looked at her in this way. He couldn't get Queen off his mind and envisioned the stripper who was giving him a dance as Queen. He watched as she walked toward the bouncer and how her ass was so well rounded. He could see himself all in her at that very moment. He was getting hard just from his view. The stripper girl was no match for Queen and she knew it. "Why won't you go ask her for a dance?" the angry stripper said as she picked up her dollars and made her way to someone who was willing to pay her some attention.

Queen had an ass so big that you would never want to leave her. With her slim waist, she stood at five feet two inches and her body measurements were 36-24- 40. She was pure perfection and didn't have to indulge in the common trend of ass shots and surgeries. Her silk-pressed wrap bounced with every step. Queen never needed makeup because she had a natural beauty; a little lip-gloss was all she needed.

Birdman waited until Queen walked past before reaching for her hand. "Damn, Queen. I never knew your ass was so fat. I'ma have to make you mine." His soft touch caught Queen off guard.

She had to keep her game face on though because she knew what kind of man she was dealing with. Queen kept it cool and flicked her hair back. "Nigga, stop playing so much. Did you talk to Red? That nigga owe me fifteen thousand!" Queen only wanted to talk straight business.

"Nahh . . . I ain't hollered at him, but he will pay you though. Don't worry about that, and don't ignore what I just said." Birdman tried to use a firm tone with a serious face. The pure sound of his voice sent chills down Queen's spine. It was like some real *Fifty Shades of Grey* type shit. His words were true and she knew it, but she also knew better than to let him know.

Queen tried mustering up all of the courage she had to put some truth in her words. "Boy, you're not even in my league!" she said in a very sassy way, practically taunting him with her good looks and her charm.

He hit her with his famous head-cocked-to-the-side— this gesture insinuated that she stop playing with him and get real. He kept it cool though. Now standing with his right hand clasped in his left one, he said, "Since I came in the picture, I know your salary has quadrupled!" He was so confident when he spoke. How could any woman deny him? Queen was trapped, and she didn't even know it.

Still trying to keep the upper hand in the situation she said, "That may be true, but you're not the only one who I supply. Oh, and I know your money is up too. The chips will always run in!"

And of course, his smooth self would have a comeback. "Well, you should know you're not my only supplier option. I chose you for a special reason."

Queen was now slightly turned off by the last statement. "You know who I am, The Queen, and where I'm at. To get me you will have to treat me like the queen that I am." With that said, she walked away and with all of her ass to follow. She had to get away from him. Yes, he was fine, but he chose her? What the hell did that mean? Had he been watching her? So many thoughts started to race through her head. Queen was always so damn paranoid that anything out of the way had her feeling uneasy. She freed the thought from her mind and shook it off. "Hell, I know he ain't the police, so fuck it! I'll give it a go. What's the worst that could happen?" She mumbled all of this to herself, but boy was she wrong. She would love this man like no other, but she had no idea what he was really capable of.

A few months passed and with time they were inseparable. Queen had it bad for him. He must have been putting it down, or all of the money they were bringing in together could have had something to do with it. Out of nowhere I was told to call him godfather. His kids became my sisters and brothers. And in one snap, we were a blended family.

Queen was so caught up that she started to dress his daughters and me alike. I didn't complain because they were the siblings I always wanted. Queen did a good job of blending our families together. We all went to the same private school. We were like a big Brady Brunch family.

We did everything together: vacations, family outings, and holiday gatherings. Whatever a family typically did together, we were doing it. It was never a shortage of people, money, food, or anything else. Every Friday he faithfully gave all of his kids, nieces, nephews, and whoever else was around him at the time, fifty dollars. This may not sound like much, but at the age of seven and eight, getting that kind of money every single week was like getting gold. And it didn't matter what he was doing, he made sure that everyone got his or her fifty dollars every week; no one would be left out.

Birdman hustled hard and made sure that everybody ate. He took care of people even if they weren't his own family. In his eyes he felt that if people were taken care of, then they would protect him with their life if need be. Hence eliminating snitching and robbing. He had a following that was more like a cult. They never complained or wanted to fight and who would? When a nigga was dropping it down like he was, it would be stupid to start up pointless drama. There was only one woman he trusted enough to leave all of his money around, and she would also be the same woman who would create a place for his kids to call home. Birdman had a big heart, but had one downfall though, and that was popping pills and drinking liquor. In my eyes, his downfalls turned him into the devil because it caused him to do some very evil things. I swear when these wicked comforts were in his system, he didn't even look like the same person. It was as if someone else had control of him.

Birdman was very serious about sticking together and instilling in all of us the importance of family. At least once a month he would make it a point to link us all up and do something as a group.

One of our outings consisted of going to the Michigan

State Fair. For this particular outing, there were literally fifty people, and we were all piled up in fifteen different cars. That's just how we rolled out! I distinctively remember Birdman leaving early that day, but he did that sometimes. He would foot the bill, play a little, and then leave to make moves. He didn't like to stay in one place too long. That would give any of his enemies an advantage, so he was in and out. I was always aware of my surroundings so I noticed everything. When people were coming and going, I always noticed. My mom didn't go on all of the trips, and this was one of them that she missed. We had a very good time at the fair, but I couldn't wait to get back and hopefully lay in the bed with my mom.

I rode home with Uncle Lee, Birdman's brother; he had one of the fastest cars I had ever ridden in, a 2000 Audi S4. Matte black with rims that shined like no other. The Audi's headlights were ice blue, and its fog lights were sky gray. His windows were perfectly tinted; anyone would have thought that the president had to have been riding shotgun. I would always feel like money just from riding in it, and this is how you knew everyone on Birdman's team was eating. Everyone around me had the most exclusive yet somehow low-key cars. I looked forward to turning fifteen because I knew for sure that I was getting a brand new car similar to the ones Uncle Lee and Birdman drove. I couldn't wait for that day to come!

As we were approaching my block, we saw a strange looking lady running down the street screaming, "*Help me!* He's trying to kill me!" Since I always paid close attention to detail, I could tell that she wasn't a bum. Her presidential Rolex was shining on her wrist. Minus the rip in her shirt and her hair all out of place, she looked very well kept. "We have to help her!" I screamed to Uncle

Lee. I felt the need to help the lady and had not the slightest clue that she was actually my mother. As we drew closer to her, I realized she wasn't just a well-kept lady, she was my Queen. She was bleeding from her head and looked like she didn't even know who she was. I immediately went into a panic.

Now for the third time in my life, I watched my mother go through yet again another tragedy. Uncle Lee was trying to keep me calm, but the blood running from her head was very distracting. I thought I was going to die in that moment, but there was something different about what was happening this time around. Strangely, I didn't cry; I couldn't cry. Whenever these events took place in my life, I would cry on spot. I was either in shock, or my once pure heart of love and happiness was beginning to fill with hatred and coldness. Is this what all-normal kids have to go through? Is there something that I'm doing wrong? Can I at least go one year without seeing something so brutal? I wasn't sure exactly who I was questioning, but I wanted answers. I was tired of living in fear. I was convinced that one day I would come home and Queen would be dead.

She must have known it was Lee's car coming up the street because she was headed straight toward us. And once she reached us, she started banging on the window as if she wasn't aware if people were inside. The hole on the side of her head was gushing out blood fast. We needed to apply pressure urgently, because she would lose consciousness if we didn't. Blood was everywhere! She had blood all over her white Gucci shirt, which was ripped half way off. I saw the lace bra beneath the shirt was also spotted with blood. It was starting to look like a great day gone wrong. I was only nine, and I had already seen too much in my lifetime.

Finally, she managed to get in the car and sat right beside me. "He pistol whipped me!" she said, in a delusional state. She had so many blows to the head that her words were slurring. I thought that being whipped meant that he attempted to shoot her but missed. I had no clue that he really just took the butt of the gun and repeatedly hit her in the head. What kind of crazy person would do this?

Lee and I were still unaware of who her attacker was. "Did somebody try to rob you, Queen? Are you okay? You get to see their face?" Lee was already in attack mode and was ready to get shit handled and fast. He was seconds from making the call to put the news out there, but the words that Queen would speak next would haunt me forever.

Lee reached to grab his phone, but Queen grabbed his arm. "Lee, it was your brother. It was Birdman!" Queen's head was hanging low with a look on her face that I couldn't quite make out. She was hurt but still in love. She didn't want anything to happen to Birdman. Even in a near death experience, she was willing to protect him. She didn't want anyone outside of the car to know what happened, and that's just how Queen was. A real trooper who pushed through all of the drama in her life. It never fazed her.

The call that Lee was about to make was to Birdman, so he placed the phone back down and headed to the hospital. "We have to take you to the hospital; your head looks really bad!"

Queen and her damn paranoid self hated people in her business. She knew if she went to the hospital the cops would come asking questions. And the number one rule to the game was: never snitch. And she wasn't about to start now. She made her bed and was now forced to lay in it.

"No, I hate hospitals. Just take me to my cousin's house, and I can stay there for a couple days. The neighbors probably heard me screaming and called the police. The cops will be lurking the hood for a while. If I go to the hospital, they will come there too!"

Lee wasn't listening to her because he could clearly tell she was in need of some medical attention. As I sat in the back of the car, Uncle Lee got out for a second to grab a rag out of his trunk. When he came back, he told me to put the rag to my mother's head and hold it really tight. I held the rag as tight as I could, but by the time we pulled up to the hospital my mother lost consciousness. Once they got her to a hospital bed and hooked her up to an IV, she woke up and was ready to make a break for it. By this time, our cousin Tonya was there with us. After Queen was admitted, Uncle Lee rushed right out of there. He knew the cops would come to ask questions, and he didn't have any answers.

Queen woke up to two black eyes and her head fully wrapped in bandages. She had to get fourteen stitches in her scalp. She looked around the room, and I was sitting next to Tonya looking back at her. She wasted no time. "Tonya, get me some shoes. I have to get up outta here." Queen's voice sounded like a frog. She was attempting to pull the IV out and lift herself up.

I could feel her pain and mimicked her facial expressions unconsciously. "Are you okay, Queen? Be careful," I said. *Wasn't this supposed to be the other way around?* Queen was supposed to be taking care of me. Nevertheless, it was always just the two of us, so we took care of each other. It was the only way to survive in our single parent household.

Tonya was upset that Queen was so eager to leave. She knew that Queen wasn't feeling well and didn't want her to leave the hospital. "You need to lay your ass back down. The doctors haven't come back with the scans; we don't know if you have any internal bleeding or swelling."

"I feel okay. My head hurts like shit. I got money in these streets! I gotta get the fuck up out of here. You know these white people will be all up my ass with a million and ten questions." Queen wasn't playing anymore. She was about to break out of the hospital. Queen got up and slipped into her all white Gucci slippers with the two GG's placed perfectly between her toes. "Come on, Magic. Get your stuff. Let's go!" Queen didn't even take a second to breathe in between her words; she was ready.

This time, neither of us attempted to stop her. She meant business, and we weren't about to be on her shit list like the doctors and Birdman. We grabbed our belongings and started to make a move for the door. As we walked through the hospital, the doctors tried to stop us. However, Queen had already instructed us not to look back and to keep moving. She walked through the hospital with dried blood on the side of her face. It was very humbling to see her like this because she was always very well kept.

Today, she just didn't look like herself. No matter what Queen may have been going through, she always kept on her game face. Her head was still held high, all of her luxurious jewelry was still perfectly positioned, and her crystal white Chanel bag draped across her shoulder. And just like that, she walked past the guards, nurses, and doctors with a look of death in her eyes. They knew better than to try to get her to stay. It was no stopping us, so they looked the other way.

Around 4:00 a.m. we finally arrived to our cousin

Tonya's house. Although Tonya stayed downstairs in a two-family flat, she also owned the upstairs, in which her daughter Keisha lived. Queen and I ended up staying upstairs while Keisha slept downstairs with Tonya. The only problem was that Keisha had a waterbed. Yes, it sounds cool, but it was no match for Queen and me. I sweated all night. The night was filled with constant tossing and turning. Images of my mother with her head blown off kept replaying in my dreams. "Nooo! Why would you do this to her?" I pleaded in my sleep nonstop.

Queen was awakened by the noises I was making and jumped, ready to reach for her pistol. The fight between her and Birdman had her on edge. What the hell was Queen really into that would cause her to always be so damn paranoid?

Realizing that no one was in the room but the both of us, she placed her gun back on the dresser and turned to wake me out of my sleep. "Baby girl! Are you okay?"

"Mommy, they are going to kill you, aren't they?" I asked, shaken up from my dream.

Queen was concerned and wasn't quite sure why I would think this. "Baby girl, no one is going to kill me. Sometimes adults have disagreements and things escalate."

"No one should get so mad that they would do what he did to you. I *hate* him! Why would he do that to you?"

As always, she was taking up for people who had done her wrong. "He didn't mean it; he wasn't himself. You will see when you're older that people make mistakes, and they don't always intentionally mean to do certain things."

"How is that even possible?" I questioned. That wasn't a mistake. And I hated that she equated getting pistol whipped to making a mistake.

"Baby. That's not important. What's important is for you never to let a man treat you like that. No matter what happens to me, promise me that you will never let a man put his hands on you?"

Here she goes with her infamous contradictions. How can she expect me to do things differently when all she ever does is cover up situations? Queen always acted as if shit didn't happen. *Is she playing mind tricks on me? Does she expect me to always have a mind of a child?* You can't preach one thing, do something completely different, and expect me not to choose the latter. She needed to be a woman of her word. She needed to make me a visual learner and stop trying to enhance my listening skills. All you have in this life is your word and how you act on it. Queen was failing miserably!

5
Dear Mama

After many failed attempts at winning me over, Birdman finally got back on my good side. Before I knew it, we were all back together like a big happy and normal family. Their fight had been pushed to the back of my mind, and it had started to fade away. I was forced to make a promise to my mother that I wouldn't tell his children what occurred that night. They looked at their father as a saint, and in their eyes he could do no wrong. Their precious thoughts were wrong, and I wanted so badly to tell them that he was the devil. I didn't care what my mother said the night we stayed over at Tonya's house; she had to be crazy if she thought I would be okay with what he did.

One day Birdman took the whole gang to Joe Dumars' Arena. I loved going to that place because there was so much stuff to do. We could ice skate, play basketball, play games, play laser tag, rock climb, and so much more. We would always start with eating together, and then we would go our separate ways. Of course most of the boys went straight for the basketball courts, and the rest of us went to the game room. Before parting ways, Birdman gave each of us twenty dollars to spend on games and whatever else our money could buy. He then placed the remainder of his money in one of his younger daughter's pockets. Since he was about to play basketball, he didn't want to lay his money around the court. Off we went to have some fun.

Forty minutes into the fun, most of us were all dried up in the cash department. We headed back to Birdman while they were in the middle of a heated game. He went into Carmen's pocket and passed us another twenty-dollar bill. Again, we left and tried to hold on to what coins we had on our game cards. I was doing well and didn't need any more money. However, a few of the others who didn't make the first trip to get seconds were now all out and ready for more. Carmen handed them all another twenty a piece without speaking with Birdman. We all laughed it off and continued playing. I never asked for any extra money because I played off of the forty dollars that we all got before departing ways.

Once the basketball game finally came to an end, Birdman came to look for us. We were all just about ready to turn in our tickets and pick up some prizes to take home. As we gathered our belongings, Birdman went to count his money and discovered that he was short much more than he expected. I don't know how much he was short exactly because I didn't pass it out. Guess who was the person that they decided to blame it on? Me! You have to be fucking kidding me. I already had enough drama on the side with this man; the last thing that I needed was for him to think that I was a thief. Hell! He deserved to be shorted for sure, but what did I look like taking his money? I knew what he had done to my mother, and I stayed clear of him. I was terrified of him, but apparently so was everyone else. I assumed fear was why I was lied on. When one of them got a whooping, he made all of them pay. They knew he wouldn't hit me, so it seemed best to place the blame on me. What they didn't know was that Queen would beat the fuck out of me to the point that I would be black and blue. My one beating could never equate to seven of their simple spankings. After Birdman conversed with Carmen off to the side, he headed straight for me. And it was at that point that I knew what was about to go down.

Birdman sat me down on one of the benches by the exit doors. His face was cold, and it looked as if he had a dark cloud over his head. I didn't have a clue how much money he was out of, but I knew that he was really angry. I was convinced that one of his kids was pocketing the shit. It couldn't possibly be this serious. He handed out money like penny candy, so why was he so furious? I should be able to get away with murder, considering that I was keeping his dirty truths a secret. I held in the fact that he had a serious problem with his hands and how they somehow liked to land on my mother. I couldn't believe this was happening. At this point I was extremely angry, and he was about to push me over the edge. "Magic, did you tell them to spend my money without asking?" Birdman asked, in a very stern tone.

After confirming my suspicion, my anger grew and I wanted to beat the fuck out of them. "NO! I didn't! She went in her pocket and started handing them money. I never even touched that money!" I was sassy in my response, but I was honest. He didn't believe me though. He knew that I disliked him somewhat, so he figured I was trying to get some payback or was being rebellious due to my feelings toward him.

"You know if you were my kid that I would whoop you right here in front of these people. You're not though, so I'll let Queen take care of that. If you ever steal from me again, I'll personally take care of you. Understand?" He spoke in a very low but assertive tone. His tone of voice didn't matter because flashes of my mother's bloody face started to come across my mind, and I was ready to explode.

"Oh, just like you did Queen, huh?" Birdman was shocked and embarrassed; he couldn't believe the words that came out my mouth. I honestly couldn't believe those words surfaced either. The words just slipped out, but seriously, who did he think he was to threaten me like this? Did he think I forgot what he liked to do as a hobby? Young or not, I didn't appreciate it, and I wasn't going to let anyone talk to me like that. My smart mouth would always get me into a lot of trouble growing up. I really didn't know how to bite my tongue. If I felt a certain way, I would be sure to keep everyone on the same page. I spoke whatever came to my mind and without thinking.

Shaking his head in a slow but almost motionless way, he managed to say, "Kids should stay in their place, and your smart mouth will get you into a lot of grownup trouble. Keep that mouthy shit away from my kids." He got up, and I slowly followed as we all headed to our final destination.

When I got home, Queen was there waiting with belt in hand. She wasted no time whooping my ass, and you can guess how the rest went. She hit me until I begged her to stop. I would never cry, so she would continue her charade until it was clear that she got through to me. I guess she thought crying or begging her to stop meant that I fully understood my wrongs.

Once again, shit was back to normal, and the routine was like a broken record. The cycle of events just kept happening. It would be good for weeks, and then something bad would happen. It took me some time to mentally process the endless cycle. When time permitted for me to embrace the inconsistencies, I found myself back with everybody like everything was cool.

It was a hot summer day, and we were all at Birdman's house. He had a three-story home in West Bloomfield with six bedrooms. It was a true beauty. We would always enter through the four-car garage. Once we entered, the very first room in view was the family room, and it had a series of flat screens. They could play one channel at a time, or you could watch multiple shows at once. With the large family he had, it was a great setup. My favorite part of the room was the built-in wall couch. It lined up along the walls of the entire room. You could pull from the bottom to turn it into a sleeping space. It was the only room where we were allowed to do as we pleased. Most of the other rooms were off limits to us. Birdman had the most ostentatious furniture. There was one other room that we were allowed in, but only when Birdman conducted his family meetings, nothing more. Even with Birdman's house being so spacious, there was only one place where we loved to spend most of our time. We loved the backyard! The backyard had a slide, trampoline, swings, and swimming pool.

On this day we were all playing in the swimming pool. We were jumping off the top of the house into the thirteen-foot pool. It was great. I loved spending time with all of my sisters and brothers when there wasn't any tension in the room. No matter what happened, we would make up like family was supposed to. I knew it was only a matter of time before something else would happen, and I hated not being able to totally enjoy each present moment due to the fear of the unknown.

All of the girls were coming to my house for the night

so that we could have a girls' night. I noticed over the past couple of weeks of visiting over to Birdman's house that Queen hadn't been around. She missed us and wanted to spend some time with just the girls. I was super excited and hadn't been home in a few days; I couldn't wait to sleep in my bed. We packed up all of our belongings, put on our shoes, and headed through the garage to hop into one of Birdman's trucks.

We were cruising down the freeway leaving from West Bloomfield. We were all bobbing our heads to Tupac's, "Dear Mama.".

Lady . . . Don't cha know we love ya? Sweet lady.

Dear Mama

You would have thought that we actually knew what the heck Tupac was talking about. We just felt good, so we were moving to the beat. Once we approached the 7 Mile exit, we turned right and met Queen at a Mobile gas station. I hopped out the car, very much excited to see my mom. It had been almost a week since I last saw her. "Mommy, I missed you!" I said, squeezing her as tight as love would allow.

She had a way of brightening my day a couple of shades even if my day was going great. She was my mommy, and I missed her beautiful face. "I missed you *more* baby girl. Y'all get in the car. Let me talk to Birdman right quick."

Carmen, Candace, Katrina, and I all hopped in my mom's new Yukon XL; she had a thing for big trucks. Short words were said between Queen and Birdman, but the exchange didn't seem hostile at all. Once we were all in the truck and a short distance away from the gas station, my mom picked up the phone and either spoke directly to Birdman or left a voicemail.

"Thanks for bringing my kids. I've missed them. We will see you soon." Queen hung up the phone after sounding very thankful.

We headed south up the Southfield Freeway toward 96. Queen had a sound system built in her car, so the whole car would vibrate to the beats of the radio. We were heading back to our jam session but this time with TLC, "No Scrubs."

A scrub is a guy that thinks he's fly
And is also known as a buster

We were singing at the top of our lungs, when suddenly, Birdman came flying on the side of us demanding that my mother pull over. He scared the shit out of me, and I instantly peed my pants. He was practically inches from hitting us. "Momma, stop him! I think I peed my pants!" Queen was scared too, so it wasn't much she could do to help me at this point. What the hell happened between them from the time that we pulled off until now? Why was he so angry?

Birdman's face was red; that's how flustered he was. He wasn't even light skinned, yet his eyes and skin were blood shot red. His veins were trying to pop out of his head. "Roll the fucking window down!"

In an attempt to defuse the situation, Queen yelled to him. "Birdman, what are you doing this for? Not in front of the kids. Please, they don't need to see this." She was begging him to stop. He wasn't going to quit anytime soon though. He was driving so crazy and was swerving in and out of lanes. My mother tried to speed up.

He picked his speed up to try to cut us off so that we would be forced to pull over. "Man, pull the fucking car over!" he yelled, trying to be heard through all of the wind and distance that Queen kept trying to create. Queen just wanted him to stop, and we were all so scared. After doing ninety-five miles per hour on the freeway, she pulled over and he slowed down to pull his car on the left side of ours. Still parked in the far right lane, he hopped out of his car and ran up to Queen's window. My mom locked all of the doors. One of the windows was a little cracked, and he managed to stick his arm inside of the car.

"Open the fucking door, Queen! I'm not fucking playing with you!" he insisted, while banging on the window. If he would've continued with this, I was sure he would have broken the fucking window.

I thought this was it. I thought Birdman was going to get my mother to unlock the door, and then beat her right here on the side of the freeway. I could see him throwing her in the middle of traffic, so that her cause of death could be accident related. All kind of things were running through my mind, and I was scared shitless. *Why is he doing this with us watching? Maybe he will just slap her up a bit and go home.* Whatever he was going to do, I wished that he would just get it done and over with. At ten years old, I had already witnessed my mother in the hospital from being beaten by this man that she loved. What was he going to do to her this time? Birdman reminded me of the scary things that I saw on TV. To me, Birdman was a big ol' monster that wouldn't die off the movie.

Still remaining calm, Queen wanted to just get us home. "No. You're not about to do this in front of the kids." She was trying to put the car back in drive and pull off.

"These my fucking kids! Open the door!"

"Please, Daddy! Stop!" My sisters were screaming in the backseat, but he didn't pay them any attention. I was sitting in the passenger seat soaked by my own pee, and shaking uncontrollably. My eyes twitched.

Why me?

Birdman grabbed Queen's freshly done ponytail, and this would be the only time she ever wore weave. As he snatched her ponytail, he started to repeatedly bang Queen's head against the steering wheel; causing her to bleed from her forehead. With each bang the cut was growing deeper. At that point, she thought if she unlocked the door, then he would set her free and stop this madness. The craziest part was that cars kept whizzing by, and none of them noticed that something was wrong with this picture. I secretly prayed the police would pull up, help us, and take Birdman.

A very demanding and impatient man was outside the door ready to kill us all. "I'm not fucking playing with you. Open the fucking door!" He yanked her ponytail one last time.

The girls screamed in the back and my mom begged him to please stop. Queen finally unlocked the door. He jumped in, pushing my mother over to the seat that I was already in. "Get over there with your daughter. I'm gon' kill you tonight, so get a good look at her." Birdman spat on my mother before pulling off.

He left his car on the freeway in the middle of the road. This man was a complete lunatic. Not only did he leave his car, but he also left it running. His car was blocking a functioning lane on the freeway. I bet he wouldn't be the one to go back and get it, despite the fact that he left it. The police would be all up his ass. I'm sure the car wasn't in his name, so it would never even trace back to him anyway. Where was the police when you needed them?

Why hadn't they rolled by? Why couldn't they have been at the right place, at the right time? This was all too much.

We were flying toward my house and Birdman was punching and hitting Queen repeatedly. She was sitting in my lap and was trying to protect me from his blows. He hit her over and over again in the face. He even tried choking her with one hand. She tried to fight back, but there wasn't much she could do. The look in his eyes made my body tremble. It was as if I was watching the devil beat my Queen, my mother. Once we exited the freeway and the car came to our first stoplight, Queen jumped out and ran up the street. We were stuck in between cars, so we couldn't move. Queen was banging on random car windows, begging for anyone to please let her in. Most people just locked the door and acted as though she wasn't there. She began to run down a residential street and started banging on their doors. Someone must have let her in, because by the time the light turned green, she was nowhere in sight. We drove around for about an hour before Birdman finally gave up and drove all of us to my house. Once he walked all of us up to the door, he stopped and began to apologize. I guess he had time to calm down. His normal colored skin had returned, and it looked like the devil had left his body. He started to really see us, his victims.

"Girls, I'm very sorry that I did that in front of y'all. You know I would never hurt you guys, and I didn't mean to hurt Queen. I love y'all more than life itself and would do anything to protect y'all from something like this. Please forgive daddy. Promise me you will never let a man do that to you." Birdman pleaded for our forgiveness and even shed a few tears.

We all stood with blood shot eyes full of tears. The only person who could get anything out was Carmen.

"Why Daddy? Why did you do that?" she asked, still crying. He had no answer. He just hung his head held low and sighed. He knew he messed up big time.

"Please forgive me! I promise not to ever let you witness anything like that again." He was still pleading.

Since those were his kids, they didn't need much more than that to reassure them. "We forgive you!" All three girls sang in unison, still crying and still scared. I, on the other hand, wasn't going to break that easy. He had to think that I was stupid. This wasn't the first time he pulled a stunt like this, and I was certain that it wouldn't be the last.

"I promise not to have y'all witness this ever again," he tried to reassure them, but was only rearranging the words to his meaningless apology. How about you control your anger? How about you promise to never do this again? Birdman would stay true to his word. We never did witness him laying a hand on Queen, but he would still beat her while we weren't watching.

Waiting for my approval, he just had to ask, "Magic, do you forgive me?"

You have to be shitting me! Of course I don't forgive you. "No! I *hate* you and I hope you die." I gave him a piece of my mind with the most hateful voice that I could muster up. He started to cry again and asked all of us to go in the house. I think those words really stuck with him because I can't recall another time he hit my mother. I don't remember much else of that night. Elle was inside waiting on us, but was confused when she didn't see Queen. I guess Birdman told her what happened after putting us to bed.

The next morning, I jumped up and realized that I slept in Queen's bed last night. I slept in her bed so that I could see her when she came home. I didn't remember being awakened, so I started to panic and thought that maybe she didn't make it home. I turned over, looked to my right, and there she was! My Queen was right next to me. I cuddled under her just so that I could smell her scent. Her flesh was warm, and I was the happiest kid ever. I was appreciative of the moment because I wasn't a motherless child. I could see her. I could hear her heart thump. I could make more memories with her. God saved her life.

Life went on as usual. The notorious cycle ran its course, although the rotation was consistently failing. We kept riding a destructive Ferris wheel, and we would ride no matter its condition: good, bad, great, good, bad, and great. It seemed like bad shit was just meant to happen. However, sometimes I did ask for it. I was a very smart girl, but like every other kid, I still did and said some bad things.

One day while over to Birdman's house, we were all in the girls' room playing. Birdman came down the stairs in the finest suit that I had ever seen. His suit was sky blue with gold buttons and it fit to perfection. He wore matching gators, which were his favorite. Birdman didn't wear jewelry since he wasn't a flashy guy, and with all of the bad shit he was doing, he knew it wouldn't be wise to draw unwanted attention. I knew at this point not to mess with him. I couldn't help my mind from drifting as I noticed my sisters and brothers looking at their father in awe. *Ugh!* I swore to my mother to never tell his children about the aftermath of Birdman beating my mother for the first time. They were all clueless to what their father really did. I believe they thought he was a carpenter. Whatever the case was, I knew he wasn't a carpenter, not if Queen was dating him. Their lifestyles wouldn't have matched if he were a carpenter. Aside from that, he was the man who repeatedly beat my momma. They always pretended that night on the freeway never happened. It was so weird for me because every time I saw him, I replayed the incident in my mind.

He always attempted to keep me happy and make me smile when I was around him, and I did my best to remain calm and play along. "Hey, my big girl!" Birdman had the biggest smile.

His efforts just weren't enough. "Hey." My response was very dry, and I was not excited to see him at all.

He was about to make his exit. He leaned down to give each of us a kiss on the cheek. "All right, y'all be good while I'm out!"

My smart mouth self never knew when to keep it closed. "He is going to get some pussy!" I whispered to the girls.

We all laughed and somebody out of the group said, "Ooohhhh I'm telling!" I didn't think she would really tell until the next morning when my mother was there to give me what I had coming. Her hair was tied to the back, her jewelry was off, and she stood over me with a switch in her right hand. I had no idea what was about to happen.

Queen was on fire! She couldn't believe I would ever make such a comment. What the hell did I even know about getting some pussy? Who taught me that phrase? Not only was she mad, she was embarrassed. She thought she was doing a fine job raising me, but clearly she had some work to do. No kid should speak in the way that I did, and now I had to pay for it.

"Magic, get up and go in the fucking bathroom!" Queen spoke sternly and was ready to inflict pain. I looked back at the girls while they whispered. *Damn! So they really told on me? Fuck 'em.* I was about to take this ass whipping like a real OG. And from that point on, I would always have trust issues. Like really? You bitches tell on me when I was only joking. What about the slick shit y'all say? Do I go running to y'all daddy? I was really mad, but tried to play dumb like I didn't know what was going on.

"Ma, what's wrong?" I asked.

Queen wasn't buying it. She knew what I said, and she was here to show me. "Just get in the fucking bathroom. Bitch, you think you grown? I'm gon' show you what grown gets you." She pushed me in the bathroom. "Take your clothes off." Queen was ready to do some serious teaching.

As I began to strip, the hits started coming. Once the hits started, they felt like they would never stop. I didn't cry though because I couldn't. My heart had started to grow colder the older I grew. My mom would hit me for anything. I was hit for pencil marks on my pants, breaking something that she only paid fifty dollars for, moving my body the wrong way, not answering a question she knew that I had the answer to, bringing home anything less than a B, and the list goes on. She feared that I would end up like her, so everything that was wrong in her eyes received some form of punishment; no matter how small. By this time, I just stopped crying. The last time that I could recall crying was when I watched her get beat by Birdman. This day was really different, because it wasn't your average whooping. My mother was beating the shit out of me. It felt like she could have killed me.

"Bitch, you think you grown? You ain't gon' cry?" Her voice woke me from my thoughts. And as I looked down at my body, I could see blood. She had never made me bleed before. This was something new. I guess I didn't respond in the way that she wanted, so she went for blood. I was so numb that I didn't even feel the pain. She began punching me in my chest and still no feeling. Everything was moving in slow motion. I could see Queen's arms swinging, her mouth moving, and spit flying all over the place. I wanted to smack her like Elle did her that one time.

She was determined to get a tear out of me, but I told myself that I was done crying. "I'm gon' beat you until you cry!" She was determined to force some form of emotion out of me.

"No, Mommy! Please stop! I didn't mean it." I started begging for her to stop. I figured since I couldn't shed a tear, that maybe if I showed her I was scared, then she would stop. I honestly just wanted her to get it over with since I saw the blood dripping from my body.

The beating lasted for another ten minutes. I guess she got tired since I never gave her the fucking tears she asked for. I loved my mother dearly, but the constant beating made me grow to resent her. The resentment was how our relationship started to break. It would take years for us to form a solid bond where we would actually get along. I loved my mother because she gave me life and did everything to keep that life comfortable. However, I didn't like my mother as a person. She wasn't someone I would want to be friends with. We saw things differently. She didn't have to beat me for me to turn out better than she did. I had no desire to be anything like her.

I couldn't go to school or take a shower for a week. The marks on my body were so brutal. I thought I hated my mother for what she had done to me. I didn't think I deserved what she dished out to me. I knew people whooped their kids, but what she had done was downright abuse.

If being abused at home wasn't enough. I was starting to fear ever being at home. I guess it doesn't pay to live in the hood and have money because our home had become the target for burglars. We were having break-ins at the house on a regular basis. One day we were out late leaving the hair salon, and Queen got a call from the alarm company stating that someone had just broken in. We rushed to the house to see what was going on. We beat the police, but we missed the predators. The side door was cracked and broken glass was everywhere. They must have broken a window to get in and exited through the side door.

Queen rushed up the steps to her bedroom once she finished checking downstairs to be sure that the burglar was gone. She had 'Baby' in hand, ready to let one loose. "Stay right there, Magic." Her jewelry was still in place. Her petty cash was gone, but they didn't take the duffle bag of cash she had on the top of her closet shelf. All of her mink coats were gone. That was really strange because whoever did this seemed to have come by with only a few things in mind. The fact that they didn't take anything else troubled her. It was time to move. Queen was furious! "Oh, these bitches knew where my shit was? They couldn't have been in the house more than five minutes. They knew exactly what they wanted and where to go." Queen was pacing back and forth and talking to herself. Instantly, Queen knew it was someone that she knew. No one else would just pass the jewelry box up leaving about $350,000 worth of jewels. They probably knew that her one-of-a-kind jewelry would be hard to get rid of.

Queen was fed up, and it was time for a change. "That's it, Magic. We are moving the hell out of this city!"

All the events leading up to this moment caused me to self-reflect. I was an emotional wreck. I kept a strong exterior going, but my inner self was never at ease. How can such a young life feel so old? I felt like my body was walking through life, but my mind and everything else was standing still. I constantly replayed all of the traumatic events in my head. Would I die one day soon because of Queen's fucked up life? Whose job was it to protect me if Queen couldn't protect herself? And as usual, there were so many unanswered questions. How could I tell my friends that the girl with this fabulous life was really brokenhearted, and she wished that she had their parents instead of her own? She longed for the parents who worked a day job and had dinner ready by seven o'clock. I hated myself sometimes because I didn't have an outlet, and I didn't know how Queen would react if I told her this. So I went through life scared and ashamed of how my home really was. On the outside looking in, I had everything, but the reality was that I was drinking from an empty glass. I knew I needed something to replenish me, but my glass was never filled. I was always hoping that I would wake up with a mother the next day.

A real one!

6
Finally Out of the Hood

She moved us out of our memory-filled home, and we began our new journey in Southfield, Michigan. Queen was going through some things mentally and was excited for the move. Not only were there break-ins at our home, but Queen recently visited a psychic that told her Elle would get into some trouble that she wouldn't be able to get out of. The physic also stated that someone who my mother wanted to die would be killed. Surely, it was two weeks later when Elle was pulled over while driving to Arizona with drugs in her possession. She would be serving a ten-year federal prison sentence. A man who raped her in her childhood years would also turn up dead just one week later. A change of scenery was so necessary.

I loved our new home. It was stunning. You know Queen had to get it all the way right before we moved in. All that we packed from our last house were our clothes, jewelry, and our diamond chandelier. We left everything else. If we were starting over, we would be starting new too.

As we pulled up to the all brick home, I could only smile from ear to ear. Our home was so big and so pretty. The two double doors that led to the entrance of the house were immaculate. I couldn't wait to get out and see what the inside looked like. We pulled into the circle driveway, and I hopped out of the car. I ran up to the door like I had a key, but the keenness to see what was beyond the doors forced me to rush. Queen couldn't do anything but smile. She was proud of herself. She hustled her butt off to be able to provide for me, and it was now paying off. Watching me light up like a Christmas tree was all the confirmation she needed. Everything Queen did was over the top. She was even planning a big twelfth birthday party for me. Things were finally looking up. I hoped that our lives would finally be normal and with no more drama; especially now that she wasn't seeing Birdman anymore. It's been months since I've seen him around.

When I opened the doors to our home, the chandelier hung right in the high ceiling of the foyer, with the spiral stairs that led to the four huge bedrooms. There were stained gray wooden floors, and I had never seen anything like it! I thought that wood only came in brown. This was the first time that I had ever seen anything so beautiful. Queen went all out to make this house our home. The kitchen was made for a true chef. It was laid out with marble countertops, which held all stainless-steel appliances. Everything in the kitchen was stark white except the black ceramic floor. This is where I would grow my passion for cooking. Finally, I made it through the house and upstairs to my new room. When I walked in, I couldn't believe my eyes.

The first thing I noticed was my king-size bed. I couldn't wait to lie in the bed, because I felt like a grown-up with such a big bed. The walls were a peach color, and they matched the carpet. I had bed posts that touched the ceiling with sheer white drapes that flowed across them. My bedding was very mature and fun at the same time. My cheerleading trophies were lined across the walls on shelves. She kept my stuffed bears because I loved them, and they had their own section in the corner of the room, perfectly positioned. She mounted a flat screen TV from the wall. These televisions had just come out, and I had one in my room! I felt like a true princess. I ran to hug my mom, giving her confirmation that I appreciated everything she had done for me.

Finally after a few months we were settled in our new home, and it was time to get ready for my twelfth birthday party. Still unaware of the magnitude of the party, I just figured it was going to be big. Queen got us tailor-made gray and pink suits. This would be the first time that I wore heels, and I was excited. While I was getting dressed, Queen was at the venue getting everything in order. Around six thirty in the evening, I heard a horn outside. Autumn was there with me, and we ran to the door together. Oh my god, I couldn't believe it. It was a stretch Hummer limo outside ready to take me to my party. What made it even better was when I stepped inside of the Hummer, all my close friends and family were already in it. This was going to be the best night of my life!

Once we arrived at the party, we were damn near partied out from having a blast in the limo. I was the first to get out, and when I walked in I had to stop in my tracks. The venue was absolutely breathtaking. It was truly amazing to see all the centerpieces with my face and a crown. With diamonds spread around the table, well not real ones of course, but you get what I am saying. There were balloons and streamers everywhere. There were huge blown up pictures from my younger years hanging from the ceiling. It was beautiful! The place was packed, and I had a million presents stacked to the ceiling. This would be a night I would always remember.

Tiara and I literally danced the whole night. When we opened gifts, my momma had to present hers in a major way with a heartfelt speech that would send everyone to tears. I received a rose gold set that included earrings, a bracelet with my initials engraved and diamonds all around it, and a cross necklace. The party favors that she gave out were candy and bottled waters all wrapped in pictures of me. There were other little things that were given out so the night could be remembered.

The night came to a close, but I would forever keep all of those loving memories near and dear to my heart! Queen was the best and she did any and everything to make me happy!

Shortly after, my private school had turned into a charter school, and my mother was fed up with their stupid rules. The teachers started to suck, and she was better off letting me go to a public school in Southfield. No more private schools for me. I was going to middle school, and I was prepared for an adjustment. I guess you can say new school, new me! It was a completely different life hopping from a charter school where it was only one class for each grade, to it being multiple classes for each grade. To make matters worse, the Southfield kids were even different. These kids knew all about the clothes and expensive shit. I, on the other hand, would wear it and didn't know what it was. You better believe them bitches noticed me though.

During this transition is when I started to notice what was really going on with Queen. She was starting to drill into my head things to say if the police ever came looking for her.

"Magic you know what to say if the police show up. Right?"

"Mom loves you no matter what happens to me."

"If I go away. You know what to do to take care of yourself."

These were her daily quotes to me. Then, people were always stopping by our house and leaving with garbage bags full of something. I always knew my mom was into something, but I just didn't know what. Once we bought the new house, I knew that what she did wasn't legal. She had safes in the ground and was always hiding things in them. I knew if she got caught doing whatever it was she did, that she would go away for a really long time. She would come in the house on her drunken nights trying to program me with the right answers. "What the fuck you gon' do when the police come here asking you questions, Magic?" She would literally be inches from my face. If she ever stuck her tongue out, she would've licked me.

"What are you talking about? I don't know," I would say in a very sleepy and confused voice. It was late! I swear I thought Queen was on drugs sometimes. There was never a dull moment with her. When she was drunk, it was not always a pretty sight to see. She would come in and bitch about anything. If I weren't so terrified of her, I would have tried to fight her back. She was always like a bull in heat, so no one should have ever messed with her.

Of course my responses were wrong. "No, that's not what the fuck you're going to say. You tell them that I work with computers and that's all you know." Who the fuck did she think she was fooling? This lady barely knew how to turn on a computer, let alone work on one. I'm sure if the police were watching us, they knew damn well that she wasn't a technician. It was all ridiculous and plain stupid.

Whatever, lady, if that's the lie you want to tell. "Okay, Mommy. Can I please go to sleep?"

Finally, my first day at Thompson Middle School had arrived. I was used to wearing pleated skirts with the matching sweaters every day at my last school. With a less strict dress code, I chose to wear khaki pants and a white blouse. Not quite of their standards there though, so I was sticking out like a sore thumb, but I did have on my brown Louis Vuitton Damier shoes, belt, and purse to match. Although I had on designer shoes, that didn't change much. I was a nobody to them. Before I came along, there was only one girl there who had it all and her name was Sonny. She had all the girls following her as if she was the Queen B.

Sonny and I ended up crossing paths because we had similar schedules. She was in so many of my classes. It wasn't until one of the girls from her crew spoke out of line that we would physically meet. In transition to second hour, some girl stopped me dead in my tracks. "Are those Sonny's glasses you have on?" Tammy asked in the most dry and sarcastic way ever. Her nosy ass was referring to the platinum Cartier frames perfectly positioned on my face. *Why the hell would I have on another bitch's glasses? Who benefits from that?*

I was so upset that I wanted to slap that 'ho, but that would have taken me out of my character, and I wasn't going to let her do that. I decided to keep it cute. "First, I don't even know who Sonny is. Secondly, you should be more concerned about what you have and not what I have. I got my own shit. I don't need to wear anyone else's," I explained to the dumb girl who should've asked Sonny if it was okay to speak anyway.

Feeling stupid, she walked away saying, "Oh, my bad. They look just alike." Tammy's voice was fading as she walked away.

Was she the only person who can wear some nice frames? The nerve of these fucking people!

Later that day, Sonny came up to me to make amends for her friend's foolishness. "Hey. Magic, right?" she asked.

"Yes, what's up?" I shot back, uninterested in anything that she had to say. Tammy had pissed me off, and I wasn't looking forward to any more drama for the day.

"I just wanted to apologize on my friend's behalf. She didn't mean any harm. It's rare seeing someone else around here of my caliber. I'll pay respect where it's due, and you deserve it. You always stay in some fly shit." Sonny's voice was so peaceful.

Completely taking me by surprise, I didn't know what to say. "I respect you for that. You stay in fly shit too. We shouldn't be competing against one another, we should shut this school down together!" And from that moment, I had found my crew and we were as thick as thieves.

They didn't know the magnitude of how much wealth I actually had until I invited them over for a birthday gathering. We never put the gifts up until New Year's Eve, so my Christmas spread was still laid out. "You got all this stuff for Christmas?" Sonny asked, in a very confused state.

Inside I thought, *Yeah bitch, you not the only one with the money.* "Yeah, every year it gets bigger and bigger!" One of the few big gifts that I had gotten for Christmas was a diamond ring with princess cuts. The top stone was about two carats, and I had another three layers of small princess cuts. The ring was bigger than what most married women wear. Besides the jewelry, we had a huge couch in our living room that wrapped around in a U-shape. My mom said I had too many clothes to wrap, so she would use the couch to place each outfit with its matching shoes, purse, and belt. It was unreal; I didn't think anyone could ever have a Christmas like mine. It still amazed me how much my mom really did for me all of the time.

During this time, I was getting used to my new life. On April 4, 2004 at five in the morning, Queen was just getting in from picking me up. I had a cheerleading competition that took place in Cincinnati. Her phone rang just as she was about to get in the bed. I'm not sure who called her, but the words she would hear next would forever be in her head. "He's gone. They shot him!" Queen instantly dropped the phone, and suddenly she couldn't breathe. The world had stopped spinning for a few moments. This had to be a dream. Not him. He was untouchable. He always had an army with him. Where were his protectors? Why did God take him? What about his kids? God! No. Not him. Please. Not him. Why God?

Birdman had been at Starters all day, and it was his favorite spot. He never sat in one place too long, which is why his long stay seemed peculiar. From sun up to sun down, Birdman sat there drinking. Now this man knew the many things he was into, and if word got out that he was lounging around all day in the same exact spot, someone might try to sneak him. There was a B2K concert going on this day, and he bought tickets for all of the kids to go. He even bought one for me, but he didn't know that I wasn't in town. He called all the kids up to Starters just to chat with them. They didn't see it as strange then, but it sure seemed strange as they replayed the day back in their heads. Birdman had even called Queen on the phone and asked where I was because he wanted to see me. They all sat there talking, laughing, and enjoying what would be the last time with their father. And as Birdman finally got up to leave, his killer would be waiting for him outside. Whoever killed him had to have known him well. As the killer attempted to approach Birdman, he was heading over to greet them. However, instead of being greeted with a handshake, he was greeted with four bullets. He died right in front of his favorite spot and in front of his children. How tragic. There was no need for the ambulance to come because he died instantly.

Queen was hurt beyond words. No matter what he had ever done to her, she loved him. If she weren't so worried about him flipping out in front of me again, she probably would have still been with him. He offered her a life with him. He wanted her to be the one that he would come home to, but Queen wasn't ready for the responsibility that came with that. If something were to ever happen to him like what took place that day, she would be responsible for his mouths to feed. Queen wasn't a half stepper, so she would want to go all out for them just as he did. She knew she wasn't capable, but never wanted to let him down.

As much as I would have liked to dislike him in that moment, I was hurt too. No matter how much you dislike a person, you never want to hear that they are dead. I loved him very much, but I just hated what he did to my mother.

His home going service was the most elaborate funeral I had ever been to. A horse and carriage carried him. The family rode in Bentley stretched limos. They even had a fabric flower made with Birdman's name on the back of it to represent one of his favorite basketball team's—the LA Lakers. They released a lot of doves. I thought to myself that the doves had to be carrying Birdman's soul to heaven and was there really a heaven for a G like him? There were thousands of people there to pay their respects to a man whose legacy would forever remain in the city.

The same night, the block had a party in honor of him. They had a makeshift stage brought right to the hood. There was a group of local rappers who performed a song written in memory of Birdman. There had to be over two thousand people piled in on one street. The street was cloudy from the amount of weed being smoked. Birdman had a true cult. One of his men said, "Ah Dee Ah" and one after another, his brotherhood started to chant. There were so many drunken people on the block that I was scared things would turn violent. But to my surprise, there wasn't any of that. It was all peace and love in honor of the Birdman. Rest In Peace was all that I could say. I was still in shock and very much worried about my Queen. She was set free of the beatings, but the pain of his death would haunt her forever.

Once life got back to a normal program, I would go over Sonny's house daily after school. Sonny had an older brother who was cool with Ace Jr. and a guy named Blu. He was without a doubt, the biggest player that I had ever seen. He was my brother's best friend, and they had a group called the Cash Out Boys. They were some reckless dudes. They did everything from fighting niggas, going to jail, to fucking all 'hos. They would get hotel rooms just to pass a girl around. The shit was sick, and I ended up being one of the many girls who would get trapped in Blu's little triangle of love.

Blu wasn't even good looking to me when I first started dating him. His swag though, had me on another planet. I never met anyone like him. He could have four girls that he was fucking all in the same room, and you wouldn't even know it, or if you knew it, you more than likely wouldn't say shit. He was telling everybody something different, and they all thought they were the only one he was really fucking with, so they just kept their mouth closed.

He was in the ninth grade and had just broken up with his first puppy love, Rhonda; that girl was crazy as hell. She would stalk all the people he talked to and would harass them over the phone. She even lit a bitch's car on fire. She was insane. Rhonda had no limits to what she would do. I, on the other hand, never acted in such a way. When Blu did shit while we were together, I either handled it with him, or did some shit to get even. I was rolling with it, or I wasn't. It was just that simple. The way our relationship unfolded was crazy. Make sure you hold on because it's about to get pretty crazy. Let me tell you about it!

We would all meet up over to Sonny's house after school since we all were pretty much in the same circle. As long as I answered my phone when Queen called, I could hang out as long as I wanted. My mother never really had rules for me as long as I did what she said and when she said it. She really didn't care to make any rules; there was no point in it.

Before Blu and I even thought about being together, he stayed on some slick shit. He would be in the bathroom one minute fucking one of Sonny's friends, and then leave out of there and come find me to ask me to be with him. This boy must have been on some drugs. It seriously took him two years of constant attempts to even get me to bat my eye. I'm sure he would have gotten to me a lot sooner, if he was really pressed. It started out as something of convenience. I was always around, so he attempted to give it a shot. The only difference between all the other girls and me was having my brother. I simply had an advantage when it came to him dating me. They were some pretty messed up boys and did plenty of women wrong, but they had a boy code somewhere along the line. You couldn't just fuck over your main man's sister. Maybe they could fuck over a cousin, or auntie, but never a sister. When Blu first tried talking to me, I had a boyfriend. This made it really easy for me to push back when he was trying to run his little game. We texted often, but that was it. I knew he was all game and no action, so I just kept it cute and never went there with him.

Summer came and it was time to devote my time to the Westside Cubs, the Police Association League, for children ages 5-15. I was a cheerleader for the A-team. That meant plenty of time with Tiara, Treasure, and Bianca. Blu was steady trying to make a pass, so of course he was still in the picture.

On the first day of practice, we were standing in formation when my Auntie Tracy came running up the field; I could tell something was wrong. What in the hell could be wrong with her? Practice wasn't over for another hour. She was all out of breath before whispering in my coach's ear. They pulled my cousin Marie and myself off the field and to the side. What she said next caused me to simply faint. "Magic, your mother has been shot—but—" She couldn't even finish her sentence because I was already on the ground passed out.

When I made it to the hospital I saw my grandmother sitting down, but she wasn't saying anything. I went up to her and asked where Queen was, but she wouldn't talk to me. "Hello! Can somebody please tell me what is going on?" No one was listening to me. I just started to roam the halls to search for her name on one of the charts hanging on the door. Finally I came to her room, but it was completely empty except for her body stretched out on the bed. No monitors, no nothing. She didn't even have a pillow under her head. I rushed over to her and tried to feel her pulse. There wasn't even a heartbeat. Oh no! My worst nightmare was coming true. They finally got a hold of my Queen. She was dead! Noooooo . . . God why? Please bring her back to me!

The sprinkles from the water that my coach was throwing on me finally woke me up. I was out for about two minutes. It was only a dream, but it felt so real. I was now scared shitless to even walk in the hospital. "Lord, please watch over her at all times, Amen!"

Ace was already there when I arrived, which was strange. I hadn't seen him in a while. We spoke on the phone, but he lived in Kentucky now and barely made trips to Detroit. Luckily he was here this week and was able to be there for Queen. As soon as I walked in, he greeted me with a hug. I could tell he had been crying; he hated to see Queen go through this. "Baby girl, are you okay?" Ace was concerned about me.

"Yes, I am fine now that I know Queen is okay," I assured him with a head nod.

"Well, that's good. Daddy is gon' try to be around more to protect you and your mom. It's just been a lot of crazy things going on. I hate this all happened in front of Vicky's house. I wonder if this had something to do with me." He went on to explain, but perhaps said a little too much.

"Wait. This all happened over at Granny's?" I was confused. *What was Queen even doing over there?*

"Yes. Don't you worry your pretty little self about it! They've already been taken care of," he responded with a very serious face. He was giving me way more information than I think I needed to hear. He was basically confirming that he either killed them, or had someone else do the job.

Queen was up and was happy to see me. "Magic, sorry you have to see me like this," she said, very disappointed.

"You have no reason to be sorry. I love you. Rest up so you can get better." I reassured her that no matter what happened that she was my mother and I loved her. As long as she was home when I woke up, we were good.

7
Love Triangle

The end of the summer approached quickly, and I was headed to Southfield Lathrup High. After all of the drama with Birdman's death and Queen getting shot, it was time for a new start. It was time to meet some new people and get into some teenage trouble. It seemed as if all of the boys at school were trying to holla at me, and I think it had something to do with my body. I prided myself on my body and keeping it toned and in good shape. I had a nice round butt, flat stomach, and the perkiest titties ever. Even though I was very petite, I had a body of a true dancer. No, not like a stripper, more like a ballerina.

It was nice out and I wanted to get away and do something, but the only thing to do on a Saturday was to go to the Southfield movie theater. Any and everybody would be there.

I had decided to text Tone, who was my boyfriend at the time. I liked spending time with him, although he was a true womanizer. Our families were real tight. They loved me and my mom loved them. He was so fine. It started out as a crush, but over time it grew into something bigger. He never pressured me for sex, and I respected him for that. Whenever I decided that I was ready, he was confident that he would be the one that I would give it up to. My mom tried to teach me to save the cookies, which was what my mom called my vagina. She told me to only let someone very deserving have it.

Magic: *Let's go to the movies*

Tone: *Cool. Let's go around 8.*

The text message alert that was set for my phone broke my thoughts.

"Ma, can you drop me off at the movies? I'm meeting Tone," I asked Queen in the sweetest voice.

"Yes, what time?" she responded carelessly.

"Around seven," I said with a grin. I wanted to get there a little early so I could have time to chill with all of the people. It was Saturday, so it was going to be crazy, but who I didn't expect to see that night was Blu. I knew I needed to stay far and clear of him. He was bad news and I could tell.

I was playing one of the games in the game room minding my own business. Then suddenly I felt someone grab around my waist. "Hey, Magic!" a playful voice spoke from behind me.

I didn't need to turn around to see who it was because I knew who the playful voice belonged to. Not taking my eyes off the game, I spoke in a cold tone. "What do you want?"

Blu immediately swung me around so that he could look me in the face. "Why you being so mean? I'm just trying to be your friend." As soon as we looked into each other's eyes, sparks started to fly. He looked at me as if he could see into my soul. He was a little older and a bit more experienced in a lot of areas. I could tell he was genuinely just trying to get to know me better.

So I tried to keep it cool. I didn't need him to know that I was more interested than ever to get to know him too. "Besides the fact that I have a boyfriend, I don't want to be mixed up with all your drama and your 'hos. I would have to be your one and only if you want to be with me," I explained. At this point I had the upper hand when it came to him. He was always begging me to be with him, but I only pushed him away. I was the first girl to ever make him work hard, so he was falling for me and he hadn't even realized it yet.

Just as Tone was walking up, I gave Blu a nice friendly hug and a pat on the back. "Nice seeing you. I have to go. Tone is here," I said with a smile, walking away. I made sure to leave him with something to think about.

I was really excited to see Tone and made it obvious by the cheesy grin slapped across my face. While hugging him I said, "Hey! I missed you. It's really nice to see your face."

"Missed you too, but what was up with you and ol' boy?" He was more concerned with why I was just in Blu's face. I couldn't blame him for being mad; Blu was all in my space, but I wasn't even thinking about him like that. Whatever the reason, it didn't matter to Tone. He was slightly pissed.

"Who? Blu? Oh that's nothing, just some friends catching up. You ready to go see our movie?" I was trying to assure him that he had nothing to worry about, while quickly changing the subject. He never questioned me again.

There was a week left of summer, and I hadn't seen or heard from Blu. He crossed my mind often, and I went over Sonny's house hoping he would be there. I was bugging out over nothing. I just wanted to be around him, and I didn't know why.

It was the last Saturday of summer, and Sonny and the girls came over to my house. We chilled and talked about how much fun high school was about to be. We all planned to go to Lathrup except for Sonny.

The next morning when they were gone, I noticed that my fucking ring was missing. I searched my room high and low looking for it but to no avail. All I could think about was Queen killing me. *I need to find this fucking ring so I do not have to tell Queen*, I thought. Today wasn't going to be a good day. Once you wake the beast up inside of Queen, there's no putting her back. I couldn't find the ring, so I tried to prepare myself for an ass whooping as I made the walk down our long hallway leading to her room. As I walked down the hallway, I glanced at all of the pictures my mother had of me posted on the wall. There was one picture from every year of life; she truly loved me. It was just real tough love, but that's all she knew.

"Hey, Magic. Ready for high school tomorrow?"

Getting straight to the point would be my best method in breaking the news to her. "Ma. I got some bad news."

Then out came the beast. "What the fuck did you do now, Magic?" Queen was already yelling, and with so much anger. She was like a ticking bomb. One faulty move, and the lady would just blow!

My head was held low. I was trying to show my remorse as best as I could. "My ring is missing."

That wasn't good enough though. She didn't understand how I could possibly lose my ring. "What the fuck do you mean it's missing? You lost it?"

"No. I placed it on my Bible and now it's gone." I was

on the verge of tears. How could my friends steal from me? I would never do that to them. If they wanted to wear it, all they had to do was just ask.

"So you let them thieving bitches take it from you? You know better than that, Magic. *We trust no bitch.* Everybody in life will want something from you. You have to be smarter than them and keep your shit tight." She started with one of her many lessons.

"What's they number?" she asked. I gave her Sonny's number. She called right then and there.

"Hello?" Sonny answered, not knowing who the caller was. "Let me speak to your mother!" Queen spoke in a very stern voice.

"May I ask what this is about?" Sonny responded with an attitude.

"Listen, little girl. I'm not a fucking kid. Put your damn mother on the phone!" Queen obviously didn't feel like playing.

"Hold on a second." Sonny's voice was now a little shaky.

"Hello?" Sonny's mother answered.

"Hey, how are you?" Queen asked, trying to keep her composure.

"I'm great. What's going on?" the lady asked.

"My daughter's ring is missing, and I have reason to believe that your daughter and her friends took it!" Queen was pissed, but tried to disguise it.

"Listen, bitch! My kid don't have to steal shit from you or anybody else!" Sonny's mother said.

"Okay, I was trying to be nice about it, but since you want to call me bitches and shit, if my daughter's ring don't find its way back to my house, I'm coming to find all you bitches," she yelled and hung the phone up.

I never spoke to them again. About two weeks later I would find my ring as I was cleaning up. I know someone had to put it there because it was under a hundred stuffed animals, which was a place that I never touched. Somebody was planning to come back for it, but luckily I cut them off before they could.

The first day of high school had finally arrived, and I was so excited. I had my hair freshly done, a nice pink and white nail set, and everything I had on was new; even my panties. This was a big day for me. I was supper excited about what would happen within the next four years. Life was getting fairly normal. I cheered, hung out with my friends, dated, and no more drama with Queen and her lifestyle. Only drama now was teenage stuff: boys, gossiping girls, and school. While I was preparing for school, I randomly got a text from you know who. It was Blu of course, and I was trying my best to let him know that I wasn't interested.

Blu: *Have a good first day of high school. I will see you later.*

Magic: *Thanks, but I have no plans on seeing you. Stop texting me.*

School was great and a lot of people from Thompson were there, so it was an easy transition. It was much bigger than my middle school and was sectioned off by classes. The building had four main hallways and of course, the freshman had the worst one. There was no place to actually sit, and we were in the very back of the school. By the time I walked to the end of the hall, it was time to head to my next class. I didn't really have this issue though since my god brothers, Birdman's sons Bruce and Wayne went there. They were cool with all of the seniors, so even on my first day of school I was chillin' with the big dogs. I had all AP classes and was over them already. The only people in my classes were geeks and weirdoes. The best time of the day for me was lunch, dance, and between classes when I got to sit on the heaters in the senior's hallway. Of course the guys were already trying their luck, but I was Magic and none of them could even get close enough to figure me out.

Transitioning into high school was easy. I was the girl everyone wanted to be friends with. I rocked the hottest shit, and everyone was looking for me to be on his or her team, even if it was only to make them look better.

Later on that day, my dad was outside of the school to pick me up with Ace Jr. When I hopped in the backseat, there he was sitting right next to me. What was he doing here? He had this planned the whole time? How did he know they would be coming to get me?

"Did you have a good first day? I told you that I was going to be seeing you." Blu laughed hysterically.

I didn't like him at all because I knew he wasn't any good for me. Yet there was something about him being there, and in that moment chills were shooting up my spine. It was such an awkward feeling, and I hated it so much. I had a boyfriend, so there was no reason he should've been able to do this to me. My body would always respond to him in ways that I couldn't explain. Just from him sitting next to me would have me in a complete daze. I guess some men just have that effect on you.

After that encounter, we talked fairly frequently, but with me never initiating the calls. I thought it was cool for him to be the one chasing me. Although I was constantly dying for his call and would practically check my phone every few minutes. I knew this was wrong on many levels. I was clearly in a relationship, and Blu had women everywhere. I could never figure out how he did it. Maybe it was his self-confidence, because for me that was the biggest turn-on. What I liked most about him was that he never stopped trying to pursue me, even with multiple occasions of me telling him no. It must have been a turn-on for him too. He probably felt the energy that I felt when we were next to each other. It felt as if we were meant to be together or something.

I was with Tone for convenience; we grew up together and it felt comfortable. It wasn't until Blu came along that I knew we just didn't have that spark. It just wasn't there, well not for me at least. Tone was a good guy though. He would have never disrespected me, or intentionally done anything to hurt me on purpose. However, I was so drawn to the bad boy mentality in Blu. It drove me wild.

Blu's name popped up across my screen. My crazy self was so nervous that I started to fix my hair, although he couldn't even see me. "Hey, Magic! What you doing?" His tone was soft yet slightly seductive.

"I'm at home chillin'. What's up?" As usual, I was trying to sound as cool as I could.

"Yo momma home?" he asked, still sounding seductive.

This was a weird question. What was he trying to do? I'd never had real boy company, so I was kind of scared to tell him that she was gone. I know that if I told him Queen was away that he would basically think that I was extending an invitation to come over. What's the worst that could happen? I knew he wasn't coming for sex, so why not? "Naw, she gone. They went to the club. Why?" I asked.

"Because I'm outside. Open the door," he said. *Oh shit! I look a mess. Should I let him in? Leave his ass outside?*

What if my momma comes back? Oh, I wouldn't hear the end of it. I couldn't believe this was happening. Maybe he was just talking shit. Why would he just pop up at my house. I've only had one boy over, which was Tone, and my mom was always home. This was a big mistake and I knew it. "So are you gon' let me in?" I forgot he was on the damn phone.

"Yeah, I'm about to open the garage door." I felt like a kid at a candy store. *Blu is here at my house to see me?* The rush flying through my body was massive. I didn't know what it was that I was feeling. I had no idea what was happening to me. The man that I had no interest in whatsoever was making my body feel so different. I'd never had these feelings before, and I was afraid of what I would do with them.

He walked in wearing a dark blue Polo jacket and True Religion jeans. He had on a fresh pair of Air Force Ones and smelled of his Gucci Guilty cologne. The scent would cause me to melt to my feet. I had never looked at him and felt turned on, but on this day I was turned so far on that I could have given him some right then and there. Of course, I was in the house lounging, so I was looking a mess. Before I opened the garage, I put on a beater with some black cheer shorts. I guess you could say I was asking for it, but I just wanted to at least look decent before I opened the door.

With my fourteen-year-old frame, I had natural porn star titties that bitches dreamed of. I knew this because all of my friends said so. I never had to wear a bra because they sat up so perfectly. My stomach was ripped, and I could wear nothing but panties and look damned good. My best assets though were my eyes, some thought they were just big, but most men thought they were the prettiest big brown eyes they had ever seen. They could never tell me no. I loved my body. I didn't have a big ass like Queen, but I had a nice shape. I knew if I just flaunted it a little that I could have Blu in the palm of my hands. I wondered how long it would take him to know that I would be his. He knew way before me. I wonder what gave it away?

"What's up, my baby?" he said as he leaned in to give me a hug. Oh, how tempting it was, but I resisted. I pushed him away, trying my best to resist his touch.

"Boy, what are you doing here?" Making his way through the door, he signaled if it was okay to come in. I shook my head yes, and we made our way to the den where I always liked to hang out.

"To chill. I've been thinking about you. I wanted to see you. You've been trying to play all hard to get, so I needed to see you in person," he said.

"Have you forgot that I'm in a relationship?"

"Thanks for the reminder, but no I haven't. That's not important to me though. I know the feeling you get when you're around me. And I know it feels like we should be together. I'm sure you don't feel like that with him, so he's irrelevant to me."

"Wait a minute. Don't you have a girlfriend? I think her name is Rhonda. She already calling and stalking me. Do you really think I want to be a part of all of that? I don't argue with people about what's mine. I know you might do your dirt, but you would have to let it be known that I'm the one you're with."

"First off, that bitch Rhonda is crazy. We've been broken up for about a year; she just hasn't gotten the picture. Since I'm not with anyone right now, she still feels like I belong to her. She was fighting people in front of my momma house and all kind of crazy stuff. She so disrespectful I can't even mess with her like that."

"Whatever, Blu! I'm sure you will be with her later." I wasn't going for his bullshit. I knew what he was about. I knew exactly what he wanted, and there was no fooling me.

"That's not true. There's something about you, Magic, that makes me want me to be your first everything. I mean *everything*." We sat there for another hour or so just kicking it. He asked me about school, dating, and hobbies.

I asked him what his plans were after graduation. He was a junior and graduation would be approaching soon. These weren't typical questions that a fourteen year old would ask, but with a mother like Queen, I always had to think years ahead. It was time for him to go, so I walked him to the door. He asked for a hug. I was comfortable now and he made me want to kiss him, but I resisted and gave him a nice long hug. I tried to keep the memory of his smell in my brain because it was quite heavenly.

"I'm gon' give you three weeks to break up with that boy of yours. You will be mine!" he said with so much confidence. How could any woman deny him? He walked away right after he spoke, not caring what I had to say. He left me straight speechless.

A month or so had passed and Blu and I were still kicking it. I still wasn't his girl. Tone and I weren't exactly dating, so I considered myself single and I was ready to mingle. I decided to add another piece to my own little love triangle. A guy at my school named Mike slipped me a number about a month into school and told me to give his boy a call. I never intended on using the number. However on some random day, leaving from a competition, I was sitting in the room bored. As I was looking through my phone, I came across the name "Ghost." It took me a while to put it together, but then it clicked. *Ghost's number was given to me months ago. Let's see what he has to talk about.* I was feeling myself this day, so I figured what the hell. There wasn't too much not to like, so it would be a win for him either way.

He picked up on the second ring. "Hello?" he sounded like he was in the middle of something.

"Hey. You busy?" I was acting as if I wasn't a stranger at all.

"Naw, why? What's up? Who is this?" Ghost asked.

"You told Mike to give me your number. Shouldn't you be expecting my call?" I quizzed.

He sounded slightly frustrated with my stalling tactics. "Man, tell me who you are, and I will tell you if I have been waiting on you."

"It's Magic!"

"Oh shit! Mike! Guess who this is on the phone?" he asked, yelling to his friend. I should've known they were going to be together. Mike gave him my number because Ghost was asking if there was somebody at our school for him to talk to. Mike was gon' give it a try, but I knew his girl. He figured he would put his mans on, so he gave Ghost a chance to talk to me.

"Who? Who?" I could hear him asking in the background. This was so funny to me for some reason. They sounded like some kids on a Guess Who show or something. Next, he was going to figure out if I had light or dark hair? I laughed so hard to myself.

"Magic!" he said to his friend. He was now returning the conversation back to me. "Well, it only took you a year to use the damn number. I gave up on hearing from you," he said, over exaggerating the time frame of his wait.

"More like a few months. So what's up? How are you doing?" I got straight to the conversation.

"Good. I'm glad that you called." We talked for about thirty minutes. I found out that he was a senior and he went to school with Tone and Blu. I never should have talked to him once I knew this. I should have known nothing good would come from this. Then I thought selfishly for a second. I was young, beautiful, and I wasn't fucking any of these niggas, so why not do them the way they do us? We started talking on the phone and texting all the time. Ghost got suspended from school for a couple days, so he picked me up and took me to lunch one day.

He pulled up in his new silver BMW 350. It wasn't an older one either; it was brand new. I couldn't believe it. He was only in high school and had a lavish car. I just kept thinking, *What is this man into? Maybe his family has money.* There was no way this man was riding around in a brand new car while he was in high school. I was so nervous to go with him because I never did things like this. My mind was racing the whole time that I was with him. I couldn't even eat my Wendy's. He was a very cool guy though. We never got out the car, but even though he was sitting, I could tell he was tall. He had on a Detroit fitted hat with tan shorts and a blue shirt. Ghost was light-skinned with a little bit of acne, but he was still very attractive. He was very different from anyone that I had actually talked to. Not only was he the oldest guy that I had ever talked to, but he was also very smart. He had his own shit: car, house, job, and money put up. He took care of his business and that's what I liked most about him. He wasn't for any games. He knew what he wanted in life and what he wanted in a girl. He wasn't quite ready to completely commit to one girl, but when and if he decided he was ready, he would know how to treat her. When the time was right, he would do what was right and marry whoever the lucky girl would be.

I'd always been real nosy when it came to men. I wanted to know everything, and I was never afraid to be myself. The radio station that was on was killing my vibe so I went to change it.

"Never touch a man's radio!" he said, moving my hand and switching back to what he was listening to, I had to laugh at myself. Who did I think I was to just get comfortable in his ride?

"Never tell a woman what to do," I shot back. I started to go through his glove compartment and armrest, just snooping around. That really pissed him off.

"I've never met someone who just gets in someone else's car and starts fucking with shit. Are you the police?"

"Don't ever disrespect me like that, sounding so stupid! I was raised to hate the police." I was looking at him with my big, bright eyes. His slight irritation and tension easily evaporated. I damn near skipped the rest of the day and we sat in the car and talked for so long. He was so cool. It was as if he had known me for years, and I could tell him anything. During our first conversation, he got so much information out of me. He couldn't believe that I was still a virgin. Most girls my age were good and ready by the age of fifteen. He had a way of getting any personal information out of me. I guess that tactic came with growth, and he wasn't looking for anything temporary. He needed to know whether the relationship would go further, or if he should just stop now to prevent a waste of time. I must have made the cut because as I exited the car, he shouted behind me. "Magic, it was a pleasure! I look forward to doing this again soon!"

I was jumping up and down on the inside. "Sounds good. Talk with you soon," I replied.

Christmas break was approaching, meaning my birthday was around the corner. I was turning fifteen. I didn't get my car that go round, but I was sure next year that Queen would have something big planned. Blu started being more aggressive, and he wasn't taking no for an answer when it came to me being his girl. One day without thinking, I said yes, and from that point on I would always be referenced as, "Blu's girl." Before any of that could last long, my little love triangle would catch up with me.

8
Trust Issues

Officially I was with Blu, and Ghost was cool. I placed Ghost in more of the friend zone. I always knew Blu wasn't good for me, but the way I felt around him had me dying to give it a shot. Ghost and I would talk about everything and everybody. He was my 'cool man,' and I used to say this because you couldn't catch him without a hat on. He even had extra ones in the back of his car window. When I rode with him, the ride was always so smooth.

Being with Blu was a constant battle because although he respected my boundaries of not having sex, he made sure to feel me up every chance he got. I remember when we were sitting in a private room at the public library and facing the glass windows, we could've been seen by anyone who walked by, and he was caressing my thighs. He even tried to rub the cookie through my school pants. He would sometimes kiss my neck in a spot that would seriously make me want to drop to my knees. Blu's touch alone made me weak. I could only imagine how his soft tongue touching my body in places that I didn't know existed would feel like. Blu was the drug that I would never come down from.

Although no one really knew of my relationship with Blu, it was real, I guess. I'm not sure why I agreed to be his lady when I knew in my heart that he was going to ruin everything that I knew about life. He would be the guiding light to some of the worst stages in my life. I continued to talk with Ghost a few days after I agreed to be with Blu; he asked to come over. I was at home with my cousin Nique and Bianca.

Nique and I were super close. We did everything together from birth. I loved my cousin to the death of me. I was always so excited to have her around. Even though she was only a few years younger than me, I always felt the need to protect her and be a good example for her. We were all young of course, and we did some silly things together that we probably had no business doing, but we were good girls. We weren't having sex yet, and we barely went places with niggas. We knew our stuff was gold, and we didn't want just anyone to have it.

My phone started to ring. "Hello?" I was excited to see what Ghost was talking about today.

"What you got up?" He was always such a smooth talker.

"Nothing. Just chillin' at home with Bianca and Nique. What's up?" I was curious to know what he had up his sleeve.

"I. Want. To. Seeeeee-you." He slowed all of his words down to be sure that I was listening.

"Okay cool! My mom will be back a little later. So see you in a few," I said and immediately hung up. What the hell was I thinking? That wasn't a good idea. I had just agreed to be with Blu not even three days ago. *Why am I letting this man come over?* There was no good reason for it besides the fact that I wanted to see him too. All of the things that were different about us made us connect. I never felt as if I had to be someone else while I was around him. Even with the three-year age difference, we were always on the same level.

A few moments later I heard him come through the chirp on my Nextel phone. "Open the door. I'm outside!"

I did just that and greeted them as they came in. "Hey! What's up with y'all?" I didn't even shut the garage. I was acting so awkward. My subconscious screamed, "Girl! You are buggin'!"

I yelled back, "I know! Tell me about it." I finally came to my senses and shut the door and remained silent for a while to just think. Why was I so nervous? I guess I was just inexperienced in all of this. I was cool with kicking it over the phone, but having men in my house felt a little uncomfortable.

"You got somewhere my mans can chill?" Ghost asked. His question would pull me from my thoughts and place me in the moment.

"Yes, the den is right over there!" I directed him to my chill spot. The den had a 70-inch flat screen TV in it. When I watched a movie, it always felt like I was in it. As he made his way to relax, Ghost and I just chilled in the kitchen.

Ghost stared me down and nearly shocked me when he started confessing his love. "You know the whole way here I couldn't stop thinking about how you got a nigga head all gone." Of course I thought this was complete bull because he had plenty of other women to consider, but how is it that I had all of his attention?

"Ghost, I'm sure I'm just one of your many women," I responded nonchalantly. I always questioned men and their true intentions because I never knew what to believe out of a man's mouth.

"Trust me. I keep asking myself what is it about you. You're young as hell, and I'm cool with your position on not wanting to have sex. Your conversations are different from anybody else!" he confessed. "It's even better that you have your own money, and you're not needy. Not to mention your body is amazing. You're the 'it' girl. I don't plan on letting you out my sight." He added, "Before I go any further with this rant, you sure your mom won't be here for a while? I had a feeling driving over here that this might not be a good idea. Thankfully Mike was in the car with me and he talked me into coming anyway."

"Maybe you should've went with your gut," I shot back. I believed in trusting my gut. My mother would tell me this particular sense was gifted to women and was called intuition. I guess men had intuition too though, because not even two seconds into my conversation with Ghost, my phone started ringing.

Ring! Ring! Ring! Ring!

I glanced at my phone. The caller was Blu. *Oh my God! What am I about to do? Blu wouldn't approve if I told him what I was really doing. I mean, I'm not really doing anything, but he wouldn't like it.*

"Are you going to answer that?" Ghost asked.

"Naw! They will leave a message if it's important," I said.

Beep!

A voicemail alert message came up, so I decided to check it. "Magic, it's me. I want to come see you. Call me back." My heart started to race. What in the hell was I about to do?

Beep. Beep.

A text came through.

Blu: *What you doing?*

My phone being on overdrive had Ghost a little worried. "Is everything all right?"

"Yeah, everything is cool." I jumped from my seat unknowingly and started pacing. Blu was known for popping up, so I needed to make him think that I wasn't home. Ghost knew some shit was up, but if he wasn't going to address it neither was I.

"I like breakfast food. Can you make some of that?" I guess Ghost figured he would shift the attention onto something else.

"Yes, I sure can! One egg, bacon, cheese, and jelly sandwich on the way," I jokingly said. I got up from the table and made my way to the refrigerator to get all the things I needed. And as soon as I began to prepare his meal, the texts kept rolling in. I knew that I would need to respond.

Blu: *Hellloooo!!!??*

Magic: *My bad baby. I was cooking. What's up?*

Blu: *I want to see you*

Magic: *I'm at my auntie house right now. I will call you when I get home.*

Blu: *Why can't I come there?*

Magic: *I'm about to head home, so it wouldn't be smart for you to come all the way over here for a few seconds.*

Blu: *Oh okay. Text me as soon as you get there.*

For a moment I was slightly relieved. I was able to put the final touches on Ghost's sandwich, but my distance in our conversation was a distraction for him.

"Is it ready?" Ghost said, after getting a little bothered

by my rudeness.

"Almost!" I responded, but was really thinking of a way to pull all of this off. This wasn't just a sticky situation for me. Bianca was Blu's best friend's girl, and she was in my room busting it wide open for her other boyfriend. Like I said, Bianca was into things that I wasn't quite interested in at the moment. As we sat to eat our food, all that I could think about was time. *In about twenty minutes this nigga has to be gone, or I'll be a dead woman.* Even though Blu was a player, he was persistent and could be a little overly assertive at times, and this caused me to panic. Even if I was feeling bossy, I didn't want to mess up what we had going on. I told Ghost to take me to the store so I could get something to drink. Ten minutes had passed. If I knew Blu the way I thought I did, he would've been in the neighborhood already and would try to ride past my house. I didn't want Ghost's car outside in case he did.

"Hey, can you run me to the Mobile up the street? I'm thirsty."

"Yeah, let me tell Mike!" Ghost looked in on him and noticed that he was sleep. Nique must have been in my momma's room since Bianca was in mine. I ran to ask her what she wanted.

"Ay! Want something from the store?"

"Yeah, grab me a peach Snapple and some chips."

"Aw right! While I'm gone, try to tell Bianca ol' boy got to go. Terrence and everybody are trying to come by."

"Oh shit! Are you serious? That's not going to be good."

"I know, so let her know." I rushed the conversation because Ghost needed to be gone and fast.

"All right!"

While we were at the gas station, I notice the red Magnum going down 9 Mile as I left out of the store. Who did I see leaning his head far out the car to try to see if it was really me? Blu! I tried to play cool and just jumped in the car. I was praying to God that he didn't see me. As I stated earlier, they all went to school together, so Blu knew what kind of car Ghost had. So just off of suspicion, Blu wanted to know why Ghost was in the neighborhood and who was in the car with him. Instead of turning around, he kept going. I could see him turning down my street. *Oh shit!* This was not looking good. I just got into this relationship, and I was practically cheating already. I wasn't doing anything to be spiteful; I had good intentions. In my heart I just felt like Blu would never really want to be with me, so I was keeping my options open. He didn't see it that way. From that point on, trust was out of the window, but we continued to try to make it work anyway.

"Don't go down my street!" I said, hoping that Ghost would listen.

"What's going on? Are you okay?" he asked, still turning down my street. I couldn't even say anything. As soon as we turned the corner, Blu was pulling out of my driveway and was headed in our direction. As he drove past us, I ducked in hopes that he wouldn't see me. Although I wasn't really dating Ghost, I just felt so wrong.

"That's my boyfriend," I explained.

"Who? Them little niggas I go to school with?"

"I guess so. Please don't tell me y'all friends?"

"Naw. I'm cool with Blu's brother, but that's it." I felt a slight release from the anxiety that was starting to stack high.

Ring. Ring. Ring.

'My Blu' appeared across my screen, and I didn't know what to do so I let it go to voicemail.

Ring. Ring. Ring.

The phone sounded off, but this time it wasn't my phone ringing; it was Blu calling Ghost's phone. *What the fuck! He just told me they weren't friends. Why is he calling him? What type of shit they got going on?* At this point, my mind was racing a thousand miles per hour. My heart was beating like crazy. I've never really had a boyfriend, so this was all new to me. *Why am I already starting off on such a bad foot?*

"No, don't answer," I whispered as he picked up anyway.

"I got you. It's cool," he said back.

"What's up?" Ghost said to Blu.

"You with my girl?" Blu asked, trying to remain calm, but at this point, I knew that he was beyond pissed.

"Naw. I'm chilling with Mike," he lied, but Blu wasn't going for it.

"I just saw your car on her block."

"It wasn't me, man. I don't know what you talking about."

"Ay, man! That's my girl, so just keep it 100 with me."

"My bad, bro! I didn't know, but we all good though."

"One hundred," Blu said as he hung up.

The death stare that was given once he hung up proved that Ghost was upset with me. I never really told him I had a boyfriend. Well, I told him that I was talking to people, but when my relationship status changed, I didn't inform Ghost. I wasn't keeping anything a secret; I just didn't know when to bring it up. This was our first time seeing each other since Blu and I got together. When we went back in the house, I could feel the whole mood shift. He was colder in his responses. However, he remained cool. He just couldn't believe that I had managed to end up with one of them little niggas.

"Ay, Mike! I'm about to talk to her right quick, but we got to get out of here because ol' girl got a man. She was keeping it a secret," he said to Mike, waking him up. All I could think about was how I suddenly became "ol' girl." Just seconds ago I was "MyMy," which was the nickname he gave me. No one had ever used that name for me, but I must say I loved it.

We walked into one of the guestrooms to talk. I was embarrassed and shocked; my face was all flushed from the events that took place. I felt bad. We hadn't even seen each other that long before it all went sour.

"Why didn't you tell me you were seeing someone?"

"The relationship is fairly new, and I wasn't sure if he would be able to be faithful to me. So I figured I would keep my options open."

"Well, I don't play second to anyone. You will have to decide which one of us you want to talk to."

Who did this man think he was? I hadn't known him five minutes, and he was already demanding for me to choose. What did he think that I would say? "Oh, I should choose you because you call me MyMy?" I laughed to myself, thinking he had gone crazy.

"Are you smirking?" His question ended my laughter before it could begin.

"No, I was just processing your suggestion."

"I'm no hater, so I won't throw shade on that man; if you choose to talk to him, then that's that. I will respect him, and we can continue like we never met."

"Wow! That's pretty extreme. I've only known you five seconds, so I guess I'm rolling with Blu."

"Big mistake you just made. Good luck to you!" he said, getting up to walk through the doors. But before leaving, he bent down to kiss my forehead, and I could have just died right there. I couldn't believe this was happening. I was just starting to like him. He was such fun to be around and to talk to. He was my "'Cool Man," and I was going to miss him.

"Sorry!" I didn't have much else to say.

"You good. Guess I'll see you around." That was the last that I would see of him for a while.

Once I sent him on his way, I headed to my phone. I was sure it was loaded with tons of messages and calls from Blu.

Blu: *Damn, we ain't been together two minutes and you already cheating*

Blu: *Why Magic? I just want to know why?*

Blu: *Hello*

Blu: *I'm on my way back. He better not be there when I get there.*

As I read the texts once again, my heart was pounding and it felt as if it was about to explode this time. I burst into my room thinking that nigga was still there, but Bianca was lying on the bed naked with her 'I just got fucked' hair.

"Bitch, get up and get dressed. Your man is on the way over here." Her face was all confused, and she was just trying to enjoy the aftermath of a good nut. I, on the other hand, was about to lose all of my niggas.

"What you mean on his way over here?" she questioned.

"Like I said! Just get dressed before we both be without niggas."

"Give me a minute. Here I come!" Bianca was moving in slow motion. I left her to get her shit together while I went to find my cousin Nique. She was quiet the entire time, and I almost forgot she was there. That's how she was though. She barely said much. Just sat back, observed, and laughed at all our bullshit. She was down for me no matter what. She might have been younger than us, but she was the true mastermind.

I walked in and she was wide-eyed, giving me that 'bitch what you gon' do face.' "Magic, Blu on the way, ain't he?" Nique questioned.

"You know it. That nigga crazy!"

"What you think he gon' do?"

"I have no idea. I guess we about to find out."

"What about the guy Bianca had in there?"

"He gone, girl!"

"I don't think you should be hanging with her. All the bad shit happens when she around! It's like, you get into worse shit 'cause she trying to be sneaky with having all them niggas!" Nique said. She was always thinking about all the possible outcomes of the silly shit that we wanted to get into. I thought she was just over thinking things. I wished I had listened. Listening probably could have saved me from a world of hurt.

"What now, bitch? Why you dragging me out the bed?" Bianca said, storming into the room; apparently, she was pissed.

"Your other man is on the way, so if you plan to keep him, I suggest you go wash your pussy!"

"Why are they coming over here?" she asked, very

annoyed.

"Blu saw Ghost and me at the store. He's probably coming over to cuss me out."

"Damn, bitch, you got to be more careful," Bianca said in her normal sarcastic tone.

It wasn't even two minutes after going to find Nique that the guys had arrived. You better believe that Blu was on tip. "What the fuck, Magic? You already cheating on me?"

"No, it's not even like that. He is just a friend. We was chilling and went to the gas station. That's when you saw me outside, nothing more. I just met the guy."

"Man, that some messed up shit. You have no business fucking with anyone. You told me that you would be my girl. Is that not what you want?"

"Look, let's be real here. You and I both know how you roll. You not looking to be serious with me, you just want to take my virginity and be done with me. I know exactly how you operate."

"You sound so crazy! Magic, I fuck bitches on the daily. I have never pressured you for pussy in the two years we have been talking. I respect you 'cause you're my man's sister. When you are ready, you will let me know. What I have with them other girls isn't what I want with you. It's never been all about the sex. Don't get me wrong; I can't wait for you to give it up to me. I'm just willing to wait because I know you worth it." Blu said a mouthful that put me in my place real quick.

"Okay. Cut the bullshit. I told Ghost he could get lost. I chose you anyway. No need to explain the sob story." I gave him a smirk.

"Are you smirking at me?" Even he couldn't resist my sassy attitude. He didn't know it then, but the relationship we had would flourish and be one for the books.

"If I see you with that nigga again, it's over, Magic. I mean over!" Blu's face meant business.

"Man, you have a million 'hos calling me on the daily talking about you were just with them. Do I trip on you? No. Miss me with all that. I agreed to be with you 'cause I have hope that you will change for me."

"I can't say I'll change for you, Magic, but I'll always be honest with you."

"I can accept that." In my head I was thinking maybe I should have demanded more. I was the first girl to seriously make him work to even get my number. I didn't just drop to my knees because he asked me to. I felt as if I had everything I needed, and my mom was always in my head. She always told me that I'd better save the cookie because it wasn't worth the drama. So I tried my best to hold on to it. I never allowed peer pressure to manipulate me into doing something that I didn't want to do. So when he came begging to be with me, I made him show consistency.

As months passed, we worked on building up our trust within the relationship. At this point we were so young, and we thought we loved each other. It was crazy. I was skipping school just to go over to his house to chill. Ace let me have his white Volvo, so my girls and I would always be riding out. My mom wanted me to get used to driving before I got a brand new car. Whenever I was with Blu, he would purposely give me big ass hickeys on my neck, trying to prove a point to any nigga who stepped to me. I would be at school with a comb trying to rub that shit out before I went home. My mom would kill me if she saw that shit on my body. He had a strange way of showing his emotions. His dad passed away not too long before I came fully into the picture. This made him cold and emotionless. He needed to feel loved. Who knew that I would be the girl to fill that void. We spent every free moment that we could together. He was growing on me. Blu became the center of my little world. Things were really starting to look up, or so I thought.

Around this time, Bianca started staying with me. Her mother was always gone, so both of our mothers got cool too, and it just worked itself out. We ended up picking up a very bad habit from our parents. We would go to the mall and steal shit, but unlike us, our parents had the money to front the bill in case they were ever caught, and they would just pay. We never stole directly from people or nothing like that. We just took what the white man owed us, or at least that's how we saw it. We would hide all the shit in my car so our parents didn't know how often we really went to the mall. It was just so easy, so why not? I already had so much stuff, and I really didn't know why I was doing it. I guess it was because of the rush it gave me.

All my friends would come over every weekend; my house was the spot. Queen set it up that way though; she didn't want me to leave home, so she set the house up in a way that people would want to come over. We all grew so close to the point that Bianca ended up transferring to Oak Park High School, and the temporary stay with me was now practically permanent. I had a few people there that I knew, so I hooked Bianca up with them and she loved it there. We started to hang out with all of the people from Oak Park and ended up making a small circle of friends. This may have been the biggest mistake that I ever made. I opened my doors to entirely too many people. My best friend Treasure even transferred to Oak Park for a year. Treasure never moved in, but I would go get them from school all of the time. During this time, we started to smoke weed after school, and we would get into some serious dumb shit. If Queen found out that I was smoking weed, she would have killed me for real. Queen was a drinker, but not big on any other drugs. So for me to be doing weed would have been completely out of the question.

Blu and I tried to hide our relationship from my brother because Blu's rep wasn't the best. My brother wouldn't be too fond of the idea either.

"Hey sister. What's going on?" Ace Jr. said into the phone once I answered.

"Nothing much. Probably go to the movies later. You?"

"Same. I called to ask you about Blu. Are y'all supposed to be dating?"

"Yeah, to my knowledge we are."

"Magic, he's no good for you. He doesn't know how to love anyone. He's just not ready to be what I am sure you want. I know you will make your own choices, but as your brother, it's only right for me to speak my opinion."

"Thank you, brother. I really appreciate your honesty. I promise to be careful. However, I can't promise that I will completely stop talking to him."

"Just be careful because he supposedly loved Rhonda, and you see how that ended. He was never committed to her and led her on for all of those years. That's not what I want for you." My brother tried to warn me.

"Okay, I will. See you later tonight!" I said as I hung up the phone. It wasn't that I wasn't interested in what he was saying, but at the time I really thought what Blu and I had was something real. Yes, he was a player, but I knew that I had the power to make him really love me. If he never changed, then that would have been his loss. All I ever wanted was for him to love me, be devoted to me, and not be afraid to show the world that I was his girl. So if he did shit on the side and made his 'hos keep quiet, then there was no foul play.

Big mistake!

9
Becoming a Woman

I didn't take my brother's advice to stop talking to Blu, but I tried my best to be wise in all situations. Finally the day had arrived where my body was screaming about how ready it was. I was ready to give Blu all of me. Each time we would get together, I wanted him more and more. I was just frightened that once he got what he wanted that he would be done with me. Even with my mother in my head about saving the cookie, my inner goddess was screaming something completely different. Blu and I had been talking for three years and had only been together six months, but I knew today would be the day.

It started like any regular day. It was the end of April, and I didn't have school the next day because we were on our spring break. I made sure to put on my black lace panties with the matching bra. This particular bra made my perfect breasts sit high and pretty. He loved when I wore black underwear; it was a weakness of his. Before today I would do it just to tease him. He would hate it, but I guess that's what they mean when they say pussy is power. Too bad I didn't master the method. I always ended up learning most things the hard way. I wore my favorite pair of Joe jeans; they hugged my hips and ass just right. I knew off sight he would be ready to just rip them off. Although I had never physically participated in sex, I always had thoughts of it. I pictured how my first time would go. I would hear Queen sometimes late at night in the act, and it haunted me. I would turn my TV up really loud to indicate that I was up. She never knew that I could hear her; I was too ashamed and embarrassed to say that I did. On this day I wanted to push Queen's late night pleasures far back in my brain. I wasn't trying to let those thoughts ruin my own feelings toward the experience. I was expecting everything to be amazing! I would have no idea of what I was truly getting myself into.

The way Bianca would make it seem, I seriously thought it would be like gold dripping from the sky. I thought money would be everywhere while sitting high on the clouds, making endless love songs. I swore I thought it was going to be some true magical type shit. Nobody mentioned the first couple of times would suck a little. My phone rang, and I ran to grab it.

"Hello?" I answered, smiling.

"What you doing?" Blu asked.

"Getting dressed for practice. You?"

"Waiting on you."

"I'll be there as soon as I can."

"Hurry. I can't wait to see you!"

"Me either. Love you!"

"Love you more!"

My inner goddess was now completely on fire. I don't know why, but I wanted him, and I wanted him badly. Finally, I could give him a piece of me that no one in this world can say that they ever had. As I finished getting dressed, I found myself practically dancing around my room. I was looking for the right shirt in my drawer. I was a simple kind of girl and I loved a nice pair of jeans and a plain shirt. My matching handbag, shoes, and belt were all branded, of course. The T-shirt I decided on was from Forever 21 with the words 'Come get it Bae' printed across it. The thought of what it said caused me to laugh. Even I knew that I was a complete joke for wearing it. He would think the shirt was hilarious. I didn't wear any jewelry but my earrings. I was supposed to be going to practice, and I didn't need Queen trying to question me before I left.

"All right, Ma. We gone! See you later," I yelled into her room as I was heading out the house.

"Okay. Be safe. I'll be out tonight, so I'll be coming in kind of late. Make sure you text me when y'all make it in!"

"Okay. Love you, Ma!"

"Love you more, Magic."

Nique and I headed straight to the garage where the Volvo Ace gave me to get used to driving was parked. I was excited to see how the rest of the day would pan out. What if shit didn't go anything like I'd hoped? I would be really mad. As I turned the key into the ignition, I was keeping my mind positive so that the night could be all that I ever dreamed of. I pulled out the driveway trying to find the perfect tune to match my mood. As I rode down the Southfield freeway, I decided on my girl Rihanna.

Now that it's raining more than ever
Know that we'll still have each other
You can stand under my umbrella . . .

The words blasted through the speakers. I was in my

zone cruising to pick up Bianca. Treasure and Tiara would already be at practice, so I didn't need to get them. Once we got to Bianca, she was geeked up about some new nigga she met. Nique jumped in the back and let Bianca's extra ass sit in the passenger seat.

"Bitch, I'm not feeling practice today. I want to go see this one nigga I just started kicking it with. He is so fine!" She practically screamed in my ear while jumping in the car.

"Damn! Can you get in the car first before you start talking about some nigga?"

"I'm just saying, he's so fine. His name is Jay."

"Jay who?"

"He go to Mackenzie, I think."

"Oh, I think I know him! My mom is cool with his family." In the back of my mind I was thinking about how I secretly had been in love with him since we were kids. He was fine. Bianca and I couldn't agree more about his appearance. I mean real fine. He probably had all the bitches going crazy. I never mentioned him because he was a lot older than me, and I was with Blu. It didn't really matter what I thought of Jay, so I just admired him from a distance.

Bianca's ass was super geeked to hear that I knew him. She tried to push her luck. "You think you can put in a good word for me?"

"Probably not. I don't have any way of reaching out to him. I just see him when I'm out." Not that I wanted to put in a word anyway. She was already sleeping with enough niggas, and she didn't need to add one more to the bunch. "I'm cool with skipping practice because I want to go see Blu."

"Oh okay. What's new with you, bitch? It feels like I

haven't seen you in a forever. You gave that pussy up to Blu?"

"No. Do I look like you?" I said, jokingly. "But I think I might be ready." She was always straight to the point with shit, no sugar coating. At the time it didn't seem strange that she always wanted to know what was new with Blu and me. We barely talked about her and Terrence. When I brought his name up, she would keep it short and say that they were good, then proceed with her questionnaire about Blu. I just thought she was being a friend and was ready for someone other than herself to be having sex out of the crew.

Before Bianca could come back with her comments, Nique tapped me and whispered in my ear, "Look bitch, I told you to watch your back. You see all she wanna know is about you and Blu. She ain't really riding with us"

"Girl chill." I laughed it off, trying not to bring to much attention to the conversation. I loved Bianca and would kill for her. Even though the relationship started out rocky, we had a true bond. She was my sister, and I didn't think of her as anything less than just that. So it was hard to believe she would do anything to purposely hurt me.

"Whatever!" Bianca chimed back in. "You aren't ready for them big girl games. Want me to teach you a few tricks?" she joked, as she reversed in the passenger seat, straddling it.

We all burst out laughing. "You're a fool! No, I'm good."

As we headed to practice, we were cruising up Livernois getting stopped by every light. It was cool though because it gave me time to plan my events for later in my head. *"We Fly High"* by Jim Jones came on the radio and quieted my train of thought.

♪ *We fly high, no lie, you know this (Balling!)*
Foreign rides, outside, it's like showbiz (We in the
building) ♪

We were all jamming. When this song came on, everybody would go crazy; especially at the teen parties my cousins Marie, Tracy, and myself were throwing. We thought we were the true BossFam! We came up with this idea because we were more than friends; we were a family. When people saw us, we were always throwing up our B's. There were three other girls who used to roll out with us too.

But let's get this straight before y'all get to questioning how many crews I hung with. BossFam was my family by blood. Treasure, Tiara, Bianca, and Nique were my real family by loyalty.

I loved my BossFam very much. However, most times it was always a competition. They didn't like to see someone else doing better than them. They were into all that material stuff. If it came down to getting braces or getting a new bag, they would choose the bag any day. Just dumb shit! I would rather have perfect teeth, than carry around a dusty ass bag because after a few years, it wouldn't be worth anything anyway. Even though I was young, my mental state always balanced out what was important. Don't get me wrong, I liked nice shit too, but my life didn't depend on it. My momma enjoyed flowering me with those things, so it was naturally a part of me. I didn't need to compete with anyone. I was born with it. Period!

My BossFam didn't always grasp the concept that there was no need to compete. They failed to mention to the world that they weren't always the "it" kids. Vicky

Uncorrected Proof   115   Uncorrected Proof

wasn't into buying kids Gucci, Louie, Prada, etc. She may have had the money, but that wasn't her style. In the generation that we live in, kids are looked at as outsiders if they don't have these things. This concept is pretty sad and very disturbing. *When I raise a child one day, I hope I can keep him/her humble and free-spirited; not caring what society wants them to be. I have a long time before that happens, but I know I'll do my best not to let him/her be corrupted by the idea of needing material things.*

When we were arriving at the gas station, Bianca noticed that I was in my own world, so she snapped at me trying to bring me back to whatever shit she was talking about.

"Bitch, what are you thinking about?"

"Can I just be Magic for once, bitch? I was just thinking about my future kids and how I don't want them to be corrupted by society and material things."

"Hold the fuck up! You ain't even having sex yet, and already you know how you want to raise your kids?" Bianca practically burst into tears and laughter as she spoke.

"I'm just saying that we have to think about these things. With my fucked up ass family, I just want my kids to know what it means to be loved by your own blood." I guess I was sounding a little crazy talking about kids, and I hadn't even done anything yet. I had to laugh at myself as well.

"Oh okay. I see you over there on your sentimental shit. Bitch, you have a family. We might not be blood, but you're my sister."

When Bianca said shit like that, how could I ever think she wasn't down for me? How could I ever second-guess her loyalty?

As we drove to Blu's house, I went back into thinking mode. I swear I could never stop thinking. My relationship with my dad's side was really messed up. Aside from my brother and my male cousins, I wasn't close to anyone. It was like Pinky and Vicky only accepted the kids who came from one of their vaginas. If one of the men made children, they would rank of no importance. And this caused separation from the beginning. There was no loyalty between Marie, Tracey, and myself. I was always the outsider when it came to them. It may not have been the best method of dealing with things, but after a while I just stopped considering them as family. Blood wasn't always thicker than water. As much as I would have loved to be included, they had always made things competitive. Vicky made it no better; she was supposed to be the rock of the family, or the glue to bring us together. Hell! I was lucky if I received a call on my birthday. If this happened, it would be the only time that I would hear from her all year. So you can just imagine how distant the relationships really were.

Finally we arrived to Blu's house, and this would be the moment when my whole life would change. I started contemplating if I should change my mind. *Am I really ready for this? Will he finally see that I didn't want to be with anybody but him?* There were many unanswered questions, and of course, I started to panic. My stomach was turning and my palms were sweaty. I was beyond nervous.

Bianca shot straight to Blu's room with Terrance, wasting no time. She was practically a pro at sex, so she didn't need to contemplate anything. She was good and ready. She didn't drift off before taunting me. "Remember what I taught you!" Bianca was always playing around.

Blu was confused. "What she talking about?"

"Come get it bae?" he asked with a smirk, reading the print on my T-shirt.

"I figured you would get a kick out of it."

"Well, I could do more than that!"

"I'm sure you could, but let's wait a little longer on that!" I didn't want him to think he was the one calling the shots. I figured I would make him wait just a little longer. We headed over to the couch to join Nique.

Blu, Nique, and I were watching TV in the living room. He was sitting to my left with his legs resting across my lap, and Nique was to my right. I hadn't told Nique what my intentions were for coming over to Blu's house, because I preferred to tell her in the last second. I knew that Nique would try to get me to consider a million factors, and I had done enough thinking. I leaned over and whispered to her.

"I think I'm ready."

"For what?" Nique asked.

"You know. *It!*"

"Are you sure, Magic?" The look on her face was priceless.

"I think so!" I said this to reassure myself. In my head I was thinking, *Who is ever really ready for this moment? Who wants to just lose their virginity because they know exactly how everything will feel?* I imagined there would be rose petals laid out in a hotel room on my prom night, or something similar. I didn't think people lost their virginities with five people in one apartment. I loved him though, and that's all that mattered. I was about to just get it over with.

I leaned up so close to his ear so that he could feel the heat from my breath. I whispered in my sexiest voice,

"I'm ready." I had the slickest grin on my face.

"Really!" His brown eyes lit up like a kid on Christmas. He couldn't believe it. I couldn't wait to run my fingers through his braids.

"Yes. I want to show you how much I really love you!" There was so much sexual tension between us. My heartbeat was steady. I was starting to soak up my black panties.

"Okay, let's go!" He displayed a smirk while positioning himself to get up and reach for my hand. He led us to the back room. We walked past his room, and I heard Bianca screaming and moaning.

"Right there, daddy! Don't stop!" There was something about the smacking and yelling that was turning me on. Suddenly I wasn't scared anymore. I was ready to experience sex. I wanted to call him a sexy name that would turn him on. I wasn't sure what he liked to be called: daddy, big daddy, papi, or just Blu. *Aw man! I am doomed. This is going to be the worst sex that he has ever had. I don't know what to do.* I guess I really hadn't thought about it. I tried playing it off.

"Don't mind her." I needed some kind of pep talk. I wish Treasure were here; she would be able to tell me what to do. *You can do it! It won't hurt that bad. He loves you, right?* My inner person started to scream at me. *Everybody is doing it, just get it over with!*

I was so excited to see Blu. I leaped with excitement to hug him. After a brief embrace, he stepped back to admire me for a second.

He must have felt me starting to tense up because he grabbed my shoulders and spoke in my ear. "Don't worry. I got you!" he whispered as we entered his mom's room. Yes, you heard it right! We were about to enter into his mom's room. This wasn't the way that I expected my magical moment to be. However, his words were well needed, and they helped me loosen up.

He started with slow, soft kisses traveling from the top of my ear to the right side of my neck. His kisses were so seductive that I could feel my heart finally slow down. His tongue then swirled in circles, which caused my insides to release juices. I was flushed with embarrassment because I didn't know if this was normal. My thighs were soaked and he hadn't even undressed me yet.

"Wait!" I didn't know how, but words had actually managed to escape my lips. Disregarding my plea to stop, his hands were now rubbing my backside. Then he trickled his fingers just beneath my shirt. In a swift motion and still standing behind me, he lifted my T-shirt over my head. Suddenly, he stopped. *Maybe he doesn't want to do this with me. Maybe he doesn't really love me the way that he said he did.* So many different thoughts raced through my head in seconds.

"What's wrong?" I turned to finally look in his eyes. He hated when I did that. He said I had a way of really looking into his soul or something. My eyes were captivating. If I was lucky to get you to look into them, they would have you hooked.

"You wore black. You know what that does to me. I feel like you knew this was going to happen today."

"Of course I knew. Now let's get back to it." I was anxious to get it over with and see what the whole sex thing was all about.

"Whatever you do, don't do it like I'm everyone else. I want you to make love to my mind and my body. I want you to know that this is yours, and I'm hoping you will commit to being mine."

"All I can promise is that I will not hurt you." I think my love talk was not what he was expecting. I shook my head and agreed for him to continue. I made a mental note to bring it up again, but for now I just wanted him inside of me.

Spinning me once more to finish what he had started, he was now kissing my left ear just as he had done before. I had done a little too much talking, but all of those same emotions that I had before my interruptions, were starting to rush through my body again. I could feel him growing beneath his basketball shorts.

Even with my inexperience, my natural instinct was to grab and touch it. I had no idea what I was doing, but I knew he would teach me if I did something wrong.

"Oh, you know how to get the party started I see," he joked as I grabbed "The Johnson."

"I told you this was mine."

"You don't play fair, Magic."

"There are no rules in this game."

Blu slipped his fingers under my bra cup and started to caress my nipples with his index finger. He stroked my nipples up and down repeatedly. My body practically screamed for more of whatever he had to offer. My young curvaceous body was no match for this young man. I was losing and hadn't even really started yet.

"I should make you cum like this," he whispered ever so soft.

"No, I want more," I managed to whisper back.

With those words and in one motion, my bra was now to the floor. I'm sure he could see my heart pounding through my chest. I was in heat, and there was no way for me to control myself. I was excited, scared, and wet! Super wet! Kisses were traveling down from my navel to my hairline. Undoing my button and sliding my pants down, my naturally long legs would lay bare. He couldn't resist kissing them. He traced every inch with a kiss. At the tender age of fifteen, I could honestly say that I was a Bad Bitch!

"You ready, Magic?" he asked, bringing me to the floor where it was all about to happen.

"More than I'll ever be." I mustered up the courage to speak proudly.

We were on the floor. I was lying on my back, and Blu was positioned on his knees. I didn't know what was to come next, but my nipples were hard and so was The Johnson. Immediately, I could feel his tongue licking my inner left thigh.

"Ahhhh!" I moaned, trying to keep my composure, but there was no point. I had lost all control.

He began to pull my panties to the side. While placing his tongue on the tip of my clitoris, he said, "You're so wet, Magic. I think you ready. Not before I taste you though." After five minutes of constant sucking and licking on and around my clitoris, something escaped from my body that I couldn't control.

"What the fuck!" my inner goddess screamed out. My body shook uncontrollably. *Holy shit! What was that? Was that normal?*

"Magic, the taste of your cum is truly magical!"

Oh shit. That's it! That's what makes women crazy? Finally, my first orgasm! If this is what sex felt like, I will be in love.

"I want to feel you inside." I wanted more but could barely breathe.

"Be patient. I'll have my turn," he said as he stood to remove his clothes. He stood in front of me completely naked; except for his socks. He had really hairy legs, but his stomach was to die for; I just wanted to kiss every pack of his. His Johnson stood at attention and was ready to go. I couldn't wait another minute. *Oh my goodness! This is really happening!*

Now lying on top of me, he slowly inserted two fingers inside of my vagina. I was still wet, although Blu had sucked every drop of cum that left my body. Blu was trying to prepare my walls for the torture they were about to experience. Even his two fingers felt good as they rubbed my clit and massaged my walls. As he released his fingers, he placed them in his mouth to taste me once more.

"Mmm . . . You taste so good!" There was something about his tone that caused my nipples to harden again.

Now with his johnson in hand, he attempted to push the head in. I tried to keep my brave face on during the failed attempt. My vagina was too tight, and my legs naturally tried to close and push him away. My body wasn't ready, but there was no turning back.

"Relax," he whispered as he planted a kiss on my forehead. His lips moved down toward my neck. His kisses would release the tension in my body. His tactics worked because as soon as I relaxed, my legs lay lifeless, giving his johnson permission to enter with one forceful push.

"Oweeee!" I screamed, without any anticipation for what was happening. It was really painful.

"Just relax. It won't hurt. I . . . love . . . you . . ." He managed to speak in-between strokes. I could tell this was quite a job for him because the once cool, calm, collected man was now sweating showers all over me.

Yuck! I screamed in my head. *Let's take this back to the part where my insides were getting licked because this shit is gross. I can't believe people are actually in love with this shit.* By the look on his face, I could tell this was everything he expected. He was kissing me non-stop and never took his eyes off of mine. After about ten minutes, his body trembled and his eyes were rolling. I knew that he was releasing the same explosion that I did.

"You're mine now!" He said this right before he collapsed on top of me.

I didn't respond and that made him question me. "Are you okay, Magic?"

"No, honestly that was terrible. I hated every minute of you being on top of me. I know it has to get better, so I'll give it more time." I started to get up when I noticed blood on the sheets that we laid out on the floor. "Oh shit! How you gon' explain this to your mother?" I said, pointing to the blood on the sheets.

"Fuck! I'll take care of that. I'm happy though, because at least I know that I'm the only one hitting that." I wasn't surprised by his boastful rant. I knew he couldn't say that I was the first virgin that he fucked, so I guess I could deal with his prideful moment.

"Come on. Get up. It's getting late. It's time to get dressed." Talk about killing the mood. We had been lounging around chatting and admiring each other's bodies. But I guess we were in his mother's room, and truthfully, we couldn't stay there forever. My own mother would be checking for me soon.

I felt bad for leaving Nique out there for so long. As I got up with my 'I just got fucked hair' I needed to brush it back into place. I began to get dressed, but my body felt weird. It felt out of place and not at all like the body that I had grown into over the years. Was my body really his now? I wanted to scream. I wasn't sure if my scream would be filled with joy, excitement, or fear. There were so many different emotions going on, and I didn't know what to do with them.

Finally, all my hair was in its place, and it was time to slip my clothes back on. I watched Blu as he slipped into his shorts, leaving his shirt behind. Maybe leaving his shirt was his non-verbal way of letting Terrance and everyone else in the house know that he'd just got done fucking me. I guess you could say that I was a woman now. There was just too much to think of at the moment, so I decided to just head out and go see Nique.

"Hey, you okay up here?" I asked, trying to hold back my emotions. I didn't know if I wanted to jump for joy because I'd finally got it over with, or cry because I felt like a fool. *My momma told me to save myself. What was I thinking? This man doesn't love me for real.*

"I'm good! The better question is are you okay?" she said, half laughing

"Sore," I responded, giving it all away in one word.

"Did it hurt?" She wasted no time trying to get all of the details.

"We can discuss this later. I heard Blu coming in here. Just know that it wasn't what I expected it to be. Promise me you will wait?"

"I heard it gets better, be patient!"

"Let me go get Bianca. It's time to go. The sun is about to go down, and we don't have a headlight."

"Magic, you okay?" Blu asked as we were leaving.

"I'm good. I just feel weird. Talk to you later," I said,

giving him a hug good-bye. I practically raced to my car. My mind was still stuck on the events that just took place. *Wow! That really just happened.*

"Bitch, did you do what I think you just did?" Bianca's ghetto behind was practically screaming while getting in the car.

"You always trying to figure out what's new with me!" Now I was feeling slightly cocky because I thought I was grown. Something inside of me shifted, and I was now more confident.

"Bitch, you ain't a baby no more, huh?" she taunted me.

"We all have to grow up some time!" I tried to play it cool like I wasn't frightened by the thought that I gave someone my most precious jewel. Someone who I wasn't sure was worthy.

As we headed home, I started to entertain my thoughts. *Did that really just happen? Was that it? Will I ever hear from him again?* Something wasn't sitting well on my heart. Blu was known for that type of behavior. He would fuck you, and then never call you again. Was that going to happen to me? I guess I would just have to wait and see.

"You're always thinking, Magic!" Bianca's words were able to break me from my mental coma.

"Got to stay on my toes, you know?"

As we pulled up to the house, I just wanted to run to the bathroom and wash Blu's touch off of me. I felt dirty! I felt cheap! I scrubbed my legs and inner thighs where Blu did most of his kissing. I could still feel him there and reality was starting to cut me deep inside. *Why did I just do that?*

"I'm bleeding. Is that normal?" I asked Bianca.

"Panty mayonnaise! Bitch finally got her cherry popped," she said, bursting into tears with laughter.

"You make me sick!" I said, rolling my eyes. Why couldn't she just be on two for a just a moment. Bianca's ass always stayed on ten.

"Whatever! Join the club!"

Finally Bianca wasn't the only one in the sex club. She had someone to talk to about sexual experiences. I wasn't sure if I was as happy as she was about belonging to the club. Then it hit me. I didn't even use a fucking condom.

God, please don't let me be pregnant.

10
All Hell Breaks Loose

The very next day Queen decided to bring Bianca up while we were folding clothes she had just washed. "What you and Bianca do yesterday when you skipped practice?"

"Oh, the usual. It was hot. We wanted to be out in the world, so we rode around and stopped over a few people houses to chill." I started looking down at my hands and fidgeting a little. She must have noticed because her direction of questioning changed.

"Oh okay. So Bianca and Terrance are a thing. I know she probably sleeping with him. She a little hot box I heard," she jokingly said.

I was just happy that she wasn't asking me about Blu. I never knew how to lie to my mother. She had a way of sensing the truth. I most definitely tried, but maybe it was the way that I said things that would always give it away. She had an invisible lie detector. Queen always asked questions about my friends, so I wasn't surprised by the questionnaire. I felt safe when I willingly gave up the information on Bianca. Joining Queen in a laugh I said, "You know it, girl. She sleep with all her male friends."

"Magic, have you slept with Blu?" she asked, in a more serious tone, and I knew she wasn't to be fucked with right now. It was quite impressive how she just slid that into our very casual conversation. I wasn't expecting that at all.

"Naw, Ma. We haven't." She could tell in my eyes that I was lying. How did she know? She always knew something new happened before I had the chance to tell her. She would say that I was hers and nothing could get past her. It was no surprise that she already knew and just wanted me to tell her the truth. It was only one day since the shit took place. I couldn't believe that she was already questioning me about it.

"Really, Magic? You gon' lie?"

"I'm not lying. We haven't had sex yet."

"I won't get mad. Just tell me." She was doing her best to get information out of me. I should have known that it was a trap. Queen got mad over little shit, and I knew that losing my virginity would be in the category of 'big shit.' I shouldn't have trusted her.

"Yes, we did, but only once though."

"When?" Her face was all twisted up, but her voice was calm.

"Yesterday," I confessed, with my head hanging low. I knew Queen would be disappointed in me. She wanted me to save myself for my husband. I was goal-oriented and headed in the right direction, and Queen knew that Blu was the opposite. Blu was somebody who switched girlfriends more than he changed clothes. There was nothing about us that matched up. I looked in Queen's direction, hoping that she looked as calm as she sounded seconds ago. Steam was coming from Queen's head as she started to ask the next question.

"Did you use a condom?"

"Yes, mother," I tried to reassure her.

"Bitch, you're a liar and a fuckin' dirt ball!" Queen was furious, and before I knew it, the left side of my face was stinging. Her blows just started flying from everywhere. She was slapping me in my face and punching me in the chest.

"You . . . STUPID . . . LITTLE . . . BITCH. Did I not teach you anything? Do you know how many diseases it is out here?" she managed to yell louder with each blow to my face, stomach, and back. It was like Queen blacked out, and her only mission was to *attack*. Just like all of the other ass beatings that I got, I couldn't shed one tear. Even when I saw the blood drip from my lip, I just licked it. I wanted to scream and call her bitches right back, but she was my mother and I knew better than that. I wouldn't have made it out of that one alive if I had followed all the way through with what I was thinking. I kept my game face on until the beating was finished.

After the usual ten minutes, she was tired and I was done being all of the bitches, 'hos, tricks, dummies, and sluts that she could think of. Don't get me wrong, I did make a big mistake with having sex with no protection. However, I was almost positive that there was a better approach that she could have taken.

I was condemned to my room: no TV, no cell phone, and no computer. What in the hell was I going to do? She would probably take my car privileges away next. I had nothing but stuffed animals to entertain me and a pen and paper to keep my thoughts company. I decided to write a letter.

Dear Queen,

Today, April 21st 2006, I told you I had sex. Your

reaction wasn't like the typical parent who would just cry and curse their child out for not being a baby anymore. Instead you beat me and made me bleed. You called me all sorts of foul names. I was a bunch of bitches, hoes, and sluts to you. How could my own mother have such ill feelings towards me? What did I ever do to deserve this? Sure, you buy me all types of nice things, but that doesn't make up for the physical and verbal abuse. How could you disrespect the one and only human being that you birthed? Today, I'm making a vow to never disrespect any child of mine in that manner. I will never call them out of their name. I'll do my best to control my anger and not hit them. You've never taught me to wear condoms. We've never sat down and really discussed sex. If you would have been a little more approachable as a mother, then I wouldn't be so afraid of you. I would have come to you when I thought I was ready if I felt like I could. Instead I was sneaking behind your back and you were forced to pry information out of me. I would love to be able to talk to you about these things because how else can I learn? Ace is never around to do his fatherly duties, so I don't have it all figured out. When he comes around, his goal is to always make it fun for me. He doesn't know how to be a father. I love him to death, but even at my age, I know that life is about more than just fun times. Ace wasn't raised to be the type of father that I long for. However, he does his best. I don't fault him. At least I can say that I know he loves me. I am sure that he would have a serious problem with you putting your hands on me the way that you do. Whenever I have children, I will never mimic your actions. I want to be a mother, friend, and protector to mine. You are so cold and I am always scared to tell you anything at all. I remember when I was seven years old in the tub and I noticed that I started to grow hair down there and pointed it out to you. You went ballistic. You *called me a bitch, told me that little girls didn't have hair, and how it wasn't cute that I pointed it out. From that point on I was scared shitless of you. I swore to never tell you anything. I figured telling you things would only grant me beatings or very degrading words that I knew that I didn't deserve. I'm not a bad child. I get all A's in school. I'm not out here fucking a million niggas. I only fucked one person and you do me like this? You know what? FUCK you! You make me sick.*

With love,

Magic

It was finally Monday, time to return to school from spring break. It had also been two days since the fight with my mom. We had barely spoken since then. I locked myself in my room and only came out to use the bathroom. Queen tried to feed me once, but I turned it down; I was just that angry. I thought she was going to drive me to school since she had revoked everything else. But as I headed to her room to let her know that I was ready, she handed me my keys without exchanging a single word. I was free at last. She didn't hand me my phone, so I knew that I was still in the doghouse.

"Come straight home from school, Magic! I will know if you didn't go either!" she yelled, before slamming her door.

I couldn't stand my mother sometimes because she could be a real pain in my ass. Even though I knew she was lazy and wasn't going to be checking to see if I really went to school, I wasn't in the mood to test her. I was glad to just get out of that hell hole. I missed my school friends, and I couldn't wait to tell them what happened to me over break. I made sure to stop at Tim Horton's before school because I was starving. On my way to school, I thought of Blu for the first time since we last saw each other. I wondered if he tried to call. *Was he worried about me? Has he forgotten about me already? He probably thinks I'm ignoring his calls. I'm sure the lovely Queen called to threaten him to never call me again. Would he listen to her? I guess I'll have to try calling him off somebody else's phone when I get to school.*

"Hey, Magic!" All the people in the senior hallway yelled to me as I walked to my locker. I actually didn't have friends in my grade yet, except for the ones who went to Thompson with me. Rushing through the hallway, I spoke to everyone briefly. I didn't want to be late.

"Hey, y'all! I will see you guys at lunch. I got to get to class."

I sat at lunch with a few of my school friends, CeCe and BeBe, they were twins and I grew up with them. My mom used dated their dad when I was younger. We would always leave campus and go to Little Caesars, or the chicken and waffle spot they put on Twelve Mile and Lasher. Once I told them about my week of activities, everyone in the car dropped their mouths to the floor. First of all, they never thought I would have given it up to Blu. Secondly, they couldn't believe the way my momma acted when she found out. Lastly, they were in awe of the fact that my first encounter lasted more than two minutes. They all had very bad experiences for their first time. Fifteen minutes of sharing precise details went by, and I had them bitches wondering what it would have been like if they were in my position.

"Have you talked to Blu?" BeBe asked.

"No, my mom took my phone. Can I use yours to try to call him?"

"Yeah, go ahead!" BeBe reached in her purse and handed me her phone.

I decided to text him. That decision was a big mistake, but I wouldn't figure that out until later. You never know who your real friends are, especially in moments of celebration. You have to always be careful to measure the amount of information that you're giving away. Not everyone can take the same dosages, and true colors often take too long to show. Your best bet is to trust no bitch. They are all out to get you.

BeBe: *Hey Blu. It's Magic!*

He called BeBe's phone instantly.

"Are you okay?" he asked. Hearing his voice allowed me to relax for the first time in days.

"Yes, I'm better now. Has my mom called you?"

"Yeah, she was hurt. She cried and asked me why I did that to you. She doesn't want us to talk anymore."

"Yeah . . . I figured she would do something like that. Well, I understand if you don't want to talk to me. I'm sure that she threatened your life and everything else."

"Magic, you think your mother can keep me from you? You might have forgotten who I really am and what it is that I want from you. This wasn't a one-time thing. I want you forever."

"Well, I'll talk to you when I can. I got to go back to school."

"Come see me later."

"I'm still on lockdown! I'll have to catch you another time."

"All right, Magic." Blu said as I hung the phone up.

When I got back in the school, there was a note posted on my locker. The message read: ***head to office immediately!*** *What the fuck is this about?* When I got there, I was told by one of the secretaries to call home because my mother needed to speak with me.

"Magic, there's a health clinic on Eleven Mile and Greenfield. You need to go there after school and get checked out."

"Ma! Are you serious?"

"Do it sound like I'm playing? Take your ID and tell them you need to be checked for everything!"

"All right, Ma."

When I arrived at the doctor's office, my mind couldn't rest. My heart was pounding! Could I really have AIDS? Could I be pregnant? How could I be pregnant? Could my life really be over after making one stupid mistake? My mind and body couldn't process all of the awful possibilities. *Why did she make me come to this clinic alone?* Yes, I made a grown woman move, but I needed my mother. *If it turns out that I have something, or something is wrong, she should be here holding my hand.* This was some fucked up shit! Being a new woman was getting too complicated.

I pulled into a parking spot, but something in me felt uneasy, so I decided to find a different one.

Skkkkrrrrrrrr!

This sound was all that I heard once I hit the car to the right of me. I was backing out and forgot to look to the front. I had my head turned and was concentrating on moving backward. I completely avoided the parked cars to the left and right of me.

"Shit! I just ruined Ace's car." All of the nerves were getting the best of me. I had lost control. *What do I do now? Do I flee the scene? Do I stay?*

I decided to just pull into another spot. I was hoping the owner of the car that I hit wouldn't notice any damages to their car until they were long gone. I needed this checkup, so I had to go in here. Once I signed in, I called my mother from the office's phone and explained what happened. Queen was there in less than ten minutes.

"What the fuck, Magic? Why didn't you just leave? Now the police are out there! You know I hate the fucking police. I got to go out there and lie to them crackers and act like I did it. You not even supposed to be driving!"

"I didn't have a phone, and I wasn't sure what to do. I'm sorry! I was scared."

"Oh, now you scared? You got your nerve! Go finish doing what you were doing in there. So I can go handle this."

Two minutes later, the doctor came in and gave me my 'Negative' test results and a sense of relief filled the both of us. We got up and gathered our stuff to go face the music that awaited us outside the free clinic.

"Now when we get out here you better start crying, acting like you just got the worst news of your life. Because bitch, that's what could've happened. You got lucky this time, but you better strap up. These niggas will put they dick in anything," she coached and fake-parented me in a matter of seconds.

Once we were outside, Queen walked right up to the police officer, praying he would be so moved by my sad story so the person I hit wouldn't press charges against me.

"Hey officer, that's my vehicle. I was distracted when I got a call from my daughter. She'd just received some terrible news, and I let go of the wheel by mistake," Queen explained. "I needed to get in there and be with my daughter, so I parked anyway to tend to her." Queen was so quick with the lie. I couldn't believe it. I forced tears in my eyes to try to help her with story.

"Yes, ma'am I'm sorry to hear that! I almost called it in as a hit and run. I appreciate you for coming out here to handle this. If you will just provide the other driver with your insurance information, we can write up the report and you can be on your way," the officer explained in one breath.

It looked like we were let off the hook this time, but I knew Queen's hook just got an even deeper grip in me, She wasn't letting me out her sight for a while.

11
Now What?

Weeks had passed, and there was still no word from Blu. My mom finally calmed down, gave me my phone back, and wasn't all into my business every second of the day. Blu's disappearance had me thinking that all of the rumors about him were true. I guess once he fucks you, he really leaves you. He used me! He used me good. He took my most prized possession and left me like I never existed. My biggest fear with dealing with Blu had now surfaced. I wish Blu's actions could've been enough for me to really digest some valuable things. It would take years for me to gain a glimpse of my self-worth.

One thing that I did know was I had more pride than anything. Some people would say that I was just plain out stubborn, but that wasn't the case. I always had enough discipline to stick to my guns on things. No matter how hurt I was about the way that Blu was treating me, I wouldn't let him know. If he wasn't going to call, neither was I. After about three weeks of no Blu, I thought that I would give Ghost a chance again. Hell! It didn't feel as if I was in a relationship with anyone. Who would I be hurting? At this point, the only person hurting was me!

Magic: *Hey stranger!*
Ghost: *MyMy! Thought I would never hear from you again*
Magic: *How have you been? Lunch one day this week?*
Ghost: *Good. Yes, I'll pick you up Tuesday.*
Magic: *Cool! I'll see you then.*
Ghost: *Ok.*

Tuesday came and I was straight bugging. I didn't think Ghost would have agreed to see me considering I didn't choose him after he dished out an ultimatum. My decision cost me more than just a few weeks without speaking to Ghost, it cost me my virginity. Ghost was a good guy, and if he would have thrown salt on Blu from the beginning, I probably wouldn't have been in this messed up situation. Nonetheless, I was just excited he was actually coming to pick me up. Lunchtime wasn't coming fast enough, and I was anxious to tell him about all the shit that went down with Queen. I knew he would be a little upset to hear about all of it, but I had to tell him. He was always a good listener and so easy to talk to. It took no time to feel comfortable around him. I often thought of how it would have been if Ghost was the one that I gave my cookie to instead.

Twelve o'clock hit, and I was practically racing to doors that would free me to Ghost. It had been so long since I had friends over, or did anything besides go to school and come right back home. Yes, I was excited to see him, but I was more excited to be in the presence of someone other than Queen and the people that I went to school with.

Just as he did a few months ago, he pulled into the school's parking lot with his car shining like no other. I wanted all the bitches to see me leaving with him. I made sure to walk out with the rest of the posse. When everyone saw him pulling up, people were trying to figure out who the hell he was.

"Bitch, who is that pulling up driving in that BMW?" CeCe asked.

"Oh Ghost? That's my friend. We going to lunch!" I tried to say as unbothered as I could. I didn't need them to know how hard I was sweating him. In the back of my head I was thinking *He's mine, bitches, keep your paws off.*

"Ghost could definitely do more than just take my ass to lunch!" CeCe responded.

My insides were jumping. I was excited to be the one hopping in the car of a man who they didn't know. I wanted them to witness me being around another guy so that they wouldn't know about my stresses with Blu. In that moment, all these bitches wanted to be me. And I swear I loved every second of the long stares and wishful thinking faces. The few weeks of no Blu had me questioning my crown. Was I still the girl that people envied and hated?

Of course there is always that one person who just can't let shit go and has to know exactly what's really going on. Not that she cared, but she just needed to know for her own peace of mind. "What about Blu? You know he gone kill you once he finds this out!" BeBe managed to get a slick comment out as usual. Her tone was nasty. As she spoke, I translated what she was really trying to say: *Little bitch, you better be careful before I attempt to take this man you flashing in front of us.*

"The only way for him to find out is if you tell him! I'll see y'all later. Enjoy y'all lunch!" I skipped off to the car leaving them all behind. I didn't care what anyone thought about me at that point, and especially not Blu's ass! He hadn't called once to even see how the hell I was doing, so why should I care?

"Hey, Ghost! I've missed you." I attempted hugging him as I got in the car, but he wasn't very welcoming. I guess he was still a little upset with the way things turned out. It didn't matter though, because he was right beside me and that was all that mattered.

"Don't act like you like me now!" he said. I had to think who the bitch in the car really was, him or me? I needed to get on his good side and fast. In his mind he'd lost a girl to a lame ass nigga who wasn't even in the same league as him. *What can I say to butter this man up?*

"I do like you! I just didn't know you well enough to choose you at the time." I figured the truth would do more justice here.

"Well, you could have just said you needed more time to decide. You didn't even think twice about it. 'I choose Blu! That's who I want to be with!'" He was mimicking me from our last encounter. "Where he at now, Magic? You *still* playing games."

I was appalled at the fact that this man wasn't to be fucked with. Either I was going to seriously give him a shot, or I needed to get lost quick. He was over the kid games. All of the women around him at the time were young and full of games; he didn't need another one added to his list. I bit the bullet and took the blame.

"You're right. I can't change what I did, but I'll do my best to show you that I'm not here just to fuck with your feelings. Let's just be friends and see where it goes. I thought what I had with Blu was something worth keeping, but apparently he never intended to keep me."

Not even twenty minutes into my lunch I received a

text.

Blu: *Damn. I guess you fucking him too!*

This man had a lot of nerve. He couldn't possibly think that he was in the right to check me at all. I didn't even respond; I wasn't about to have the same thing unfold like last time. I just let the man think whatever he wanted. *How did he even know that I was with Ghost? Who told him? I swear you can't do anything these days without people trying to involve themselves in your business.* I was never the type to focus on what someone else had going on. I minded my own business and left people to mind theirs. The lunch date ended up being great! I didn't let Blu's text ruin my mood. After Ghost and I talked for a while, I was back to being 'MyMy!' We agreed to leave what happened behind us in the past and decided to just focus on getting to know one another. From that day forward, we would talk nonstop. Ghost became my best friend, and we would talk about everything under the sun.

Ghost basically lived in an apartment by himself. He started working at the age of twelve, and that's how he could afford the things that normal people in our age range couldn't. Ghost knew what was important in his life: his savings and his credit. He taught me all about this stuff. The goal was to beat the system; never let the white man own you. Make him owe you! Ghost would preach the same speech about beating the system that I basically had it memorized. Ghost was on another level! He was always doing what he had to do to live a better life than the one given to him. His mind was what I liked most about him. He had shit together and would try to enlighten me as much as possible. I remember our first official date. Well, it was more of a group thing, but I was with him and that's all that mattered.

One day all of the girls were over, and we knew that

we would be getting into something. Treasure, Tiara, Bianca, Nique, and I were all out riding my go-cart and two bikes. My momma had just left and told us we couldn't have any company over. We thought we could outsmart Queen and be a little slick. Instead of our company coming to the house, we would just meet them around the corner. Yet, Queen either left something at the house, or had a hunch that we were up to something. I saw her car flying fast down the street; she had to be doing about sixty on a residential street. Her speed came at the same time that Ghost was about to pull up. I flagged for him to keep going and immediately texted to say we would meet up later.

"Go! Just keep going," I mouthed to him as I signaled with my hands for him to pass us. Just as I mentioned, Queen was there and was ready to go off on somebody.

"Magic, you think you slick?"

"No. We are just out here riding around in the go carts."

"Whatever! Where is Tiara and Bianca?" *Oh shit!* I had completely forgotten about them. *They must be around the corner with their niggas.* What the hell was I about to do?

"I don't know. They're riding around on the bikes." She raced back to her car, determined to catch them doing something. *I hope the boys are gone by the time she finds them.* Unfortunately, Tiara and Bianca weren't so lucky. My momma caught them around the corner with boys and she caused hell.

"Y'all are not slick. Get in this fucking car and tell your little friends bye!" Queen was on fire, and at that moment she badly wished they were her own kids so she could beat their asses. Once they made it back to the house, Queen was running around trying to hit all of us. She was so mad that she told Tiara to get her shit and leave. It was so funny. And to make matters worse, while Queen was on her rampage swinging after us, she fell right on her fat ass! Her fall came after running around on our hardwood floors without shoes on. It was the funniest shit I had ever seen! We couldn't laugh right when it happened because that would have only made her more upset. Once she finished her rant, we all laughed for days about her fall.

She was always quick to get over the stuff that we did, so we decided to just strategize on another plan. Later that day we told her that we were going with our big sister Lanae. We knew that was the only way she would allow us to go anywhere. We told Lanae to come pick us up, and we would have her take us to meet the guys. The plan worked like a charm, and we had no problem tricking Queen. She had no idea what was going on and that was the very first time that she was clueless. She was so good at knowing what we were up to before it even happened.

Once we all met up, Treasure, Nique, and myself went with Ghost and two of his friends. Tiara and Bianca went their separate ways with Jerry and Reggie. Jerry was Tiara's boyfriend, who was also friends with Blu. I was certain that the night's events would get back to Blu somehow; it was only a matter of time. I didn't care what messages Blu got about me because he clearly wasn't interested, so why stress it? I was on a mission to get out of my comfort zone and enjoy my life.

We all went to the Emagine Theater in Novi. I had never been there, so it was new to me. Summer time was coming to an end, so it was kind of breezy when the movie let out.

"You want me to grab a jacket out of my car, Magic?"

Ghost asked.

As much as I would love to have his scent on me, I didn't want to act like I was cold. "No, I'm good. Let's just figure out where we're going now."

"Lucky Strike." He spoke really calm, as if he had everything all figured out.

We all headed over to Lucky Strike and were excited to go bowling and get some food. The excitement left as quickly as it came because Treasure and Nique didn't have a fake ID. I, on the other hand, always came prepared. One of my play sisters from the Cubs let me borrow hers because we looked so much alike. They were only letting people inside who were over eighteen, and we weren't even sixteen yet. With disappointment, we headed back to Jerry's house to see what Tiara and Bianca were up to.

On the way back to Jerry's, we stopped at the Coney Island right off The Lodge and Evergreen; it was the high school hangout spot. It was a place that a nigga never wanted to take his side bitch because he would get caught up for sure. I ordered my favorite meal: a grilled chicken pita with Swiss and American cheese, lettuce, and a large lemonade. Bougie ass Ghost had to request all plastic ware because he never ate off of the silver utensils at restaurants. Naturally, after watching him do this a million times, I found myself asking waiters for plastic ware as well. Slowly I was becoming the bougie bitch everywhere that I went. I swear I learned so much from Ghost, and he probably never really took heed. After we ate and paid the bill, I noticed that it was getting close to the time that we needed to be at my house. I didn't want Queen to start up her rant again, so we made our way to the exit.

On the short car ride to Jerry's place, I decided I would

be a little flirty and see how Ghost would react. "Mirrors" by Ne-Yo was blasting through the speakers, and the song had me all the way in mood. I haven't thought much of sex since the popping of my cherry. It was strange to have the same emotions I had for Blu toward another man. In that moment I wanted to feel him inside of me, taking me to new heights that I knew he could. He already proved he was more of a man than anyone I'd ever dated, so I was sure he would be a beast in the sheets.

♪ *Baby tonight let's try in front of the mirror (in front of the mirror)*

Watching ourselves make love/ Girl why don't we ♪

While the song played, I reached my left hand over to his lap and started to search for his third leg. He wasn't expecting my search and neither was I. I just wanted to show him that I wasn't the innocent little girl that he thought I was. Yes, I was a bit inexperienced, but I knew what a man liked. He gave me the "you not ready for all that" look.

I shot a look back that said "I ain't a baby." I couldn't do anything but laugh at the fact that we were having a conversation through our eyes. I really didn't know what the hell I was doing. He could've pulled the car over right here and fucked the shit out of me, but I wasn't really ready for that. I figured since we were riding solo, I could get a little teasing in. I took it a step further and placed my hand inside of his shorts. This time I could feel every inch of him through the stroke of my hand. His third leg that was once limp, stood full of life and attention. I was surprised by how hard he was. Slowly, I began to stroke his ego. His eyes seemed to have expanded as he was in shock and falling in love all at once. He was ready for whatever I had in store. I continued with slow but steady strokes. His pre cum dripped down my hand, making it clear to me that he was feeling good. I knew that I could make him explode, and I wanted to. I added a little spit to my palm because I knew that it would make the pleasure feel more like a vagina. With a firmer grip I went back to stroking, but this time I paid more attention to the head of his dick. I was ready for that moment where he would call my name out with passion and beg me for more! Just as we arrived to Jerry's house, his body began to stiffen and seemed to enlarge. He was ready to cum.

"Oh shit, Magic! Magic, Magic . . . Stop!" he said, while releasing in my hands. It was too late to stop that part now because all of his kids were swimming around in his shorts.

It was about 11:00 p.m. when we pulled up to Jerry's house. We had to be back to my house by midnight, so we needed to get a move on it. All of the lights were off when we walked in, so I figured somebody had to be getting it in. Reggie and Bianca were in the back living room.

"You ready? We got to be back in thirty minutes," I asked Bianca.

"Yes, bitch. You know the answer to that. I been did what I needed to do." I already knew what she was referring to, and I was also convinced that she probably got it in about ten times.

"All right! I am about to find Tiara. I'll meet you outside. Ghost is waiting in the car to take us back."

Tiara was upstairs in Jerry's room, so I just yelled up the stairs for her to come down because we had to go. If she had done anything with Jerry, it would have been her first time. I couldn't wait until we got back home so that we could exchange stories and share juicy details.

We both said our good-byes to Jerry at the bottom of the steps and headed to Ghost's BMW. He had to drop us off at the corner because Queen had cameras on the outside of our house. She could see who dropped us off, if he pulled up too close. I knew where the cameras pointed, so I knew which way to walk up to the house without her seeing us. Luckily, Queen was sleep when we got in, so we just rushed to my room and shut the door. I was ready to hear Tiara and Bianca's stories of the night.

Bianca wasn't as interested in what happened with Ghost and me and I was happy because finally I could have a little peace. I didn't want them to know that I had just given my first hand job anyway. I guess stories about Blu were more interesting to her. She knew Ghost wasn't the one I cared about, so neither did she. A text came through.

Ghost: *I had a great time with you MyMy. Looking forward to returning the favor! Sleep tight.*

Magic: *So am I! Good night My Ghost!* ☺

Ghost and I ended up going somewhere every weekend. When we went out to eat, he would of course always ask for plastic ware. His consistent request explained why all the females he ever dealt with were handpicked. He didn't just talk to any girl. He wouldn't just fuck girls because he could, or because it was fun. He had standards and he had to test a female to be sure he could trust her. What amazed him most about me was that I always passed the test. He could be fucking the shit out of your mind and you wouldn't even know it.

It was just when I stopped thinking about Blu's ass that he would come with his bullshit.

Blu: *I miss you*

I changed my number after the third month of not hearing from Blu and now he was calling me. How? Why? Ghost and I were just starting to be intimate. Even though we never made being in a relationship official, he was my true friend. We could call and depend on each other, and we always conversed about the most random things. The title just never felt necessary because we knew what it was. If Blu would've stayed away from the start, Ghost and I would have made it official one day. I made the choice to not pick Ghost in the beginning, and I'd dealt with the consequences of my immediate decision. I knew there was one choice that I didn't regret and that was giving Ghost a piece of the pie.

He called me over one night. "Hey, MyMy! I'm ready to return the favor that I owe you. Are you ready for some payback?" Like a kid in the candy shop, I lit up.

"Of course, what time you want me to come over?"

"Eight o'clock should be good."

"Okay. See you then!" As I hung up, my heart was racing and I didn't quite know what to expect. All that I knew was the one time with Blu. *What if it isn't what he expected? I'm sure I'm not as experienced as the other women he has dated.* Whatever he wanted me to know I convinced myself that he would teach me. He had already taught me so many other things, so I was sure there wouldn't be too much of a problem. I was just excited he wanted me as bad as I wanted him.

Eight o'clock couldn't come fast enough. Even though Blu and I hadn't spoken in a few months, I felt a strange sense of guilt. The feeling almost made me out to be a cheater. Were we still together? I needed to push the thought of guilt to the back of my mind. Tonight was about Ghost and me, nothing else.

When I arrived, I texted Ghost letting him know that I was outside. He buzzed me up and told me that the door was already unlocked. I turned the doorknob and walked into a very dark space. After a few seconds of standing in silence, I could see the light from lit candles giving me a path to follow. When I finally reached his room, I could hear that same Ne-Yo song that played through his car speakers on the night that I gave him a hand job. Those same lyrics were coming through Ghost's bedroom speakers. Instantly my insides were screaming for him to touch me. Already this experience was much better than my last sex scene. I would have never expected what was to come next.

As I walked completely in his room, he had on nothing but his Ralph Lauren boxers and a pair of handcuffs in his right hand. *Oh my goodness! What is he going to do to me?*

"Strip!" He loved the curves of my body, so it was no surprise that he didn't want to see me in any clothing.

"Should I leave my panties and bra on?"

"Not unless you want me to rip them off!" Naturally my body began to dance to the music playing. I guess the dancer inside of me was also anticipating a good performance. I began to slip out of my shirt, still swaying my hips to the beat. When I got my shirt over my head, I pushed Ghost on to the bed so that he could enjoy my show before finishing out his own plan. Even in the bedroom I was competitive. I couldn't let him 'little girl' me. I stepped out of my jeans one leg at a time and stood before Ghost with nothing but my bra and panties on. His eyes scanned me from head to toe in amazement. He was yearning to get his hands on me. I placed both of my hands on his knees and began to swirl to the ground very slow and seductive. On my way back up, I stopped to kiss his neck right below his ear. Turning around to place my ass in his lap, I danced against his third leg. I felt his dick harden against me, and it was then that I knew he was ready for me. I stepped a few inches away to continue my strip tease. Now with my backside facing him, I placed my hands on his dresser. As I moved to the ground, I was swaying from side to side. I wanted to be sure that he could see me from every angle. I started crawling to him on all fours while biting on my bottom lip. Once my breasts were right in front of his face, I released my bra to the floor. Ghost's natural instinct was to grab them. They were just right; they sat high and at attention. Ghost never took his eyes off them. He started to lean forward, but I stopped him before his lips could touch my nipples. This was my tease session, and there was no touching.

"Sorry, there's no touching in this game!" I said.

"You don't play fair," he responded.

"When it's your turn, it'll be your rules." I slipped out of my panties and stood with nothing but the skin that I was birthed in. He moaned at my perfection. I signaled for him to stand, and I took my rightful place on the bed. I was ready for him to give me every piece of him. "Go ahead! Show me what you got."

As he stood, I couldn't help but notice that his third leg was pointed toward me. He took my right arm and cuffed it to the bedpost.

"Well, since you like to play games, guess what? There's no touching for you either. If you can't comply, then I can't play nice."

"Whatever you say, My Ghost!" He started licking on my nipples, flicking his tongue fast, and soon after came the sucks. This seemed to have instantly gotten me nice and wet. Moving to my neck, he kissed me just enough to have my body practically pleading for him to slide in me. "I want you."

"Oh, baby, in due time." He reached for the drawer to

his nightstand and pulled out the infamous gold wrapper; he tore it and placed the condom on. I watched his every move as my body cried out for more pleasures. He gently rubbed his fingertips from my hairline down to my navel. He passed straight to my cookie hoping that I was already wet. He had no clue that I had been dripping through his sheets for the last five minutes. The touch of my juices satisfied him. He slid his third leg in with so much force and determination. He was sure to make me feel him just as I asked.

"Ahhhh!" I screamed with both pain and pleasure. It was something that I had never felt before. Each stroke was harder and more intense. He was completely lost and in his zone. Ghost laid his chest next to mine and put his lips on my neck. He kissed me repeatedly and then whispered, "MyMy, turn over!" I did as I was told. I was now totally exposed on all fours. He had a view that no one else ever had. He was about to take me from behind.

"You ready?" he asked.

"Yes! I need—" And before the last words could escape my mouth, he was in and thrusting against my ass. He moved fast, and I could hear my ass slapping against his thighs. He reached for my breasts as they hung, waiting for his touch. Ghost grabbed my waist tighter, and I could feel him stiffening inside me. He gripped my ass with both hands as the strokes slowed down. One minute later, he exploded and collapsed on top of me.

"MyMy, I'm never letting you get away!" Those words were music to my ears, and we would be inseparable from that moment on. Now what am I going to do? Could I really get over Blu and be Ghost's girl?

12
Guess Who?

"Bitch I'm gon' kill you!" a voice on the other ende of the phone said to me before pressing the end button.

The past few months I'd been getting weird text and phones calls. They would text from an app that showed random numbers. Saying, "Oh you think you got money and can't be touched?" I didn't tell Queen because I knew she would have security walking me to the bathroom. I just figured it was one of these jealous 'hos looking for me to react. So I didn't feed into it. I just continued living, and whoever was watching could keep on.

Ring! Ring! Ring!

I figured it was yet another prank call. I answered my phone without knowing who was on the other end. A voice that I hadn't heard in months was just a speaker away. It was now August, and I was about to start my sophomore year. I paused. It felt like a ton of bricks were sitting on my chest because I couldn't seem to breathe anymore. The thought of him was just finally starting to escape my mind. I was just beginning to accept that he used me. I counted my loss and decided that moving on would help me break even. Somehow all of the self-motivational speeches that I fed myself turned into a blur.

"Magic, why haven't you been answering my calls?" Blu's voice brought back all of the emotions that I desperately tried to tuck away. It only took a few seconds for me to notice that I was his again.

"I thought you got what you needed. You can't pick and choose when you want to be with me."

"Your mom was threatening my life. Ace Jr. asked me to just leave you alone. I thought I was doing right by letting everything die down."

"If what my mother was going to do was a concern, you should have let me know. Wanting to let things die down doesn't justify you ignoring my calls and texts."

"I'm sorry. I seriously wasn't trying to hurt you! Are you home?"

"Yes. Why?"

"I'm outside. Is your mother there?" Blu loved that popping up shit.

"No, but I'm not letting you in. I don't really want to see you."

"Man. Come outside!"

"No, Blu! You haven't been thinking about me for the last few months, and then randomly decide to pop up. You can't expect for things to just go back to normal."

"Magic! Please come outside. We can talk about it, and I'll try not to hurt you again."

It didn't take much convincing to win me over. I was ready to run outside as soon as I knew that he was out there. "Here I come!"

I walked over to the mirror to check my appearance. I thought about rushing, but I wanted to take my time and make him wait outside. For months I had waited to hear from him, so I didn't mind making him wait at all. My hair was in perfect condition, and my ass was looking just right in my sundress. I grabbed my lip-gloss from Victoria's Secret out of my purse and applied it to my lips. Lastly I went to find my Gucci thong sandals to slip them on.

As I exited the garage, I walked as cool as I could to his car. He was parked directly across the street and in some type of minivan. I could see him smiling at me, and I instantly forgot that it had been months since the last time that we saw each other. It felt like we had never missed a beat or a day without seeing each other. He had the most perfect smile that I had ever seen. How could such a grimy looking guy have the best teeth in the world? I melted instantly. He always had a way of getting my entire body to scream with excitement. Not even Ghost could do this by just looking at me. I needed to keep my game face on, so I pretended that his presence didn't affect me. I wasn't paying any attention that I was wearing a sundress and black panties. I wore the same black panties that served as a magnet to The Johnson. As I was walking up to the car, Blu could already tell how the night would end. I was giving him the "Don't even try it" look.

Blu immediately tried to get on my good side by spitting his game like wild fire. "I missed you so much. What you been up to?"

"I can't tell. Haven't seen or heard from you in months."

"I can show you better than I can tell you."

Trying to keep my composure and not give in, I shot back. "I'd rather not!" I knew damn well that I wanted him just as bad, if not more. I knew that he was only outside of my house because people were starting to talk about me being Ghost's girl. Blu was a man built with too much pride, and he wasn't going to let anyone else claim me. He felt that he needed to reclaim his territory and quick before Ghost and I made anything official.

"What color panties do you have on?" Blu completely ignored my last statement.

Fuck! I couldn't tell him that they were black. "White." I decided lying would be best.

"Let me see!"

"No! This isn't a question and answer session about my underwear. What did you come over here for?"

"I came to make sure that you were still mine. I really do love you, Magic. I can't lie and say I wasn't out here doing me for these last few months. I can't lie and say that your mother was the reason you hadn't heard from me. I was scared. I was actually catching feelings for you, and I knew that I couldn't be the man that you deserved. Your brother would kill me if I hurt you the way that I hurt these other females. I'm ready to try to commit and be whatever you need. I can't stop thinking about you."

His confession was all that I needed to hear. Without a solid male in my life, I was doomed to fall for anything. I thought I had learned my lesson fooling around with this man the last time, but he was my drug. I was hooked. I was a real fool in love. When I gave Blu my cookie, I knew that I would do anything for him, and nothing was different in this moment. Even with the passing months of heartache, I was his and nothing could change that. He knew of my heart and loyalty and that would be our biggest downfall. He was sure that what happened didn't matter because with one phone call, I would be right back to being Mrs. Blu.

"So, do we just go back to how things were?" I wasn't sure of how to go about our next move.

"No, we do it better!"

I felt safe. I went from standing outside of Blu's driver's side door to sitting in the passenger seat. I stopped pretending and put away my defense mechanisms. When out of nowhere, Blu's face was underneath my dress. He was removing my black panties with his teeth. Oh my God! It should have been illegal to have felt that good. He was the only man who ever tasted me, and I loved his hunger for me. He knew just what spots to touch. He knew when to lick, what to suck, when to rub, and how to use his tongue for penetration. He must've loved the way that I pleaded for him.

"Magic, I need you!" he managed to say in between licks. And just as he was finishing his statement, my juices burst out everywhere. *How did he do this? What the fuck was that? That has never happened to me before. Did I just pee on myself? How did it just sprinkle out like that?*

"Get on top!" he instructed, after pulling his pants down to his ankles.

As I straddled him while he sat in the driver's seat, I reached for the lever to recline his chair. I acted as though the position and location of where we were wasn't new to me. I had never been on top of anyone, and I had never had sex in a car. Blu had a way of making sure that everything he did with me was my first time.

"Oh, you've had practice?" Blu had to question me for his own self-conscious.

"No. You have a way of making me act out of character. Now sit back and let me ride in peace."

Before sliding into my wet pussy, I thought that I

would taste him for once. I wanted to blow his mind like he did mine. I always wanted to give him something that he would never forget; something that he would never want to leave. I wasn't quite sure how I was actually going to be the best at giving him a blow job; it would be my first time. Although I had been sexually involved with Ghost, he did all of the work.

I placed my right hand around his johnson and held it firmly. I had experience with giving hand jobs, so I figured that I would keep those techniques in mind and go from there. I started with slow strokes to get him wide-awake. Once the wetness from his pre cum touched my fingers, I covered his johnson in it. I got on my knees and turned my body in the direction of Blu's right shoulder all while staying in the passenger's seat. I was positioned face to face with his johnson and paused. I gave a perplexed look, but tried to disguise it by quickly rubbing my completely dry nose against my forearm.

"You sure you ready for that?" Blu smirked.

I began to kiss the head, slow and soft. I was barely touching his johnson so that anticipation would arise within him. I wanted to make him beg. I wanted him to want me. As he squirmed beneath me, I knew that he was enjoying every second of my teasing. I began to lick right below the head with the tip of my tongue.

"Magic," he whispered in ecstasy. I knew I had him right where I wanted him. I sucked him up and down slowly while occasionally trying to put all of his johnson in my mouth at once. I decided to slob a little and give all of my attention to just the head. His Johnson stiffened in my mouth, so I released him. I was really turned on from all of his moans. I was able to straddle him and slide onto him without any hassle. The wetness from my cookie and the saliva from my mouth made it an easy task.

"Oh shit, Magic! You have the best pussy!" He was basically petitioning for more of me. Blu led the way during our initial sexual experience, but for the first time, I was in control. I took full advantage of having things done my way. I fucked him slow and steady. His cries of love were turning me a notch higher every time he moaned. I started to feel my own build up. I began to pick up the pace in order to match my own desires. And just as I was about to explode, Blu started to squeeze my ass. This was an indication that he would be climaxing soon. Together our bodies began to jerk; driving the lever to his seat to adjust without us moving it again. I was holding on for dear life. I couldn't help but dig my nails into his back. My climax was so intense that I had to scream out.

This was the first time that I was able to anticipate myself coming I could feel it searching for an exit. "Blu, I'm cumming."

"Baby, I want to feel you cum on this dick!" Those were the words of my undoing. We climaxed together and it was like 'blue magic.' Still inside of me, I lay there on his chest and just listened to his heartbeat. We were both out of breath, and all that I could do was accept Blu as my addiction. *How will I ever come down from the high that he gives me? How does he make me feel so good and so bad all at the same time?*

He began stroking my hair and lifting my chin so that I could look into his eyes. "Magic, I promise I'll do my best to be what you need me to be. I don't love them other girls. It's all a game. My niggas be doing it, and it's just something to do. I have way more respect for you."

"I'll have to see it to believe it. I love you, Blu, and I don't ever want to feel the way that I've felt over the last few months."

"I heard you were occupied, so you couldn't have been

that hurt."

"I hope you didn't think I would wait around forever."

"Well, you know what to do now. I don't want to hear of him again." Blu the man was back and in full takeover mode. He never liked to see me with anyone besides him. He would dog me out and cheat on me, but he didn't want anyone else to have his position. Blu was quick to call and blow somebody's phone up over the mere thought that they were dealing with me.

The next day everything was back to normal between Blu and me. He was back to doing all of the tricks that originally drew me to him. He was calling me every second of the day to see what I was up to. I still needed to break the news to Ghost. He was my friend amongst everything else. We never let sex complicate our friendship. We genuinely enjoyed each other's presence, and there was nothing complicated about that. We never bore any kind of title but knew where we stood. He wasn't a man to wear his emotions on his shoulder, but I knew he had feelings for me, although he never verbalized it. Eventually, he would speak on his feelings, but not until it was too late. I wouldn't find out how he truly felt about me for years. I thought we were both just enjoying the moment. Since I had messed up the first time, I figured there was no hope for us being in a committed relationship. So whenever Blu came knocking, I was always willing to open my door to more hurt and lies. It was a mess. I was wrapped in a love triangle, and I had no clue which way to turn. Ghost had it all, but Blu was my kryptonite; I could never say no.

Weeks passed and I had started to cut back on the time that I spent with Ghost; sending him right into the arms of yet another crazy girlfriend. The word was getting out about Blu and me, which meant that bitches were not feeling it. I received countless calls from girls, and even when Blu was with me they would ask to speak to him. How in the hell did they even get my number? I can recall one particular day when I was at home chilling, and Blu had planned to come over later. I received a disturbing phone call that altered my entire mood.

"Hey. Is this Magic?" the unknown female's voice questioned.

"Who is this? What do you want?" Instantly I was upset because I already knew what it was about. There weren't too many people calling my phone that I didn't know, so I knew that it had to be about Blu.

"I didn't call to argue. I just want you to know that Blu is deceiving you. My name is Asia, and he's my boyfriend." I couldn't have heard her correctly. There was no way that he had someone else out there claiming him. I mean, I knew that he would be fucking a couple of people, but there was no way that someone else could be claiming him. No way! It didn't make sense.

"I'm not sure what kind of games you're trying to play, or how you even got my number. Whatever Blu told you about us, believe it. I will not sit on the phone and explain myself to you or anyone else. What I do know is that he for damn sho' ain't claiming you either. Have a good day!" After enlightening Little Miss Asia, I hung up. I prayed she never called my phone again. I couldn't believe my ears. I might have sounded strong on the phone, but my heart was weak. I never imagined that I would hear those words. It felt like ten people were standing in front of me pointing and laughing. I was never the type to argue over a man. I'm not saying that I wouldn't fight someone, or put them in their place when needed. I just wasn't the type to just show up to your house, bust windows out, key the exterior, or slash tires.

That was just too irrational to me. I felt Karma was real. I knew that whatever a person sowed, they would also reap those same fruits, so I always tried my best to do well by others. I've made mistakes and did some things that I knew were wrong, but I never tried to intentionally hurt anyone. I was going through my own mental issues, and I coped with them differently. The female that called my phone was on another level, and I knew that I couldn't believe Blu. I wondered what lame ass excuse he would use this time. I was too steamed to call him.

Magic: *You need to get your hoes in check! No bitch should feel as though she's welcomed to call and question me. PERIOD!*

Blu: *Magic, what the hell are you talking about?*

Magic: *Don't play dumb. I can't deal with you and your lies. You can save that shit for the next bitch. I'm done.*

Blu: *Man I'm on my way.*

When he arrived I gave him the rundown of what happened, and he assured me that none of the things that Asia spoke of were true. He claimed that Asia was delusional and everything else. She was just another victim of his cherry-popping streak. He took about ten different female's virginity. He was playing a sick game with all of us. I didn't break up with him, and I never heard of the girl again. I'm sure he was always fucking with her, but I couldn't prove it.

13
Boss Moves

The time finally came for me to get my new car. I was turning sixteen, and we had been car shopping for about a week or so. I decided on the Toyota FJ Cruiser. It was silver with an all-white top. At the time there were only fifty made in the USA, so I was practically the only bitch in Michigan with one for sure! My aunt had one in Florida, and she was sure that I would be the hottest bitch in the city if I got it. So since it was a limited edition and niggas weren't hip to it yet, I got it. My momma instantly dropped twenty thousand on it. And just like that! I pulled off the lot in my brand new car.

The FJ was like a ghost machine. The inside was all black and it had a sunroof, of course. The best part of the car was the suicide doors. They haven't made any trucks to date with those doors. It was crazy! I knew that when I pulled up, everyone would know who I was. I got the car two weeks before my birthday, so I couldn't drive it yet; it was sitting in the garage. At the time, the only people who knew about my new car was my family. But of course they couldn't let me shine. It was maybe two days before my birthday, and I got a call from Tracy.

"Hey! I'm on your side of town, and I'm about to stop by." Her call was strange because she never came to the suburbs unless I was having a party or something. I knew some shit wasn't right. What was she doing over here? Her birthday party wouldn't be for another month. Anyway, my cousin Tracy pulled up and told me to come outside. What do I see her sitting in? It was a brand new Dodge NITRO truck. Guess what color it was? SILVER! You got to be kidding me. So now when I break out with my shit, niggas would think that I was trying to be like her. When in actuality, she was really sweating my every move. I couldn't believe she had the nerve to come over here to show the shit off.

"Oh, that's nice, looks very similar to mine," I said with a hint of sarcasm. I was upset. Why did it always have to be a competition with my family? I just wanted to live my life and be loved by them. But instead, I would spend my entire life fighting a silent battle with them. It was like they hated me from birth and that wasn't changing. I just needed to learn to deal with it and move on.

"Yeah, that's all they had. I got it today."

"That's cool! Well, if that's all you came over for, I got some stuff I need to finish before my birthday dinner tomorrow. I'll see you there."

"Okay! See ya later!"

Oh, I couldn't believe that bitch. I wasn't going to let it ruin my day. It was my big day, and I was sure that Queen would be doing some over the top shit that would put all them bitches to shame. So screw them! No matter what, I would always be a step ahead of them.

My day had arrived, and I didn't know what to expect. My mother rented out a room at Andiamo's and all of my closest friends and family were there to celebrate with me. It was about fifty people in my party. I wore a brown leather Arden B jacket with nothing but a bra underneath. I matched it up with a pair of True Religion jeans and some brown wedge heels. I was told not to put on any jewelry, so I had on a costume pearl necklace and bracelet. I figured Queen had something up her sleeve because she never told me not to wear any jewelry to a big event. She was always big on appearances. I could never leave the house not looking my best. She would beat me like I stole something.

"Magic, you're a lady. Ladies don't go weeks without getting their hair done. Ladies do not wear mismatched panties and bras, that's dirt ball shit and you're not a dirt ball." She meant well, but she was a strange woman.

All eyes were on me when I walked in. I had my hair in one of Shannon's infamous ponytails. There was no one in the state of Michigan that could do hair like her. She was a gift sent straight from God. I loved every time she touched my head. I would always leave her chair feeling like a million bucks. I walked around greeting everyone at the table and thanked them for coming to celebrate with me. It was great. Queen was running around doing what she does best, bossing people around. My aunt Ann walked in and placed sixteen crisp hundreds in my left breast pocket, and they were all signed by my little cousin RJ.

"Baby, you're a star and should be flooded with money! Happy Birthday, baby girl!" Oh, I loved when she came around because she was so full of life. One thing for sure was that she loved me. She was so bossy, and I would always say when I grew up that I wanted to be like her. You never caught her slipping. She wore a different floor-length mink coat every day of the winter. She was just that bad! She wasn't even my blood, but she treated me better than the rest of my real family.

I was just starting to warm up, and the night would be full of surprises. I ordered spinach dip for my appetizer, but when my plate arrived there was a large black leather box instead of food. Not realizing what was inside, I tried to send it back. The waiter assured me that it was mine. *Oh shit! What has Queen bought now?* I had already gotten a car and a shit load of clothes and shoes for Christmas. *What could be in this box?* As I opened it, I could do nothing but cry. It was the diamond heart necklace that I picked out just a week ago while at the jewelry store. I couldn't believe it. She told me it was too expensive and that I wasn't going to be able to get that plus the car. But of course, she was going to get it. I only turned sixteen once, and I knew Queen wanted nothing but the best for me. It was a beautiful princess cut, heart-shaped necklace; the ticket read fifteen thousand. *Wow! Queen out did herself again!*

"Thank you, Mommy! I love it. I love it so much!" I jumped up and gave her a hug.

"You're welcome, baby, but we are just getting started."

Just getting started? What more could she possibly give me? The night was going beautifully and everyone there was enjoying themselves. Of course we were footing the bill, so niggas were ordering all kinds of things: lobster for everybody! When the main dishes were said to be on its way out, only my plate came. I was bragging that my food came out first without paying attention to my plate.

"Magic, look at your plate!" Queen tried distracting me from teasing my guests.

Oh shit! Is that a watch on my lobster tail? Not only was it a watch, it was a beautiful diamond bezel Rolex with a peachy rose-colored face. My mouth flew open in complete shock. I wasn't expecting this at all. I had no idea what Queen was up to.. Of course I wanted one because she had one, but I figured that I would get it when I turned eighteen or something.

I wasn't the only person in shock. I could see all of the hate on my cousin Marie's face when I noticed the watch. She looked disgusted. Her face was turned up so bad. Her nose was touching her eyebrows. Jealousy was written all over her face, I couldn't believe a person who had the same blood as me could dislike everything about me. It was just sick. It wouldn't be until after the photos from my dinner were developed that I could really see her disgust that only a camera could capture. Nothing else mattered in that moment. I was the luckiest girl in the world, and no one could steal my joy.

"Mommy, you didn't! How could you keep this from me?" I practically yelled at her. She was so slick!

"Welcome to the club, Magic!" Tracy said. She had to chime in to remind us that she had one as well. *We get it already! Your mother buys you shit as well. Kudos to you, Tracy!*

"I had no idea!" I replied. I've never even looked at one before at the jewelry stores.

"I did, girl! You're in the big leagues now!" Tracy was still talking.

I responded with a smile. I really didn't feel the need to entertain her right now. It was time for dessert and Aunt Ann had another surprise up her sleeve. "Baby girl, your pockets are looking a little off."

"Huh?" I questioned in a very confused state. I already

had the money that she gave me in my left pocket; there wasn't any money missing. I hadn't touched it since she placed it there, so how were my pockets off? I was so confused. Ann tilted her head to the side a bit while tapping on my right pocket breast.

"It looks a little empty on this side. Let me fix that." She pulled out another sixteen crisp hundred-dollar bills and placed them in my right pocket. "Now, that's much better, baby girl!" Aunt Ann was a true boss. She dropped thirty-two hundred dollars on me like it was nothing.

After cake and ice cream, it was time to open gifts. Everybody had cameras out, so I knew it wasn't the end for surprises. They all knew something that I didn't know.

I got to the last box and it read: LUXURY FURS. *Oh my goodness! No she didn't!* She couldn't have gotten me a car, watch, necklace, and now this? There's no way Queen could afford this. She didn't even go to work. *What the hell does she do?* My young mind wasn't ready to even know. I just knew whatever it was that it kept her on edge most of the time.

When I opened the box, it was a gray and white mink jacket. The fur was so soft and delicate to the point where I could've just slept with it as a blanket. Queen truly made this my day. I felt like a queen myself. With a mother like Queen, what else could a girl ask for? I was on cloud nine, and I had no one to thank but her. She made all of it possible. I'm sure Ace had some input, but this was all Queen's doing.

The night came to a close, and I needed to thank everyone and make my exit. There were a few parties that night, and I was trying to make an appearance somewhere. I couldn't let my outfit and all of my jewels go to waste. "Thank you so much, everyone, for this beautiful night. I am blessed beyond belief. I love you all so much, but it's time to go. I want to do hood rat things with my friends."

The room burst into laughter, and everyone started to gather their things to make an exit. "Wait, wait, wait. Magic, there's one more gift!" Ann was practically screaming in order to get everyone's attention.

"I didn't see another gift!" I said, searching for it on the table where I pulled the rest of the gifts from.

"Here it is!" She handed me a small box as she spoke. I already had a ring, so what was it? As I opened it, my eyes virtually jumped out of my head. *No fucking way! This was the best birthday ever!* Inside the small box were custom heart earrings to match my necklace. Not that chip diamond shit either; it was pure clarity. The princess cuts were shining. I immediately slipped off the earrings that I had in for my new ones. I felt like the hottest thing walking.

Tears started to fall from my face. I was in disbelief! My mom and aunt really outdid themselves. "Thank you! I love you both very much!" I hugged them tightly and made my exit. It was time to blow the joint and get out into the world. I was bound to run into Blu, and I was sure that he would be trying to make me go home with him. I was ready too. Hell! Whoever crossed paths with me would want to stop me just to know who I was! I felt like a true star, and I was ready to show it off.

I was flying up the Lodge with my girls, and we were jamming to the radio. We stopped at the store to grab a bottle of Moet with one of our many fake IDs and were heading to the party. Of course the party was eighteen and up, but we were already set. When we pulled up, we noticed people pointing in our direction. Most people had never seen the FJ up close, so all eyes were on us. Once I stepped out of the truck, everyone's head turned. I was breaking necks this night. It wasn't because I had on a skimpy outfit, but because my diamonds were in fact shining bright. The suicide doors didn't make getting out of the car any better. We parked right in front, so that I could toss the keys to the valet man.

"Sweet ride, kid," he yelled behind me.

"Don't get lost in it!" I shot back with a smirk.

Not only were the guys watching us, but the bitches were lurking too. Some instantly wanted to fight me just because they were jealous. Others wanted to be me so they silently prayed to God to honor their wish. Bitches were funny to me. I realized that the worst bitches were the ones that always wanted to be around just to see all that I had. They were the bitches who had a little bit themselves and felt like they needed to hang with people who they thought were on their level. This concept was stupid to me because I would never befriend someone because of social status. I would rather be around a person who was genuine than someone who only cared about dressing up and couldn't care less if the next bitch snuck me. People will befriend you because of your assets, and that's the Detroit culture. I believe in loyalty, and if a person didn't like one of my friends, then they signed up to not like me too.

The party was where the Southfield Bad Girls Club found me; they were all there that night. I guess they noticed me and were ready to invite me into their crew. I only knew them by association at that point and never had conversation with them.

The Bad Girls Club consisted of a few females. Jamie was probably the craziest of them all because she loved to fight. She loved it so much that she would kick your door in for looking at her wrong. She was very pretty though and always rocked the latest stuff. Jamie stayed fly as hell. Raven was the loud one who had manly facial features. She couldn't dress to save her life, but she was down for the cause. She did have nice things, but she just pieced the shit together all wrong. Blu's ex-girlfriend, Rhonda, was a part of the crew too. There were about four others that belonged to the club, but they really didn't cause noise like the other three. They had a rep in the city, and people tried to stay clear of their path. There was always some shit going on with them.

Jamie approached me and made small talk. She commented on my outfit and said we should link up sometime and the rest was history. They were sleeping over, and we were getting into all kinds of trouble: stealing, drinking, smoking, fighting, and so much more. It was like I went from good to bad overnight. I still had my same friends, but I was starting to spend less time with them. The Bad Girls Club was more convenient to hang with because they lived near me, and most of them had cars or access to one. This was a benefit because I didn't need to go out of my way to pick anyone up. It was a crazy time for me. I was slipping down the wrong path and fast. The only person that was capable of saving me from falling into a dark hole was me.

On top of me falling off my square, Queen was going through it herself. She had just got word that she was mentioned on some paperwork by someone who was serving a life bid. The shit had her straight scared. Some snitch ass nigga was sentenced to life, so he decided to tell on all of the females in the game so he could get less of a sentence. He ignored the rules of the game. If you can't do the time, then don't commit the crime. They threw decades at him, and he snitched like a bitch. If Birdman were still alive, none of that shit would've ever happened. He would have sent a team to kill him, and his snitching ass would've never made it to the stand.

Four other women were on her case and the rest were men. The paperwork stated that they had multiple business exchanges of a large amount of money and cocaine. My mom wasn't referring to the local police, she was talking about THE FEDS! I guess my mom was a big timer because I only saw them on TV. My mom was really into some deep shit that I would have no idea of. She was freaking out. She wasn't going outside, and she even changed all of her numbers. Queen completely isolated herself from the world. I was ordered to go to school and go straight home. She always felt like people were watching, and she was right. They had been staking our shit out for months.

Queen was ready to pack up and go, but she knew that wherever she went trouble would only haunt her. For the first time in her life, reality had really settled in, and she knew that she was going to have to go away. All she could think of was me. What would I do? Who would look after me?

All of these questions wouldn't be answered until she was forced to do the time and leave me with nothing. No one was prepared for the events that took place; it was a roller coaster that I never wanted to ride.

14
BITCH

Even with all the bullshit happening with Queen, I was still living my teenage life. By this time there was nothing anyone could say to me about Blu. He was very much a part of me and all mine. Anyone who came within fifty feet knew this. There was no excuse for the people I loved and called my friends to think anything different. They should have known not to mess with him.

One night everybody was out partying except me. I'm glad I followed my first mind to stay home. It wasn't like I wasn't allowed to go anywhere, but my mother was on an all-time paranoia streak. The Bad Girls had decided to link up and go out, and Bianca was with them. She made sure to get in good with them, so that I didn't have to be around for her to hang. I was seriously starting to think Bianca wanted my life. She simply envied everything that I had. They were all riding in the same car, wilding and clowning as usual. They were driving in circles outside of the club that they had just left. I don't know all of the details, but I did know that Raven was hanging out of the side of the car window. When the driver made a sharp and fast turn, Raven flew out of the car.

They couldn't believe what had just happened. When reality sunk in that Raven was hurt and bleeding, they all rushed to her to try to see if she was okay. She wasn't responsive, so they called 911. Just about everyone was under age, so many people made their escape before the police could get there to send them all to jail. Bianca was crying and screaming hysterically. It was all too much for her. Everyone was running wild, and it looked like a scene straight out of a drag racing movie. As the police approached the scene, Bianca jumped in the driver's seat and drove away to make an exit.

When the police arrived, only Bianca and a few others were left there. They weren't concerned about the alcohol possession consequences, because Raven was their friend and she was in a puddle of blood. Silent prayers were said, and they all promised God to never drink if He brought Raven out of the situation alive. The many lies we tell God in the midst of wanting a way out! Most people tend to do right, but it's just funny how we always want to do right *after* getting ourselves into trouble. The ambulance arrived and rushed Raven to the hospital. After applying pressure to her wounds and keeping her stable, they eventually made it to the hospital. She was rushed to ICU where they would later find they had to keep her overnight and her recovery would be fine.

Everyone was able to finally breathe.

Later the following day I received a text from Bianca.

Bianca: *Hey bitch! Are you going to the competition?*

Magic: *Yeah. You?*

Bianca: *I want to. Can you come get me?*

Magic: *Yes I'll be there in an hour.*

Bianca: *Cool. See you then!*

No sooner than I arrived did she come bursting in my

car on cloud nine. *I wonder what nigga she fucked last night that got her all happy and shit?*

"Bitch, what's up your ass? Who got you acting all brand new?" I was trying to get the scoop.

"You'll never believe my night. When the whole thing with Raven was over, I called that one nigga that I was telling you about from Mackenzie. We went back to his spot and fucked all night. It was the best sex that I ever had!"

"Damn, bitch, you stay fucking somebody new. I'm glad that somebody is getting some because Queen has my ass on lockdown. She thinks that we're being watched every second of the day. I was so damn happy to get out the house today. I can't wait to sneak off to see Blu later."

"Magic, you know he's no good for you. I don't know why you even waste your time!"

"He's good *to* me. I have no real complaints."

"Don't say I never told you so!"

The conversation ended after Bianca gave her pitiful advice. We continued living our daily lives as normal. She started to spend less time over. I hadn't thought much of it because I needed a break.

While out shopping at the mall with Queen, my best friend Treasure called.

"Heyyy . . . Magic." She paused. "Are you . . . are you busy?" She didn't sound like herself. Her voice reverted to that of a small child. I knew I would have to make her get to the fucking point. *What is up with her tone of voice?*

I brushed it off and gave her a little time to get it out. "At the mall. What's up?"

"Well, are you sitting down?" She was talking a little

higher than a whisper and sounded as if she was about to start crying. *Did someone die?* I didn't know what to think.

"Treasure, what is going on? No. I'm not sitting, but what's up?"

"Bianca fucked Blu."

Click!

The line went dead.

I didn't know who was more scared, her or me. Why the fuck would she say that and then hang up. There was no way that her statement could be true. I thought Bianca was fucked up in the head, but not delusional. What seriously could possess her to do such a foul thing? Once I was able to wrap my brain around the situation, I needed Treasure to give more details so I tried calling her back.

She picked up on the first ring, "Are you okay? I'm so sorry, Magic, that this happened to you. You really don't deserve this." Treasure was so sympathetic that I would have thought she slept with him. All I wanted to know was how. I was standing in the middle of C'est La Vie aisle completely still. Anyone looking at me would be sure to come over and ask was I okay? It felt as if I saw a ghost. I went to find the nearest bench.

As I took my seat, I took a deep breath and finally found the courage to know what took place. "Treasure, how do you know this?"

"Her sister Ashley told me. She didn't know your number, but she knew what Bianca was doing was wrong and that you needed to know. Bianca told her it happened the night of Raven's accident!"

"For whatever reason she called Blu to pick her up from the hospital. He did and they ended up at the spot. He tried putting her on the couch. When she got bored in there she figured she would spice it up. Took her clothes off and walked in the room where he was. The rest you know is history. So basically she did all this shit on purpose." Treasure explained all in one breathe!

Instantly my phone dropped to the floor along with my mouth.

I was with that bitch the very next day, and she told me about having sex with another nigga. All this time she was talking about Blu? Fuck! This bitch is cut off! Period! I'm done! I burst into tears right in the middle of Fairlane mall. This was the first time my heart ever ached over a man who I thought loved me. Why me? Who would have ever guessed? Two of the most important people in my life went behind my back and betrayed me.

"Hello! Magic, are you okay?" Treasure screamed through the phone, snapping me from my daze.

I picked up the phone to try to explain what was just confirmed. "Bitch, we saw each other the next day, and Bianca told me about a new nigga that she fucked, and she never mentioned Blu. WOW!"

"You have to be fucking kidding me? She's not that low of a person. No way!"

We were both in denial because she was our friend, and we trusted her. When others wouldn't accept her, we did. We would go to hell and back for her. How could she? Treasure was ready to fight, and all I wanted to do was cry. I was crushed. I needed to get my shit together before Queen saw me. I knew she would want to know everything, and I just wasn't ready to tell her. I always had a forgiving heart, but if I let her know of the situation, then she wouldn't be as forgiving. I didn't want to ruin her image of either of these people. Deep down in my heart, I knew that one would stick around, and Queen would never understand that.

My heart was big and all I ever wanted in life was to love and be loved. I could be the biggest bitch in the world, but whenever I let a person in, it would be hard to let them go, regardless of their doings. It was as if I was meant to love people, so for this to have happened to me, I would never quite understand why. At this point I should have completely cut them both off and never looked back. A person will only treat you the way that you allow them to. And if you forgive them once, they will do it again. However you decide to handle any situation, be sure that the journey always leads to loving yourself more and letting shit go!

Once I got out of my feelings, I made a call to Blu. He picked up on the second ring.

"Is it true? Did you really disrespect me like that?" I was trying my best to hold back my tears. I didn't want to give off the impression that he had broken me in more pieces than he could imagine.

"Magic, what the fuck are you talking about?" His aggression told me everything I needed to know. He had slept with the person that I once called my sister, friend, road dog, etc. How could he?

"Oh, you gon' play stupid, I see. Lose my number, bitch, and continue to fuck Bianca!" I hung up and turned my phone off. I didn't want to talk to anybody else for the rest of the day. Fuck everybody!

Ironically, as I was searching throughout the mall for Queen, I ran into one of the infamous Schoolcraft Street niggas in footlocker. When I was exiting the store, he called out to me.

"Magic, where you going, pretty lady?" I was a sucker for a nice smile, and Black had one of the best! His teeth were so white and straight that his smile would cause any woman to fall to his feet. He was a bit short though, so that was a slight turn off. However, Black was the one guy Blu asked me to never talk to, no matter what happened with us. Black had already slept with his two previous girlfriends, and he refused to lose another one to him. He made me promise to never do the same. Of course I had every intention on listening to him, but in this moment I wanted to hurt him like he did me. So I was quick to agree to a date just to piss Blu off.

"Oh. Hey, Black. What's up?" I said, already flirting.

"Nothing much! You still acting funny? When you gon' let me take you out?"

His questions were music to my ears. "How about this Friday?"

"Sounds good! What's your number?"

I gave him all ten digits.

"Cool. I got you locked in. I'll call you a little later."

"Okay. See you soon."

Bianca and Blu could have each other for all I cared. There were too many niggas out here for me to be stressing. Now I felt like I might be able to win the game.

14
Guilty

A couple of days passed, and I was finally ready to turn my phone on. It almost shut back off due the amount of texts and voicemails awaiting a response. I had over fifty texts and voicemails from Blu; Bianca even called few times. *What the fuck did they want from me?*

Blu: *Magic, it's Blu. Call me.*

Blu: *WTF! You playing games now?*

Voicemail: "Hey, it's Bianca. Can you please call me when you get this?"

Blu: *Magic, fuck it. You don't want to talk. I will stop calling you*

Bianca: *Are you okay?*

Voicemail: "Man I didn't fuck her. Please return my phone calls."

Blu: *I love you!*

Bianca: *Please call me!*

Blu: *I rode by your house. I didn't see your car.*

The messages seemed to never end. These two guilty

motherfuckers just weren't going to let the shit go. They made their fucking bed, and it was now time to lie in it. It was Friday and I had a date with Black, so I wasn't ready to entertain either of them.

Black and I had plans to get together around three o'clock, so I had a few hours to make it to the shop for a quick press and curl. It was nine in the morning, and as long as I came in washed, Shannon would for sure squeeze me in. Whenever she touched my head, I was bound to break necks. The way my hair would sweep across my face was like pure magic.

I made it to the shop just in time because Shannon had a last minute cancelation. So I was able to slide right in, get a quick press, and head out of there. I was now heading to the mall to see if I could find something that I wanted to buy. I was sure it was something in my closet that I could have worn. But I had some spare time, so browsing couldn't hurt.

Around noon I pulled into the mall's parking lot, but suddenly I had a feeling that I shouldn't go in. My feet didn't want to move. It felt like God was holding me at my ankles. You know how the devil works though! He was already on one of my shoulders chanting for me to move anyway. When in fact he already knew that I wasn't ready to face what God was trying to protect me from.

I went straight upstairs to Macy's to the jean section in the back. I hadn't bought a new pair of jeans in a while, and I knew Joe Jeans had to have something new. I found two pair of jeans that I was in love with, so I went to the changing room to see which ones would fit the best. I decided on the dark blue pair with the rips at the knees and patches on the thigh. They fit my hips perfectly, and I knew that these were the jeans to wear today.

As I was exiting the dressing room, the other pair of

jeans that I didn't want dropped out of my hand. As I bent down to pick them up, I bumped right into Bianca.

"My bad. I didn't see you there," I said as I rearranged the jeans in my arm. I looked up to give the lady eye contact and show respect, but instead I instantly grew angry. I wanted to scream and fight, yet I didn't want to make her think that she had won. So I kept my poker face on as always.

"It's cool!" She hadn't notice that it was me yet. "Oh my God, Magic! I've been calling you."

"Yes, I am aware."

"Well, bitch, why haven't you answered? You mad about something?" she asked, still not catching on that we weren't friends.

Is she really trying to play me like I am a fool? I guess she wasn't going to admit to anything until I questioned her first. "Listen, I don't have time for your lies. If you want Blu, you can have him. I have a date that I need to be heading to. Y'all can be miserable together for all I care. Just tell him to stop calling my fucking phone, and you can just act like we never met. Have a good day, Bianca!" I walked away, more hurt than angry. I was never the type to fight a woman for a mistake made by a man. If I wasn't going to fight him, then there wasn't a need to fight her. I could hear Bianca crying for me as I walked to the register.

"Magic, I'm so sorry. I didn't mean to do it. Please let me explain. It's not what you think!" She managed to speak through her tears. I never looked back though. The bitch could choke and die on them sorry ass tears. I was heartbroken, and by the time I reached the car, I noticed the tears running from my own face. How could someone you trust with your life harm you in such a way? She was my sister, my friend, my ride or die. Now she left an empty hole in my heart. I would never trust the same. I would always have a wall built around my heart. I would never *ever* trust a female around my man.

When I made it home, I only had an hour to shower and get dressed. I had to make it quick. Once I got out of the shower, I found the perfect shirt to wear. It was a cream color and hung off my shoulders a bit. I paired my shirt with the Joe jeans I bought from the mall. I searched for my Cartier burgundy gym shoes, belt, and shoulder strapped purse. Since the buckle was gold on my belt, I decide to wear my rose gold jewelry collection. I was all ready to go. I let my hair down, applied my favorite lip-gloss, and it was time to head out.

I turned down Black's street around 3:30 p.m. and shot him a text letting him know that I was outside. He asked if we could take my car since his car was kind of hot, so every nigga in the city knew about his red charger. I agreed, although what he failed to mention was that my car was just as hot as his. When people saw my car, they knew it was mine. So either car could draw attention. We would be noticed either way, but I guess he wasn't the only one trying to get back at somebody. We were all playing a game, and it was just a matter of time before we would find out who won.

We drove out to Novi to see a movie. After the movie he asked if he could drive since my sense of direction sucked miserably. He practically had to drive through me on our way to the theatre. Keep in mind that I was only on the date because I wanted to piss Blu off. I knew that all I needed was for one person to see us, and I would have succeeded with the mission.

Black had his own agenda. All that he had to do was to get caught driving my truck, and the world would think we were fucking. It was a genius plan, might I add, because the shit worked! What he didn't know was that I wanted the exact same thing out of the deal. He thought he was playing me, when in fact I was playing his black ass.

As Black drove, I noticed we weren't going to the place where I picked him up. Oak Park was starting to look more like the Schoolcraft area. And that's when I knew his plan. My insides were jumping for joy! It was the summer, so niggas were bound to be hanging outside. Everyone in the city knew that I was the only bitch around with this car, so there was no way that the plan couldn't work.

While I was in the movie I received a text from Blu stating that he wanted to see me. I told him that I was on a date and would call him later. Something in my heart already knew that he knew what I was up to because I had already told Bianca. He was just trying to get it out of me before he went off.

Blu: *That's cute. Come see me when you done. I'm not even mad at you.*

Coming up on Schoolcraft and Southfield took me out of my thoughts. We turned left and just like magic, Asia was standing there on the porch with Black's sister. We continued to drive past them, but before we could turn down another street, my phone rang. Guess who it was? Blu! We both burst out laughing.

"Damn! We couldn't even make it down the street!" Black said.

"You know how this city do. They love this type of shit."

"Yeah. I don't know why the hell Asia is even over there. She been calling me, but I didn't think she was gone pop up in my hood."

"These 'hos are crazy. She's calling and snitching to Blu about me, but came to see you. Like, can I live?"

"Yeah, that's crazy. Well, you can drop me near Mama Vic's house, and I'll call you later. Don't go getting into any trouble. I enjoyed my time with you. Maybe we can do this again."

"I would love that!" I responded, knowing damn well that I had no intentions on taking him up on his offer. I did exactly what I wanted, and now Blu was somewhere losing his mind. First it was Rhonda, then Asia, now me? Black was back dooring all his women. The only difference was that Black would never get the pleasure of fucking me. He wouldn't need to though because that one date made Blu mad enough.

"Talk to you later, little lady!"

"Okay." I hopped over from the passenger side and into the driver's side, closed my door, and pulled off fast. I was so excited that my heart was racing. Blu was finally getting a taste of his own medicine. He finally knew what it felt like to be betrayed. Now I was ready to face him. He had been calling nonstop since we rode past Asia, so after about the fourteenth call, I answered.

"Magic, what the fuck! You fucking Black too?" It sounded as if he was about to cry. I couldn't believe my ears. I had to see this shit for myself.

"Come on now. You know me better than that. We just went on a date. What's up? What do you want from me?"

"Magic, I just want to see your face. Can you please come see me? I'm over Dre's house."

"I'll be there in fifteen minutes." I hung up. I knew this was a bad idea, but deep down inside I wanted to see him. No matter what he did, I loved him. I just wanted him to get his shit together already. I had high hopes that this little scandal would knock some sense into his brain.

When I pulled up, he was already on the porch. He was standing there looking homeless: dressed in black basketball shorts and a white tee. His hair was in desperate need of some attention. He just looked rough and not himself. My doors were locked when he came to reach for the handle.

"Magic, open the door. I'm not even mad." He was trying to convince me.

For a split second the thought crossed my mind that he could try to fight me. "No Blu. I know you're just saying that." I've never even come close to fighting him, so this was all new to me.

"Open the door!" he demanded. His tone was full of anger and irritation.

As I went to press the unlock button, a laugh escaped my lips. I was unaware that the match he tried to light had been lit. As soon as the door unlocked, he was punching me in my stomach as if I were pregnant. If I were pregnant, he was sure to have killed it that day. "Yoouuu fucking bitch! How could you do this to me?"

"Blu, please stop hitting me!" I scratched his face. "I should be mad at you. You fucked my sister!"

"Man, that bitch came on to me. If anything, I did you a favor. I showed you she ain't shit!"

"Fuck you!" I said as I spat right in his face. "I hate the both of you, you dirty bitches! Y'all are made for each other!"

He took his right hand and wiped my saliva away. Then using that same hand, he slapped me so hard across my face that I could feel my left eye instantly swell up and my spit resting in my eye. I grabbed my face and began to cry. I had been holding it in too long. How did we end up here? Why are we going through this? Just weeks ago we were in love. Now here we are fighting and crying. What is really going on? Once he saw my tears, he stopped his ranting, and the pain started to sink in. He was hurting too. He was hurt that he hurt me and hurt that I hurt him. We both were soaking up pain. Then he embraced me like never before. He climbed into the passenger's seat to grab me and placed me on his lap. "Magic, I'm so sorry. I never meant to hurt you!"

"Look at my face, Blu! What am I going to tell my mother?"

"I'm sorry!"

"Just get out my car, Blu! This will be the last you see of me!"

"What? Are you serious? Why are you doing this to me? Do you like to see me hurt?"

"No, but you don't love me, and I have to accept that." My words triggered something in him.

"Even if you didn't fuck that nigga, you should have because I'll never trust you again."

"Yeah, you're right. I should have! Bitch!"

His hands were now wrapped around my throat. I wasn't able to scream for help, but luckily Dre looked out to check on us and came to rescue me. He pulled Blu from me and held him down. "Dog, you can't be hitting on a girl. Magic, leave now while I got him."

I managed to shut my door and pull off, but I wanted to kill him. I turned around and drove straight toward him with no intention on stopping. He was either going to move or get hit.

"MAGIC, WHAT THE FUCK ARE YOU DOING!"

he screamed as I raced my vehicle toward him. Lucky for him, he was able to get out of the way. I needed to get the hell out of there before I ended up in jail.

By the time I made it home, my eye was already blackening, and the imprint from his hands was around my neck. There was no way I was going to be able to keep this from Queen.

So much was going on that I had completely forgotten about my phone. Queen had been blowing me up all this time and had already called my uncles over to figure out a plan. If something happened to me, she would be ready to start a war. She thought maybe I was robbed or in an accident. She wasn't prepared for what really happened though. Nor would she have ever imagined that Blu would be the cause of all of this.

As I walked in the door, she was there with her phone in her hand; she was most likely calling me because she hung up when she saw me walk in. "Magic, where the fuck have you been? I've been calling you for two hours now. I got your uncle J-Bone on the way because I was worried."

I was trying to hide my face, but when I looked at her to answer, it was too late. "What happened to your face, Magic?"

"Nothing. I got into a fight. It's okay. I'm okay!"

Queen wasn't buying my bullshit. "You let some bitches jump you? What do you mean you got into a fight?"

"No. Blu. He hit me. I went on a da—" I couldn't even finish my sentence before she cut in.

"I'm going to kill him! Where does he live, Magic?" She went soaring from zero to a hundred real quick.

Even after he did this, I was still trying to protect him.

"I don't know. He just moved into a new apartment."

"Where? I'm not going to ask you again!"

"I don't know the address. I just know how to get there."

"What's the area?"

"Seven Mile."

"And what, Magic? Don't play dumb!"

"Telegraph."

"Okay, get your ass in the car. We are going over there. You better not let him know that we on our way." Queen was angry, and I knew she meant business. I was mad at Blu as well, but I wasn't ready to see him die. I knew my uncle J-Bone and his crew didn't have anything to lose, so if they found him they wouldn't hesitate to put one in his head. I wouldn't want that kind of tragedy on my conscience or my heart.

Magic: *Whatever you do don't go home! Please!*

Queen went to grab her gun, and we were headed to his house. I prayed that he would listen to me and not go to his house.

We arrived there in five minutes at the max. "Which apartment?" Queen was hungry for his ass.

I hesitated to answer because I wasn't ready for something bad to happen to Blu. The sun had just fallen and suddenly it was pitch black; only the headlights from the car were visible. I whispered as low as I could, "Three C."

She called J-Bone who had been waiting for her call. He pulled up with four others dressed in black. They hopped out of the car and came to my door.

"Do you want this man dead, Magic?" my uncle J-Bone asked.

I looked at him and I knew they meant business. "No." I instantaneously burst into tears. I hated Blu, but I didn't want to be responsible for his death. This was the moment that I realized my family was full of killers and drug dealers. There wasn't one sane person in sight. I literally had people who would kill for me, and it was a power that I was afraid of.

"Okay, but I'm still going to fuck him up!" He was serious; nobody would mess with his family. Uncle J-Bone and the rest of the crew made their way to the apartment and up the stairs. They kicked in the door, but could only find an empty apartment with no Blu in sight.

Thank God! I thought. As bad as he deserved his ass whopped, I loved him too much to be the one responsible for it.

Magic: *STAY AWAY FOR A WHILE THEY WILL BE WATCHING YOUR HOUSE!*

Blu decided to go out to his dad's house in Ypsilanti for a couple of days until it all blew over. My mom took a trip out of town for a few weeks to clear her mind. She was being mentioned on federal paperwork, a guy put his hand on me, and she couldn't make any money due to the fact that her every move was being monitored. It was all too much, and she needed some time to think and reevaluate life.

I was there left alone and of course, since there wasn't anyone to lean on, I fell back into Blu's arms like nothing had ever happened. I went out to Blu's dad's house, and we made love for three days straight. I should have broken free when I had the chance. Blu knew that he had me. Even after the fight and him sleeping with Bianca, I was there. Choosing him would be my only option.

15
All Things Go

June 7, 2007
One month later . . .

Beep! Beep! Beep!

The sensors located outside of our home were suddenly going off. The motion detectors must've alerted my mother before anyone could even reach our front steps. Queen made her way to my room fast with only seconds left to try to prepare me for what was about to happen; she shook me as if I wasn't already awake. I slowly squinted at the bold red numbers on the clock; it was four in the morning. "Baby, get up, get up!" she said, her voice a little louder than a whisper.

"What's wrong, Mama?" I asked.

Moments later, the Feds came in and everything changed. They came in with guns in hand pointed directly at us.

My heart nearly still itself as I panicked; the red beam was pointed at my head. I managed to whisper, "Please . . . please don't shoot."

"That all depends on if you listen to my directions, now get on the fucking ground!" He must've heard me. They were ready to take me out, so I knew there was nowhere to run. Oddly, my mother had prepared me for this day. I just didn't know when. All the preparation in the world couldn't have changed my thoughts or emotions. This was a living nightmare. They searched our house for what seemed like hours. I now lay face down on the ground looking through the doorway of the kitchen. My mother was in clear view, and my eyes were locked in on her. Why wasn't she saying anything to me? I needed her to tell me everything was going to be okay. Her head hung low, and silent tears streamed down her face.

"Ma, don't cry. It's going to be okay," I tried to reassure her. "I love you, mother. They can't hold you down forever."

"Stop fucking talking! You need to be praying that I don't find anything in this house, GR." The black officer used her street name, so we knew someone was indeed talking.

They ended up empty-handed after about twenty minutes of tearing our house to pieces, breaking all of our valuable stuff, cutting our mattresses open, and flipping over all of our furniture. Queen wasn't dumb enough to keep drugs or any money over ten thousand dollars in her house. Once she got wind of the Feds watching, she completely closed up shop. She made no phone calls or anything; she was practically living in a dark room for weeks and too scared to come outside.

"You got lucky this time, but if you want to be here for your daughter, you will need to tell us what we want to hear." The black officer tossed a card toward Queen's feet as they all made their exit.

Queen just burst into tears. I ran over to hug her. I

didn't know what to do. She thought she would be killed if anything, but never prison time. She really didn't see anyone snitching on her, forcing her to be sent away. We didn't know when they would be back, but we knew they would. She was sure their next encounter would end with them placing her in cuffs and taking her away.

"Mommy, are you okay?"

"Magic, I'm so sorry that you had to witness that. I only wanted your life to be better than mine!"

"It's okay. I'll be fine. You raised me right. I won't let you down."

"We need to find you an apartment and get it paid up, so that you will have somewhere to stay. I don't know when they will be back, but I'm sure the time is coming. When they do come, make sure you only open that piece of paper when you've exhausted every single option. Make this the last resort. Promise me that. Guard this with your life. I don't even want to know where you've placed it."

"Okay, I promise!" We never spoke of the paper again. I knew the perfect place to hide it, and no one would ever know. I wondered what the key led to. I wasn't going to open it unless I needed to. I would keep my word.

For the next couple of months, my mother was doing all that she could to get things in order for her exit. Since the phones were tapped, she decided we needed to visit Elle to get some advice in person.

Elle was so excited to get a visit. She hadn't gotten one the whole time she was locked up. She was starting to feel abandoned by all of us, but everything that we did or didn't do was with good reason. Queen was distraught and needed some guidance. "Ma, what am I going to do?"

"Before we get into that, let me show my grandbaby

some love. Hey, Magic! I've missed you!" she said, hugging me tight.

"Hey, Grandma. I've missed you too. Been a long five years. I'm all grown up now!" I tried lightening up the mood.

"I know and you're even more beautiful than I remember," she said, breaking our embrace and looking me over. "Now, back to you Queen." I knew Grandma felt for Queen if nobody else in this world did.

"Listen, baby, doing this time will be hard, but you can't open your mouth."

"Ma, but you know those charges are not all mine." Queen was angry because although she did a lot of things, most of her charges were lies.

"Listen, Queen. You knew what you were getting yourself into when you signed up for this. You heard what I said! Keep your mouth closed."

"I hadn't planned on saying anything, but I want to be there for our baby Magic."

"She'll be fine. She might not be a Johnson, but she got us all in her blood. Keep a package safe for her. Understood?"

"I'm already on it. I love you, Ma. I'll see you on the other side. Be strong in there."

"I love you more, Queen. Be safe!"

After the visit, I felt as if Queen was preparing to die. She was literally getting all of her affairs in order. She was making calls and taking notes and so was I. She hadn't even left yet, and I was starting to feel abandoned. She learned who was snitching and was on fire. One of the men was someone she let into her home when he had nowhere to go. She considered him her brother because he was tight with Birdman. If Birdman were alive, none of this would be going down. Everybody who crossed his path feared him, and they knew he had the power to order your death immediately, no matter where you were. He wouldn't tolerate loose lips, so everyone kept theirs sealed. Only one person had the balls to off him and to this day that person is still unknown. He probably killed himself right after taking Birdman's life. He knew his life would never be safe after he pulled that trigger.

Fall was approaching, and it was time to start my junior year of high school. Queen wasn't making much money, and all of the excessive clothes and shit was starting to slow down. All I knew was that I needed to get a new wardrobe before we went back to school. I wouldn't be caught in the same shit from last year. At this point, the Bad Girls and I were super cool since my house was the hangout spot. They were all practically staying with me. We had a lot of extra space, plus Queen didn't want me leaving her sight much. I was even friends with crazy Rhonda. Maybe I shouldn't use the word "friend" so loosely, but I thought we were friends. We didn't let Blu come between us. For the moment I was the one he was fucking with. Rhonda was cool as hell but had split personalities. We were doing a lot of crazy shit together: fighting at parties, getting drunk, getting high, and taking over the city. I was having the time of my life, but my goals and morals were slipping through the cracks of my hands.

The first day of school approached and we decided to skip it and go get some clothes for the semester. Jamie, Kalin, and I went on a mission. I don't know what gave us the balls, but we thought we were about to hit a major lick. Things were going well with Blu and me. He barely let me out of his sight, which meant that he would be rolling on the mission with us. At the time, Jamie was talking to G-man, so he went for the ride as well.

We went to Kohl's department store, grabbed a shopping bag from the door, and went to work. Once the bag was filled with shit, we would just pop the sensor off the bag and walk out. EASY! Well, not that day. The niggas thought it was a smart idea to pull up to the door and wait. Once they noticed that we were taking longer than they thought, they went to park again. After another fifteen minutes, they pulled back up to the door. We ran out of the store like normal. We hadn't set off any alarms, so we just hopped back into the SUV. We thought we were free and clear, so we headed to the next stop.

As we rode up Big Beaver Road headed to Somerset Mall, I slipped the three bags to Blu so he could throw them out the window. We parked and went in. We went to Express, Macys, and Forever 21. On the way out, we had a great idea to go in the Gucci store and steal some shoes. We had a bunch of bags, so they would've thought we had real cash. They wouldn't question if we could afford to buy the shoes. All three of us kept asking them to bring us more and more shoes; the floor was piled up with boxes.

Jamie gave us the signal by throwing up the peace sign on the sales associate's final trip to the back. We all picked up a pair of shoes and slipped them in our bags. We then politely got up and walked out. No one inside the store had any idea. It was easy.

Blu and the rest of the guys weren't in the car when we got there, so we had to drive around a bit to try to find them.

"Blu, where are y'all? We had to get out of there!"

"We saw the guard yell after y'all, so we just walked

to the apartment building across the street from the mall."

"Stay there. We are about to drive around and come get y'all."

"All right! Magic, be careful."

"Okay, I'm making a left turn on Coolidge now!"

When the light turned green, the car in front of us never moved; instead it started to back up. I immediately began to blow my horn and yell at the car as it was closing in on me. The car behind me was closing in too, and the car on the side of me was only inches from my passenger door. There was an island to the left side of my car, so there was no fourth car attempting to close in like the others. Before we knew it, officers all jumped out at once with guns and badges, forcing us out of the truck. *Damn!* They laid us out in the grass with cuffs on, and I knew our lives were over. We would never be able to do anything again. Queen was going to kill me. What I didn't realize until later is that an officer got suspicious about the irregular movement of my truck in Kohl's parking lot. He made a call to the police to report his suspicion. The police drove by to see if anything was happening. They were waiting in their unmarked cars to see if someone was going to rob the store, or steal clothing and then run out of the store.

Instead of Queen being fingerprinted, I was the one with fingertips covered in ink. It was me getting put into a system that the white man created so that all of our fuck ups could be recognized. Now anytime a theft happened, we would all pop up in the computer system as thieves. How would I ever get a job or go to college with this on my record? I made a mental note to myself to never steal again. If I could get this expunged from my record, I would be sure to do right with my life. They took our mug shots and asked us our ages. When they got to Jamie, she lied and said she was sixteen so she wouldn't have to go to a cell. However, this wasn't her first time being arrested, so her fingerprints came back instantly and they knew that she lying and dragged her ass right to a cell. They were going to give her a pass, but since she lied they made her stay in jail for a few nights.

They let us sit in the waiting area while they fed us Chinese food, which was their lunch, but they never got a chance to eat because Kohl's security called. My momma was under surveillance, and she didn't want to risk coming to get me, so she sent my aunt Binky. Kalin's grandma came to get her, and she was banned from ever seeing me again.

Queen was pissed! She wasn't mad that I was stealing because she knew of that habit, but she was mad that I didn't tell her my plans. If I had told her what I was going to do, she would have just paid someone to get me some clothes. I shouldn't have been risking my life when she was going through what she was going through. It was very stupid of me. Even though Queen was always claiming broke, she would never let her nest completely deplete. I was young, dumb, and hanging with the wrong people. I wasn't thinking of the consequences of my actions. I just figured I shouldn't bother Queen with my issues because she had so much on her plate. I knew she would have told me to wear something out of my three closets. This was during a phase where I was feeling myself. I was getting more attention from guys, and I was hanging with a crowd that I had no business being around. It was fun, but it wasn't worth the drama. I never did anything that I didn't want to do, but most of the risks that I was taking outweighed the rewards. I knew Treasure and my other friends wouldn't have done any of the crazy things that I had been up to.

Kalin and I were sentenced to six months of probation for shoplifting $10,000 worth of stolen items. Once those six months were completed, our records would be cleared. Jamie was still fighting the case since it wasn't her first run-in with the police. She was known for going to jail: setting cars on fire, running in people's houses, and fighting. Going to jail was a routine of hers. Blu was still fighting a case for loitering after throwing the bags out the window. They made sure to write him a ticket for that weak ass shit. G-man did some time since he had a warrant or something out for his arrest. It was sick. The police couldn't really fuck with us because we were young, but they tried to slam everything they could on the guys. If we would've just left them at home, none of this shit would have ever happened. I learned that day that one careless move could fuck up your entire life.

A few weeks passed since my jail run-in and life was getting back to normal. Our school's talent show was coming up, so my school best friend Chelsea and I decided to form a group and participate. We wanted to have the baddest show that Southfield Lathrup would ever see. We handpicked ten of the best top performers, and we spent a week choreographing all of the moves for the show. We knew it was up to us to turn the crowd all the way up.

I met Chelsea at the beginning of sophomore year. So many people were mistaking her for me and vice versa. I would get, "Omg! Have you seen that new girl? Y'all look just alike. Are y'all cousins or something?" My response would always be extra dry because I didn't like the idea of people comparing me to someone else. It took a few weeks before we even crossed paths, and I promise it was an instant friendship. It almost felt as if we were made to be friends. We were complete opposites, but we bonded on the same level. We would be inseparable from our first words in the hallway. "You're the girl that everyone keeps comparing me to?" She was the sweetest girl ever! I, on the other hand, was somewhat of a bitch. Most people didn't like me until they actually got to know me. I had the bitch resting face down to a tee. People just naturally hated me. If someone wanted to judge me by my exterior, then so be it. They didn't deserve my loyalty anyway.

Finally, we had all of the girls and guys that we wanted to participate in our performance. We practiced nonstop for weeks. December approached, and it was only one week left before the show. The night of December 4, 2007, we had a huge party at my place. All of the dancers came over to practice for the show, and my big sister Lanae was there to help. My mom invited all of her friends over too because she was cooking. Anytime she mentioned that she was cooking, there would be a party. Even the Bad Girls were there that night. We had a house full to just celebrate life.

I wasn't really in the spirit to be around all those people. So I was camped out in my room toward the end of the night. Queen and I were not exactly getting along. With all the people that I hung around, it started to seem as if she preferred having them as her kids and not me. I thought she treated them better. They all loved her, and in my heart I despised her for all of the beatings and calling me out of my name. No one could see her the way that I saw her. She was so hard on me, and I never understood why. I remember one night in particular when I was out with the Bad Girls Club, and I came in later than expected.

Nique was with me that night as we made our rounds to drop people off. I arrived home around three o'clock in the morning, which caused Queen to have a bitch fit. She knew I was going to a club that didn't close until two o'clock. I was the only driver, so what else did she expect? When I walked in the house, Queen was there sitting in the living room with all of the lights off.

She texted that I needed to get home and asked if I was okay. She heard a club was shot up downtown and needed me to come home right away. Nique texted her back and explained that we had to drop people off at home. We hadn't heard from her since, so I figured that she was cool with our arrangements. She must have sat in the house and got drunk because she was on 100 when I walked in.

"Bitch, when I call you and tell you to come home, make a way to be here!"

"I'm sorry. I had people to drop off."

"I don't give a fuck about that. When I say do something, you do it!"

Next thing I know I was waking up on the ground in the hallway with blood dripping from my bottom lip. I understand punishing your children is necessary, but there was no reason that I should have been waking up in the middle of the floor oblivious to what could've happened to me. After picking myself up from the floor, I looked around to see where everyone was. Did Nique just let me lay there all night? How could Queen just let me lay there passed out? What if I was dead? There were just too many unanswered questions. I checked my own pulse to make sure that I wasn't dead. I hated Queen for doing power-tripping shit like that! She probably was so drunk that she wasn't aware of the damage she did. I walked to the bathroom to look at myself in the mirror and see all of what she had done. She was careful not to mark my face up too much. My lip was slightly busted, but my ribs were completely bruised. I'm almost positive that she punched me in the chest and in my ribs until her fucking hand went numb. Finally I found Nique in my room. She was just waking up as I entered the room. Her eyes were blood shot red. When I got closer I noticed she had either cried herself to sleep, or hadn't been to sleep at all.

"Are you okay?"

I saw the pain in her eyes; she was hurting. Hurting for me, I suppose. After checking my wrists for a beat and looking over my face to see the damage, she finally opened her mouth. "I thought she killed you, Magic. I was so scared to even leave your room. I just cried for the last three hours. She must have blacked out or something. After she was done with you, she passed out in her room. I'm sure she doesn't even know what the hell she did to you!"

I attempted to stop her from crying because I could tell that she was scared, hurt, confused, and all of the above. "It's okay. I'm fine. She never went this far, but I'm used to her. Don't cry for me."

"But, Magic! I promise I tried to stop her, but she looked at me with eyes of death and told me to go mind my business before she did the same to me. I knew she was drunk, so I just did as I was told. You were just lying there lifeless, but I could see you breathing so I felt better. I was so scared!"

"I know you were. Listen, I promise you I am fine! Queen is just going through it right now, and this will all pass."

"You're so strong, Magic. I've always admired you for that. I know it's only a two-year difference between us, but I will forever look up to you. Thanks for always being so positive in life."

"Hey! You're stuck with me for life. As long as I am

around, we will always pull through. God gives his toughest battles to his strongest soldiers. One day my story will be told and it will change the world."

"You're so right about that. You will have one for the books. Love you, cousin!"

"Love you more."

When Queen woke up, of course she tried to take me shopping and out on the town. She felt terrible, but she would somehow try to say that I should've listened to her. "I know you were out there being fast, Magic. That's not the life you want to live. You will end up in situations you won't be able to get yourself out of. I'm just trying to make sure you never end up like me. I don't mean to hurt you!" The half apology would just make me angrier. This happened right after they raided the house, so I knew she was on edge. It really wasn't the reason that she was mad, but that still didn't mean I forgave her.

"Magic, are you okay?" Chelsea asked, snapping me out of my thoughts. I could go hours just thinking about my life and all of the crazy stuff that took place.

"Yeah, I'm cool. Is practice over? I kind of got lost in my thoughts."

"Yeah, all the girls are gone. I'm about to head out too. I just wanted to say bye."

"See you later. You know we don't say bye! That's a statement referencing forever."

"My bad. See you tomorrow. Did you sign up for that field trip?"

"Yeah, I'm going!"

"Okay cool."

I walked Chelsea to the door and gave her a hug. After she made it to her car, I shut the door and locked it behind me. Maybe if I had paid attention to the house across the street I would have noticed the random car in the driveway. The house had been vacant for years, so no cars belonged over there. We were being watched, but we had no idea.

The party died down. I had school in the morning, so I was already getting ready for bed. Jamie, my cousin Heem, and Dre were still there, so they were going to stay the night. My mom would take them to school the next day.

This would be my last normal night of life. After the party, nothing in my life would ever be the same. No one was expecting this storm to come so quickly. I know I wasn't! My birthday was in twenty-one days, and I was ready to see what another great year of life would bring. Our talent show was next week, and I had my own things going on. I wasn't ready for life to change. I wasn't ready to have everything taken from me in a blink of an eye. All I could do was look to God and ask, "WHY ME?"

16
Until We Meet Again

On December 5, 2007, the morning came and everything felt normal. I was the only one up because I had to be at school around 6:50 a.m. to make the bus for the field trip. We were going to O-tech to learn about their program. It was a special program where you could do real work and gain credits for school. You would go to O-tech for half of the day, and then come to school. It was a good program if you weren't planning to go to college and head straight to the work force.

I would always go see Queen before leaving the house. I would either go to just say bye, get money, or to just tell her I loved her. I was mad at her for my own selfish reason, so I opted out of seeing her that morning.

Once I was dressed and ready to head out, I paused outside Queen's room, but decided against going in. I headed for the garage and hopped in my car and pulled off, heading to Tim Horton's before I went to school. The funny thing is that I actually thought about Queen the entire ride to school. I was beating myself up for not saying anything to her before I left. It haunted me the entire morning.

It was 8:00 a.m. and I made it to the bus just in time, and we all headed to O-tech for a presentation and tour of the place. About thirty minutes into the meeting, my phone was buzzing non-stop. We technically weren't allowed to have phones, so I wasn't able to check it right away. After the fifth call, I figured it was important. Everyone knew I was in school so they shouldn't be calling anyway. I excused myself and made it to the bathroom. I looked at my phone and I had ten text messages and like twenty missed calls from Jamie, Heem, and my aunt Yanna.

Instantly I thought someone was dead. If it was such a big emergency, why wasn't Queen calling me? I guess she was mad that I didn't speak to her before I left. Yanna never called me, so that made me think that whatever was going on had something to do with Queen. I decided to check my voicemails first.

Voicemail from Jamie: *"Magic it's important. Pick up!"*

Next voicemail from Jamie: "Oh my god! Why aren't you answering the phone?"

Voicemail from Heem: "They took her MAGIC! Pick up the phone."

What the hell are they talking about? Instantly my heart dropped as I realized who the HER was that they were referring to. It was Queen! They came and took her away from me. My full world was now empty. The walls started to feel as if they were caving in, and I couldn't breathe. My world was crumbling around me, and I was weak. What was I going to do? I didn't have my car, so I couldn't just leave. I was stuck there for three more hours. I just wanted to go home. I wanted to see my Queen. She would be there once I got home from school. I didn't even get to tell her that I loved her. I knew that she was hurting inside.

I hadn't even realized that I had locked myself in a stall, and my friends at this point were banging on the door trying to get me out.

"Magic, what's wrong? Are you okay?" TeTe asked through the door.

"Does it look like I'm okay? The fucking cops just took my mom!" I shot back at her. That was rude of me because she was only trying to help but I was hurt. There was nothing anyone could do for me.

"I'm sorry to hear that. Please come from out of the stall, we have to get you a way home!" She didn't respond to my nasty attitude because she felt what I was going through.

I guess Yanna found out that I wasn't at school, so she had to come check me out of the field trip and take me to my car. Since she was still on the clock at work, she couldn't go to the house with me right away. She said she would be over later, but before I got out of her car she held my hand for a brief moment.

"Hey, Magic. I got you! Don't worry about all this. She will be home sooner than later, and you will be just fine! I got you!"

I couldn't really think about what she was talking about because I was too busy wondering how Queen was feeling. It really hadn't hit me yet. I really thought I was going to go home, and she was gon' be there like, "Got 'em!" She was tricky like that. Since I didn't say anything to her before I left, I was hoping that she was playing a game with me to prove that one day she would really be gone. She would yell about how I needed to appreciate her while she was around. I couldn't wait to hear her crazy rants!

As I turned the key to the ignition of my truck, I tried to convince myself that this was all a dream and I would wake up soon. I drove in silence, trying to figure out what to do. When I pulled up to the house it was quiet. Queen's car was right where it was since I'd left. I noticed all the unmarked cars I had drove past this morning on the street were gone. The street was now clear and quiet. I was so nervous to walk in the house. I didn't know if my friends were still here. I was just still. I didn't want to move, so I sat there in the car for what seemed like forever. I wasn't ready to face the truth. Through all the drama, there was only one person I wanted to talk to.

Blu picked up on the second ring. I'm sure he had already got word about what was going on and was expecting my call. "Magic, are you okay?"

"No! Blu, I need you. I can't even walk in my house."

"It's gon' be all right. I'll be there with you through it all. Come over tonight. I'm out right now. Love you!"

"Okay, see you around eight. Love you more!"

Speaking to him gave me some form of peace. The thought that I had someone to hold me just made it seem easier to deal with. At this point, he seemed to be all that I had. My grandmother Elle was already serving a ten-year sentence, and I remembered the last time she came to see me.

It was summertime, and I was over to my sister Lanae's house with Treasure and Tiara. She called my minute phone and told me to come outside. She had a croissant, sausage, egg, and cheese sandwich from Burger King, which was a favorite of mine. Elle also came with a hundred dollar minute card. I was only ten years old, so it was everything that I needed. I would have minutes for the entire month. So you know I was super excited. We sat and talked for a while. She lived in Arizona at the time, so she said she was about to make the drive there. Something in her eyes told me she didn't want to leave. She was always super emotional, so of course she cried as she was leaving. I gave her a big hug and told her that I would see her very soon.

"I love you, Grandma. Thank you for my card. I will call you tomorrow! Stop crying. It's not like you'll never see me again." Even at ten I was never one for tears. I needed her to stop because it was making things awkward. Her tears were killing my mood, and I was too pumped about the minute card. I was ready to get out the car and make some calls.

"All right, Tweety. See you soon! Be a good a girl. Remember grandma always loves you!"

"Love you more!" I said as I exited her car. Her voice was so strange. Throughout the years I had done everything with my grandma and was basically attached to her hip. She sat me in the pouch (which was a term that she and I used when I sat in between her legs to watch movies and things all day) more often than I wanted her to, but it was our little bond. It was what we did. She showed me how to order up some stuff from room service. The bill would be five hundred dollars or more, and it was just the two of us in the hotel room. Never in a million years would I have thought that she was going to be taken away from me.

On her ride to Arizona, she was pulled over with twenty kilos in her trunk. The rest is history. She was a first-time offender, and one of the men who was with her took most of the wrap. She never gave up who they were really after. The crackers gave her ten years just because they could.

Tap! Tap! Tap!

It was Jamie at my window wondering why the hell it was taking me so long to come into the house. "Magic, are you okay?"

"Yeah, just thinking about the last time I saw Elle before they took her!"

"Oh! We've been in the house waiting on you. Are you getting out anytime soon?"

"Yeah, here I come!" My body felt numb. I was there, but my mind was so far from that house. I didn't want to go in. I wasn't ready to face what had happened. How can I move on with my life without my mother? It almost felt as if she had died and was never returning. The thought that she would soon return to me is what gave me the push to make it through those doors without crying.

As I walked through the house, everything felt foreign. Nothing in the house felt like it belonged to me. It felt as if Queen was watching my every move. I was scared to look in her room. I thought looking would just make me increasingly angry that she wasn't in there waiting to cuss at me for not speaking before I left for school.

I decided to sit at the kitchen table. Everyone was still there since they didn't have to be at school until 8:00 a.m. The FBI came breaking down the door at 6:55 a.m., ten minutes after I left. Jamie and the rest of them were getting ready for school.

"Magic, Queen said she loved you and would call you as soon as she could. She also said she was so sorry for leaving you and to make sure you stick to the promise y'all made, and this wasn't the time to use it." *Oh shit! I completely forgot about the key that she gave me.* I stashed it in the ground behind Vicky's garage. It was practically an unused area, and no one ever went back there. It was the most stable house that I knew of, and

Vicky would live there no matter what. I kept the piece of paper that she gave me taped to the inside of my Bible. I snuck over my granny's house late one night and buried it deep in the ground.

"So what happened? When did they come in here?"

"It had to be about ten minutes after you left. They said they were waiting for you to go to school. They had been watching y'all for months and got y'all routine down. They didn't want you here when they took her away. Maybe they would've taken you into custody if you were here or something. They didn't even know all of us were in here. That didn't stop them though! I was walking out of the bathroom when I heard the first boom. It was so loud that it woke the entire house up. Queen came out her room crying. She could see them on the monitor so she knew the deal. That's when she said to tell you she was sorry while opening the door to let the FBI in. As she opened the door, about twenty agents came rushing in. They demanded for us to all get on the ground. They said they had a warrant for Queen's arrest. They didn't even search the house. They just kept the guns on us until they had her cuffed and in the car. I was crying, begging for them not to take her. It was crazy! All of the nosy ass neighbors were outside. We didn't know if we should tell you over the phone or not. We called Blu and he thought it would be best to wait for you to get home, but when you weren't answering, we decided to just tell you. I'm so sorry, Magic!" Jamie was finally done with the story.

I was so wrapped in my own thoughts that I truly only heard half of the story. Everyone started to chime in with their version of the situation. I still hadn't shed one tear. It was too fresh. I was still in this big house. I still had food, clothes on my back, and a car to drive. Not much changed but the fact that my mother was no longer easily accessible to me at the moment. It was a bad thing, but I was old enough to know how to survive. I wasn't so young that I absolutely needed someone to take care of me. She taught me how to up keep a home, how to pay bills, cook, clean, and wash clothes. She didn't teach me how to make money because all her ways were wrong. I didn't know a thing about credit and its importance. Some areas I lacked knowledge, but I knew what it took to survive.

Around 7:30 p.m. she was able to call. "Magic, I'm sorry!" I could hear the hurt all in her voice. She was defeated and had failed at being there for me.

"It's okay, Momma! I will be just fine!"

"I talked to Yanna, and she will be looking after you. Y'all can stay at the house for now, but you will eventually have to move with her. She will rent out our home. Magic, promise me one thing."

"What's that, Ma?"

"No kids. Go to school, and don't get married while I'm in here."

"Okay, Mother. It's a promise. I love you!"

"I love you more, Magic! Please don't forget about me and write me often, please!"

Our time was up and the phone went out. There was no more sitting on the phone and discussing our day in great detail. We needed to get to the point and fast because time wasn't on our side. She only had ten minutes, and once the phone hung up she had to wait another fifteen to call back. It was sickening already. There was never any way that I could just call to talk with her. So I made a vow to answer the phone for her no matter what I had going on since I didn't have a way to reach her directly.

It was time to head over to Blu's house. I hadn't been

answering the phone for people all day because I didn't feel like hearing people and their sob stories. Everyone always said they would help and I didn't have anything to worry about. Whatever! After a week I bet I wouldn't hear from any of them. I knew Blu was serious when he said he was going to be there for me. He was the only person I wanted to be around. I figured I could return phone calls after I had time to think. I couldn't sleep in my empty house all alone, so I packed a bag and headed over to Blu's apartment.

I walked up to his door, anxious for his embrace. Blu's head was cocked to the side. He wore his perfect smile, and his arms were stretching toward me as soon as I came in. Just being in his presence lifted a weight off of my shoulders. I felt at peace for a brief moment. His embrace meant the world to me. I instantly melted in his arms. He was my knight through all of this, and I felt as long as I had him there beside me that I was going to be able to get through.

"Baby, how are you feeling?" he asked in the most sincere voice I had ever heard from him.

I couldn't think of anything to say. I honestly didn't know how to feel in this moment. "I'm numb. Not quite sure of my feelings. I just want to lay down and be held by you if you don't mind." That was all that I could say.

"Say no more. Lay down and I will be in there in a few."

"I'm going to take a shower first," I said as I brushed passed him and made my way to the bathroom. I got the water going and began to undress. Once I was down to my underwear, I tested the water to see if it was ready. As I slipped into the shower I could feel the tension in my back slightly relax a little. For the first time all day I felt safe. I kept thinking the FBI was coming back for me. In my brain I felt as though they wanted me too. They weren't going to let a young girl be out in the world alone. The reality was that my momma was a big time drug dealer, and they didn't give a flying fuck about me. They never even asked about the sixteen-year-old daughter she had. They wanted her and nothing else mattered. I could have sliced my wrist and died that day. Why didn't they see if I was okay? As I slipped deeper and deeper into my thoughts, I must have lost track of time. Blu came in looking for me.

"Magic, I'm sure you're clean by now. Come out of there!" Blu sounded more like my father, but his demand brought me back to the present. I noticed there was still soap on my back, so I quickly washed it off and rushed out of the shower. When I walked back in Blu's room, there was a teddy bear waiting for me that said I love you. There was a plate right next to it. It wasn't until that very moment when I realized that I hadn't eaten all day.

"I'm sure you haven't had a thing to eat today, so eat!" His tone was sounding too much like my father that I almost refused. Then he paused and added, "Please!" My stomach wasn't going to say no anyway. I promise it was the best barbeque chicken pizza that I ever had from Jets. Blu wasn't a major cooker. I did most of the cooking, so I didn't expect him to make me a meal. Breakfast was something that he could handle, but dinner, not so much! The fact that he thought of me was all I needed right now. After we ate, I got under the covers and waited for him. I wasn't in the mood for sex, and I was sure he completely understood. I just wanted to be held and soaked in his sweet smelling cologne. This man always smelt so heavenly. It was truly amazing how he did it. I guess it was also because when he showered he had to repeat the process at least three times to even be considered clean.

He was so weird like that, but I loved everything about him. It wasn't long before I was asleep that my body and mind were finally able to rest.

The next morning came and I didn't set an alarm, so I clearly missed school. I guess Blu figured I wasn't going, and I wasn't about to argue with him either. I hurried to check my phone. I was sure that Queen was wondering where I was because I didn't go home last night. When I looked at the screen there were no missed calls or text messages. What the hell was going on? And then it hit me again! Queen wasn't at home waiting for me because she was in a cell somewhere trying to figure out if she was ever going to be able to come home. I was in denial that she was really gone. *This is real! Queen may never come back.* I needed to see it for what it was and move forward. Since Blu was still sleep, I thought I would get up and make him breakfast. He loved when I cooked. Since he was gentle and caring for me yesterday, I figured that I would return the favor. Breakfast in bed was a great way to start my day. In that moment, nothing else mattered. It was Thursday, so I would start fresh with school next Monday. They would understand!

For the next few days I needed nothing at all besides my Blu, sleep, sex, food, conversation and a shower until Monday arrived. Over the weekend I returned calls. Can you believe Ace wasn't on the next thing smoking to come see me? He was scared they wanted him too, so he didn't even come to check on me. Instead he asked me to drive and see him. He sent me a couple hundred dollars and told me to stay out of trouble. Great advice, Dad (NOT!). Vicky called and said that if I ever needed anything to give her a call. That would be the last I ever heard of her trying to make an effort to look after me.

My friends were all worried, so I sent a mass text to let

them know that I was fine. I called Chelsea and made sure she was ready for practice. The show was in three days. I had no time to just sit back. My birthday was in a few weeks, and I just wanted to get the semester over with so I would have some down time to think this all through. For the next week I was just going through the motions. The goal at hand now was to finish this year and make it to the next school year so I could graduate high school. Blu had pepped talked me to death and made sure that no matter what happened in the next years to come that I would attend college and walk across the stage. It was a promise we made to each other, and I was going to make sure that I followed through with it.

17
Element of Surprise

Hype Night arrived. I was so excited to get it over with. My mom called earlier that day to wish me luck. I wished she could have been there to witness it, but I would dance my heart out for her. We legit had the best performance, and the crowd went crazy. There's always at least one hater in the crowd though. Someone yelled during a skit part of the show.

"I heard she a broke bitch!" Quese yelled out to the audience, referencing me. I didn't make a big deal of it then. I took a mental note to ball on her the next chance I got. See, I wasn't one to throw what I had in someone else's face. People would test me though, and make me have to show them better than any words could amount to.

The next day I let the school speak their piece on the comment that was made. They were all whispering and making comments. "I knew she was really broke"; "Now her mom gone, she really ain't got shit!" The nerve of these people, and more than half of them didn't even know me. The other half wanted to be me, and the select few that I called my friends were riding with me for richer or poorer! In reality, I was in a way better situation than they were, and my momma was gone. I needed to step out of my comfort zone and SHOW THEM!

It was finally the end of the school day, and seventh hour had come to a close. I came to school for this sole purpose, and I didn't let anyone in on my plans. I loved the element of surprise. As everyone gathered in the senior hallway, I figured it was perfect timing for my statement to be made.

"Hey, Quese! I heard you said I was a broke bitch!"

She was completely shocked by my statement and was scared as to what may happen next. Quese knew she couldn't back down though; everyone was watching. "Yeah, I . . ." Nothing else that would come out her mouth would matter because I politely threw two thousand dollars in twenties at her!

"Bitch, where? Now go run to your granddad who picks you up and tell him here's a down payment for you a car!"

The place went crazy! I mean people were falling from the sky to pick up that money. I walked away and let them all fall to their knees. Fuck them all! I might not have Queen, but I would always be straight. Throwing that money might have put a dent in my stash, but her face was priceless. That was definitely something I needed during a time like this.

My girl Red walked up to me as I reached my truck. "Here, girl. You don't have to prove nothing to these broke bitches. They miserable and want attention." She handed me maybe a thousand dollars of my money. I guess she wasn't fast enough for the rest of it. I was grateful.

"Thanks, girl. I'm just sick of all they shit! I'm really not a bad person, but people like to just fuck with me causing me to act out!"

"No explanation needed. If you need something, never hesitate to call me!"

"I'll be sure to take you up on that offer!"

"Keep your head up, Magic!" After saying those words, she walked away. I hadn't really hung with people in my grade, so it was strange that she did that for me. We were cool, but she could have easily taken the money like everyone else. That's when I realized she was trustworthy, and she would always be a friend in my book.

It was Christmas break, and we had three weeks off of school. The feeling was bittersweet. I was happy to be out of school, but pretty sad that I had to deal with the shit at home. At least going to school kept my mind off the hard times that I was facing.

My aunt Autumn flew into town. She was currently in college and going through her own crisis. She came to try to organize my life as best as she could and prepare me for the move. She had recently given her life to Christ and made a major turnaround, so we didn't necessarily connect like we used to. I was used to the wild, carefree auntie, not this Ms. Holy Lady. I wish I could have heard what she was preaching because she could have saved me a world of trouble, hurt, and pain.

Blu wasn't as attentive the past week. That's how he was though! I mean, I guess before my mom went away we weren't on the best terms, but when she left I had been spending all my time with him. I assumed that we were in a good space. Then his calls started to slow up, and he was dodging my calls. The only thing this could mean was that he was giving his time up to someone else. I would later find out that it was a girl named Sha. I had been hearing rumors, but nothing concrete.

Four days before Christmas, Blu went to jail. He was pulled over for a suspended license, but since he was on probation for the loitering ticket crap, he had to do thirty days. And now suddenly he was blowing my phone up. I guess his women were nowhere to be found. I had to go over to his house for something, and that's when I saw the pair of Gucci shoes he had on the side of his bed. It was a woman's shoe and two sizes too big for me. I questioned him, and that's when I found out that they belonged to Sha. He was tricking on these 'hos! This gave me the "fuck it" attitude to treat him how he treated me. I wasn't sure if we were together or not. Honestly, I was confused at this point, and I just wanted to mean something to somebody.

Christmas Eve came around and Ghost and I went to eat and hang out with my brother James and his friends. Ghost had an apartment out far as hell in Rochester. We spent the night there. I woke up to Ghost on Christmas. This was the first holiday that I spent with anyone besides my mother. In my head of course, it was far more than what it actually was. Women have a way of over thinking things, and then assuming. Don't get me wrong, Ghost had a major thing for me, but Blu would never be out the picture. So it was over before it even started. I did wake up to a few gifts under the imaginary tree! We always joked about that. His place was so empty. He seriously only had a bed, a TV, and that was it! He didn't have a couch, and he only kept juice and breakfast food in the fridge. It was hilarious!

Christmas had come and gone. I don't quite remember what I did for my seventeenth birthday. I imagine I went to a club downtown and got drunk with my friends while Autumn was back at my place praying for my safe return.

New Year's Eve rolled around and Ghost said he was going to drink for the first time, so I had to witness that. My brother James got a room at the Marriott in Southfield with Ghost. They invited a lot of people there to drink and chill. Ghost insisted that I come. I brought the New Year in at church, but rushed to the room to see what it was looking like.

Once I walked through the doors of the lobby, I briefly thought of Blu and how he was sitting in a cell while I was out enjoying my life. I felt bad and I started to turn around and head home. I felt as if I should've been somewhere waiting for him to call me the next day. He had been talking good and writing me letters every day. He said that he was going to be a better man when he came out. He was going to help me get through the physical absence of my mother, and we were going to work out all of our issues. Then it hit me! What about the bitch he was buying Gucci for? He never bought me anything. I brushed the senseless guilt off my shoulder and went to the hotel. It would always be a night to remember.

By the time I made it to the room, Ghost was already drunk. Since he never drank before, it probably only took one little drink to do the job. To my surprise, he had not one but two of his ex-girlfriends there. They were both clearly making a fool of themselves. While they argued over something in the back room, I sat in the living room area with the rest of the party and started to drink.

"Magic, you see this nigga Ghost? He fooling!" James said.

"Not my business!" I tried my best not to even comment on the situation. Clearly, neither of them was of his interest this particular night. He was just trying to enjoy his New Year, but they were making that pretty hard to do. I ended up having a good time. I knew everybody there, so we started playing cards and just enjoying the night. Ghost finally escaped their trio of love and made his way back to the party.

"MyMy, you made it!" he said, reaching over to hug me. I could see the hurt in both of the girls' eyes. They spent two hours arguing and trying to get him to choose between the two of them, and he ignored them as if they weren't even there.

"I told you I was coming! I had to see you drunk. I must say, it's a funny sight to see!" I joked.

Now with Ghost just inches from my face, I could feel the fire both girls possessed. "Why they tripping, MyMy? I'm just trying to enjoy myself!" I could smell the Patron seeping through his pores.

"Well, get back to the party then. Hanging over here with me is definitely not helping." I wasn't one for conflict, especially when it came to someone who didn't even belong to me. They could argue and fight all they wanted to. I was there enjoying myself just as they should've been doing.

The drink had taken over him this night. "You think I'm worried about what they think? They just don't know I'm going home with you tonight. Ain't that right, MyMy?" He started to raise his voice.

"Ghost, you're drunk. You need to find some water and sober up." I was trying to defuse the situation.

James must have noticed me getting a little uncomfortable, so he pulled him away and he started to entertain the rest of the party. An hour passed and I was tired; it was about 4:30 in the morning. I finished my card game and started to make my exit after saying good-bye to everyone. Just as I reached the door, Ghost was on my heels. He still had two women just holding up the wall trying to see which one he was going with.

"Hold up, MyMy. You not leaving without me!"

"Are you sure? It looks like you already have people to attend to. I'm not trying to start anything."

"Listen, I'm not with either one of them, and they can argue all they want. I am going home with you. Let's go!" We were headed to the elevators. When we walked on the elevator, it was pretty full already, but just as the doors were closing, girl number one waved her hand through the gap to stop the doors from closing. She hopped on as well.

"Ghost, I'm not letting you leave this place with her! I have your keys and your phone." Girl number one looked like she wanted to cry.

"Do you see her? She has her own car and phone. I will be just fine," he said with a slight chuckle. I guess she didn't expect for me to have my own wheels.

I wasn't going to get involved any more than I needed to be. I wasn't even trying to be in this situation. I came for a good laugh and a few drinks to take my mind off my own issues. This turned into an episode that should have been on reality television. No one would've thought this was really happening. The doors finally opened, and I was the first one out. I walked at a fast pace while Ghost trailed along behind me. Girl number one wasn't too far from him.

I guess Ghost was fed up with her harassing ways, so he turned around and snapped. "Listen, I'm not leaving with you. She's not being disrespectful to you, so show Magic some respect please. Chasing us to the car is ri-di-cu-lous!" His last word was so slurred that I barely understood it. He had reached his limit long ago.

"You are not getting in that car with Magic!"

"Watch me! Now have a good night." Ghost opened the door and got in my car. He instructed that I pull off. I had never seen him act like this. Never! We ended up getting a room at the Westin and stayed the night there. Of course he woke up ignorant of his actions. I tried refreshing his memory, but he was way out of there. I still tease him about that night to this very day. It was for sure one for the books.

On the other hand, Autumn was back at the house worried about me. She insisted that I should have at least let her know that I was okay. I think people were letting me slide with stuff because no one knew exactly what I was feeling, so no one wanted to push me too far. I didn't even know how I was feeling. I just felt as if a piece of me was missing no matter what I did.

During the first year of my mother's time in the Fed joint, I was spinning out of control. I was trying to fill a void with men. It was like I had no backbone and no one to say no. I was vulnerable, and let a few weak men use me to their advantage. When Blu and I were solid, I was fine. But then he would cheat and all hell would break loose. I wanted to make him feel my pain. In the end I was the one who ended up hurting, not him.

There's no excuse for the wrong that I did during that time. I was young and I had no sense of self. I wasn't thinking about tomorrow or any consequences. I loved Blu with every breath in my body. I was heartbroken, and I didn't have anyone to help me through it. Queen wasn't there, and Ace gave the worst advice in the world. No one ever told me about protecting my worth as a woman. Honestly, I let a few people use me because I was bored and angry: angry at life, angry with Blu, and angry with Queen. I was just angry, and the only way that I thought I could express it was by getting even. Doing things out of spite soothed me. Never ever do anything to get back at someone because Karma can do that for you. Treat people how you want to be treated.

18
This Could Be the End . . .

Blu's time was served, and he was finally coming home from doing his thirty days. We had talked through our issues while he was on the inside. At this time, it was still only Ghost and him who I had ever dealt with on an intimate level. I hadn't called Ghost since New Year's though! Blu and I decided to let the past be that and move on. To make sure Blu felt more secure, I thought it would be a good idea to surprise him with something for being released.

I drove down to the county jail in Pontiac, Michigan. He was to be released at 12:00 a.m., and I was there thirty minutes early. They still didn't let him out until around 2:00 a.m. I was so happy to see him walk through those gates that I practically knocked him down when I jumped on him. He hugged me so tight, and it felt like he never wanted to let go.

"Magic, I've missed you so much!"

"Me too! I have a surprise for you when we get home."

His eyebrows raised in amazement. "I can't wait to see it!"

Still, I was a little nervous because I wasn't sure he was going to like it. "Hope you like it!"

"I'm sure I will!"

The ride to his place was so intense. Both of our hormones were racing. I would have pulled over and done him right then and there, but I was sure he felt dirty, so I figured taking a shower first would be a better idea. We had to go to his place because I had officially moved in with Yanna. I wasn't quite used to the idea of her being my stand-in parent. I honestly thought she was taking the job a bit too seriously. Over the last couple of weeks the fact that Queen wouldn't be returning home anytime soon sunk in! One day it all hit me.

After school one day, I came home and all of my mother's things were lying out on the couch with a price tag on them. A for sale sign that stated: EVERYTHING MUST GO! was lying on the floor! I was freaking out. Throwing shit at the walls, screaming and trying to find Yanna. The bitch had organized the whole thing. She was selling all of Queen's designer things for pennies. Her mink coats that she'd spent thousands on were selling for a few hundred bucks. It was sick. I was sick and ready to fight everybody in my house. People were picking through all of my stuff. I mean everything in my house had a price tag on it. EVERYTHING! Even the damn clock on the wall was for sale. My room was the only one off limits to the whole house. Everything else was up for grabs. My go-cart sold for only a few bucks. I walked in and started screaming! I was picking everything up and yelling at all the people there. "THIS ISNT FOR SALE!" To make matters even worse, when I walked down the hallway toward my room, I noticed my bathroom set was GONE—like wiped completely out. She even sold my bathroom stuff? Who would even want it? I just burst out in tears because everything I had was being stripped from me. I had lost everything: my mom, my home, and now all my mother's things were being auctioned off for little to nothing. I slammed the bathroom door and locked it. Climbed into my empty tub and just cried. I stayed in there for what felt like forever. I didn't know what to do. I couldn't believe everything I had was being taken from me. Yanna said I needed the money. Queen's stash was stolen in the midst of the drama. I had a car note to pay and it cost to live. She said so much that I went numb to it. It was truly possible to go from having everything to having nothing but the clothes left on your back. I may have started with a silver spoon in my mouth, but now it was for sure a wooden one, and it was causing all kinds of splinters along the way. This was terrible! Life didn't feel worth living, and I was so lost and confused. If I had truly known who God was, I probably would have turned to him then, but I didn't know so I started making decisions for myself. I was slipping into dark holes that had no visible exit signs.

"Magic, we're here! Are you okay?" Blu said, tapping me to get me out of my thoughts.

"Yeah, I'm fine. I was just thinking about the day I realized that my mom being gone was real and how I cried for the first time after she left. Now I'm living with Yanna, and it's just weird. That's all!"

"You're going to make it through this. You're stronger than you think. You just stay focused on what's important and that's school. Don't ever drop out. Do you hear me?"

"Yeah, I hear you!" I was more interested in him getting in the house so we could have some fun. I needed a release so I would agree to anything he said in that moment.

"Good. Well, get out. I'm ready for my surprise!"

I had completely forgotten about that, but I see he didn't. We made it upstairs, and he immediately rushed to the bathroom. I figured he would be a while, so I made him a quick meal. It was one of his favorites: fried chicken and French fries. It was quick and simple. As soon as he was finished up in the shower, I was placing his food on the table. He came out smiling from ear to ear and looking better than ever. He hadn't had a line up, nor was his hair braided. He was rough just the way I loved him. There was something about the roughness that just sent chills up my spine. While he ate, I made my way to the room to undress and wait for him. I don't think he chewed the food, because within seconds he had dropped his towel and was next to me under the covers.

"Thanks, baby, for my surprise!"

I was slightly confused by his statement because I hadn't shown him his surprise yet. "Oh, you think all I can do is surprise you with a meal?"

That same kiddy facial expression appeared again. "There's more?"

"There's always more for you, Blu. Never forget that. I'll forever belong to you!"

With that being said, he started to kiss me repeatedly. He traveled down to my happy place. I kept the lights on so he could see. As he kissed every inch of my body, he noticed it. My surprise! It did take him by surprise because he paused for a second, stunned by my bold gesture to get his name tattooed on me: "Blu's Wifey." With two wedding rings attached below it. For a minute I thought he was about to freak out, but instead it turned him on more than ever. "You do belong to me!" We made love for the rest of the night. I mean, we blessed the entire place with our presence. I felt bad for the visitors to come after the night we had. No spot was safe. Neither one of us could get enough. That's just how it was with us. We loved to feel one another, and it was like some weird obsession we would have for many years to come.

I was starting to get into a normal routine. I got a job at Potbelly's, and it was my first job ever. It caused me to be more responsible, and it helped to keep a few dollars in my pocket. I ended up having to give my truck back since I couldn't afford the seven hundred dollar monthly car note. Yanna attempted to do a good deed by putting her name on another car with a note that I could afford on my own. It worked out great. However, in my down time without a vehicle, I was driving one of her extra cars that she barely used. I would often let Blu drop me off at school so he could get out and make some money. Everything would work out fine until the day Rhonda popped up at my school. She had the office call saying it was an emergency with my mother. When I got the message to come down, I knew that it was a lie. Someone from the prison would have contacted me if there was an emergency with Queen.

I went to the office anyway. Who did I see? Rhonda. We hadn't really spoken in a while since Blu and I got serious and were practically living together. She was cool with it, until she noticed he really did love me. She couldn't accept that. She always thought he would be with her and no one could replace her. I was shocked and confused as to what the hell she was doing at my school.

"This better be important. What's up?" I asked.

"Blu is in jail, and he got your aunt's car towed. You need to go down to the police station to figure how to get her car back." Rhonda wasted no time getting to the point.

"What? How did this even happen?"

She was very short. "We were at CVS. I told him I was

pregnant and he hit me! The police came and took him to jail."

I knew it was more to the story, but whatever. At this point I was more interested in figuring out what his bond was and how was I going to explain all this to Yanna. She wouldn't be happy, and she would probably put me out. I had enough things going on. There was no way I was going to be able to make this right.

"Well, do you want me to take you down there?" Rhonda said.

"Yeah! I don't think there's any other option," I agreed, and was off to the station with her. It was one of the most awkward rides of my life. I was so upset with Blu, and I couldn't wait to get a hold of him.

When I got to the station, they said he wouldn't see a judge until the next morning, so I would have to come back. So that trip was a fail. I called his mom and broke the news to her. She was crushed yet again. We were really close, and I loved her like my own mother. She was there for me anytime I needed her. She truly loved me like I was one of her own.

Next, I had to call my aunt and confess the drama to her.

She picked up on the first ring. "What's wrong?" she said.

Seeing as though it was school hours and I was calling meant it was a problem.

"Umm I had a little issue and the car was impounded."

"How, Magic? You're supposed to be in school."

"I was in school. I let Blu drive it, and they took him to jail so they impounded the car."

"You're joking, right? There's no way you let someone

else drive my car when you're not even with them?" I could tell she was angry and confused as to why I would allow anyone to even drive her car. I can admit that it was stupid, but when you're young and think you're in love, these are the dumb things you do. This is where the trust issue began to arise between Yanna and me.

"You will pay to get it out," she said, before hanging up on me.

From that point on, she wanted me home right after school. I wasn't supposed to spend the night out with Blu. I could barely see him. When she got my car and I was paying my own bills, I felt as though it shouldn't matter if I came to her house, as long as I called to let her know that I was okay.

My life was crazy. Ace was now in jail for a crime that he didn't even commit. He was over to his boy's house playing the game and the house was raided. They smacked him with two years. Just like that! So there was no more couple hundred dollars being sent to me. As I stated earlier, Vicky never called to even see how I was doing. The people I expected the most from, never even called to check on me.

I was losing my damn mind. After Blu got Rhonda pregnant, I couldn't trust him either, but he always begged me to come back. So I did. This was why they were fighting! Rhonda was threatening to keep the baby and tried to run into my auntie's car. She was mad because he showed up with my car, so she was trying to run into it. And that was why he got out and tried to choke her up. I knew there was more to the story. I never fully trusted him again, and I let myself slip into a deeper depression. This would start the never-ending battle of our spiteful cheating. We had a toxic relationship, but we continued to hold on and drag each other through some very depressing situations. I honestly think that it would have made a huge difference in my life if I had at least one positive role model. I was doing a lot of discovering, but it would have been nice to see how someone else did it. Many of my mistakes could have easily been avoided if I had known the value of life. Instead of being beat all of the time, I could have been given life lessons.

On June 23, 2008, Queen was sentenced. We didn't have much family, so it was more so friends, my granny, and aunt who came. It was about a good fifteen people in the courtroom, all waiting for the verdict. For months now they had been trying to get Queen off. They had no physical evidence that she was involved with any drug accusations. All they had was word of mouth, but there were a lot of people talking. On the paperwork they had for her case, Queen was the only one with closed lips. People can say what they want about Queen, but she wasn't a snitch. No man on earth would make her tell on someone else. It just wasn't in her blood. She did the crime and was ready to serve the time, even if it meant leaving me out in the cold world all by myself. She was born and raised on the east side of Detroit, so clearly no 'ho was in her blood. I respected my mom for keeping her word. Sometimes I also despised her because it shouldn't have mattered what people would think of her. She had a daughter who needed her, so she should have told those crackers what they wanted to hear so she could come home to me. I guess that was the selfish side of me. If she would have done that, then her life may have been in danger. She would forever be looking over her shoulder and mine.

"Ladies and gentlemen of the court, could you all rise as the Judge enters the room," the officer stated. And on cue, all bottoms were up right.

I squeezed Blu's hand as we waited for the Judge to enter the room. He could tell I was nervous because my palms were sweating uncontrollably. He whispered in my ear, "It's going to be okay, Magic." Some tension released for me, but it didn't stop the knots in my stomach. I was scared out of my mind. Seeing Queen in those ugly jail clothes made me sick. This was all extremely terrible. Why was this happening to us?

"You may be seated."

"Are there any final words that you would like to say, Ms. Johnson before we go forth with the sentencing?"

Queen stood and turned to me. "I just want to say I never meant to leave you in this cold world alone. I always thought that I was doing what was best for you. The crime that they are saying I've committed is false. I am doing someone else's time. Judge, all I ask is that you keep in mind that I have a seventeen-year-old girl who needs me. Magic, I love you: no kids, go to school, and don't get married until I'm home." She cried the entire speech and so did I. I mouthed the words back to her.

"I love you more, my Queen!" After that, Queen took her seat and the Judge was ready to read her sentence.

"I, Judge Robert Harris, sentence Queen Johnson to 96 months in federal prison." The whole courtroom fell silent as they all attempted to calculate the time in their head. If you're still confused, 96 months is a total of eight years. She was about to be taken from me for eight whole years. With good behavior and the drug program she could be out in six. Seventeen was a crucial age for me, and I needed my mother. I was already going down the wrong track. I was able to hug her before she left and that was great. Since she was in the regular prison, all of our visits were through a glass, so I wasn't able to touch my mom for seven months. I didn't want to let go.

When we left, everyone was trying to say well wishes, but I wasn't in the mood. I practically ran to the car and climbed in the backseat. I cuddled up and just cried. Blu drove the three hours home as I drifted away in my own thoughts. Blu knew to just wait this one out. As long as he was there he was sure I wouldn't harm myself. He bathed and fed me that night. I still hadn't said a word. I eventually snuggled up under him and went to sleep. He held me close and kissed me on the forehead. "I love you, Magic. Sleep as long as you need to. I'll be right here." Nights like this made me fall further in love with him.

I had come to the conclusion that Yanna wanted to have my mom's life. Aside from her trying to run my life, she was sleeping with Queen's man at the same time. She was also lying to Queen and me about our home. The arrangement was for her to rent it out and pay the mortgage on it so that Queen could come home to something. However, she was letting it slip further and further into foreclosure. She was using that money monthly for herself. She also sold my mom's bed for free hair appointments. The lady thought she was paying for it by doing Yanna's hair for free every single week. Yanna was doing us so wrong, and we didn't even know it. I had gotten close to one of Yanna's friend's daughter, who always overheard the dirt Yanna was doing to us. She wasn't a fan of it, so she kept it real with me and let me know what was going on. When I found out what was going on, I was hurt. I felt betrayed. My mother trusted her to help with the most important task of her life, and she failed miserably. Yanna was out to get us, and I was on a mission to get the hell out of there.

Late one night I was outside in my car on the phone with Blu. He was arguing with me about something. I was trying to be respectful and just keep the conversation outside so I wouldn't disturb the peace in the house. Yanna wanted to pull her 'I'm the mama' card and felt the need to preach about listening.

The door to the house swung open, and all I could see was her Big Foot ass marching toward the car. I wasn't sure if she was upset because she didn't get any today or what, but she was tripping. "Magic, I told you to stop coming in my house late!"

"I've been here since curfew. My conversation was rather loud, and I didn't want to disturb your household!"

She wasn't listening to anything that I was saying. "Since you don't know how to listen, hand over your keys!"

I was very confused by her demand. I put the down payment down for my car, and I paid the bill. She couldn't just take my keys. "Are you referencing the car I pay for?"

"The car is in my name, and you're not welcomed to drive it anymore until you start obeying my rules."

"You know what? Fuck you and your rules. I'm out of here. You don't have to worry about me disturbing your house anymore. If you didn't want me here, that's all you had to say," I said, throwing her those stupid keys. I hated when people did good gestures, but then threw it back in your face as a constant reminder that they did a good deed once upon a time. What was the purpose if all they were going to do was take it back?

"Where are you going to go? Can't you tell nobody wants you? I was the only one willing to uproot my life and let you stay with me."

"Listen, bitch, my mother took you in when you didn't have a pot to piss in. Miss me with that bullshit. You owe us. You don't have to worry about me again!" I went in the house to pack a bag making sure to pack my Bible, and I was out of there. She thought I was bluffing about never coming back. Right then, I made a vow. *No matter how bad it gets, I'm never coming back here.*

Before I made my exit, I made sure to let her know what I needed from her. "I'll be back for my bed and the money for my car." I slammed the door and never looked back.

19
BLUE MAGIC

It was a beautiful day. Queen and I were headed to the mall to shop for prom dresses. I was finally graduating. All of the stuff I went through over the years was worth it all. I accomplished something I never thought I could do. Queen never finished school, and she wanted different for me. It was going to be a good day, but not before Queen bitched a little about what I had on.

"Didn't you wear that already?"

"Yes, and it was so cute the first time I wore it, so I thought I would wear it again." Queen didn't play that. She felt as though she bought me enough clothes to only wear them once. The only thing to be recycled was my jeans. Even then I'd better wait two or three months before I put them back on. She was crazy like that, but I loved her. I couldn't imagine life without her. She was the ying to my yang.

"Magic, you got all this new stuff in your closet and you want to re-wear outfits? Whatever, I'm ready to go. I didn't call off to argue with you about the clothes you have on."

Whew! That was the easiest argument that we'd ever had. I was just happy to hang with her. She was always so busy with her work that she never really had time for me. She was the top interior designer of Michigan and was making bank. I couldn't wait to go to school for Culinary Arts so that I could become a private chef for all her rich clients. It was going to be an amazing business.

Once we made it to the mall, I ran into my girl Red. All I kept thinking about was why was she here? It was a school day, so what were the chances of her missing school too? Not only was she there, but she was yelling and screaming at me.

"MAGIC! MAGIC! IS THAT YOU?"

It was too hard to understand what she was saying. "I can't hear you!"

She began to shake me. "Magic, wake up! Are you okay? Did you sleep here?"

When I finally opened my eyes, I realized that I was inside the school and by the band room. *What the fuck happened?* I remembered leaving Yanna's house and walking to her friend's house. It was late so she didn't answer the door. The school wasn't too far so I walked there. The band director was getting ready for a performance, so he arrived a little early to prepare, and I noticed that the door was cracked.

After replaying the events, I was frantic and ready to flee. "Yeah, I'm good. I got to go."

Red was confused. I was talking and walking in circles. She thought I was going crazy. She was afraid to leave me alone. "Where are you going?"

"I don't know. Far away from here," I said in some sort of daze.

She knew I needed someone there with me, so she

decided to tag along. "Okay, I'm going with you."

As we were walking out the building, people attempted to stop us, but I was in no mood to face people. My life was over, and I didn't have any other reason to live. My mom, dad, and grandma were all put away on drug charges. My aunt Autumn was so wrapped up in her own life she couldn't take the time to help me. I didn't have any other family that I knew besides Vicky, Marie, Tracy, and them. I promise they never called to even see how I was doing. It was sick! The people who should have cared, didn't! Maybe they didn't know what I was going through. Maybe they thought I was good, but how could they? I was seventeen with no parental supervision. I had no roof over my head, no car, just the clothes on my back. I was sleeping on my high school's floor. No one even knew. I just wanted to die, and I was sure no one would even miss me.

Red was amped and wasn't in the mood to be at school anyway. "Magic, where you want to go?"

As I hopped into her passenger seat, I reclined the chair all the way back and whispered, "Anywhere but here. Anywhere but here." I was tired and on the verge of giving up.

She started the car, and in seconds we were cruising down the same road I had previously walked to find a place to sleep. It was the first week of senior year, and no one would really be looking for us. Red, being the kind of person she was, I should have known where we would end up. The liquor store of course! For the first time in weeks, I had a laugh that was well needed.

What I didn't need was the liquor though, because it would always put me more in my feelings. I was really contemplating on ways to kill myself that night. I didn't let Red know because she would have never dropped me off later that day. We ended up doing a whole bunch of dumb shit. We got drunk and went to Fridays, Dave and Buster, and go-cart racing. Hanging with Red was always fun, and once again she proved she was a friend who was really in my corner. She had my back. Once the day ended and it was time to go back to my thoughts, I was in panic mode.

Yanna's friend, Kris, was nice enough to open her home to me, but I knew that would only last for so long. I decided to pack up, take the five hundred dollars to my name, and just go away. I had no idea where I would go, but I knew I was leaving that place for good. Blu was still mad for whatever reason, so we weren't talking. Everyone could go to hell for all I cared. I was angry with the world. My insides were on fire, but somehow I maintained a level head.

Soon as the sun started to rise, I was up. I wrote a Thank You letter to Kris for allowing me to stay there and told her that I would be moving in with Blu. I said this so she could have a destination for anyone looking for me. The last thing I needed to happen was someone trying to stop me from leaving before I ever made it out of Michigan.

I made it out of the house just before their alarms went off. I called a cab to pick me up. There were two stops I needed to make before I figured out what to do next. First stop would be to my very vacant home that I hadn't seen in three months. I still had a key, so I let myself in. The renter of the house was in the process of moving because I told her the truth about Yanna holding on to the payments. The house would be foreclosed soon. She stopped paying Yanna and moved somewhere else so that her family wouldn't end up on the streets.

The taxi arrived to my home, and I tossed him ten

bucks and asked him to wait there. As I exited the car, I felt out of place. This was no longer my home. I made the long walk up the driveway and entered the code for the garage. To my surprise it still worked. This very familiar place just didn't feel like home anymore. I didn't expect the code to work. Once the garage was lifted, I walked to the entry door using my key to unlock it. As soon as I walked in, tears began to stream down my face. The house was so empty. Aside from all the material things, it lacked life, and character. Queen had invested so much money and time into this home, and now it wasn't even worth half of what was spent. I started to walk very slowly, as if someone was in one of the rooms and I wasn't trying to wake him or her. Once I made it to the main entrance, I noticed our diamond chandelier had been replaced with a simple light fixture. *I bet that bitch Yanna took it to sell it and was blowing all of our money fast.* She was a dirty bitch and I just wanted to kill her for putting my mom and me in such a tough position. I could have done a better job of keeping all of our shit in order so that Queen wouldn't have to come home empty-handed.

Allowing Yanna to take on the task was a mistake, and now Queen couldn't even come home to a pair of drawers. Whenever her time was served, she would have to start from scratch. In that very moment I knew that I needed to make sure all things were in order with my life, so I could take care of her once she returned. I needed to take one last look at the rooms upstairs before I could depart. As I walked up the stairs, all of the memories started to flood my brain. My heart began to feel heavy. I walked into my Queen's room, and it was completely bare. There was nothing but the scraps of things that were unwanted. I put my back against the wall, and I felt all out of options. I broke down and cried for my life. I was lost in this world with nowhere to turn to. Everyone I ever cared about was locked up or dead. Those were the simple truths of the game they were in. It was very rare that someone made it out to live a normal life. Once you were in, there was no way out. After five minutes of crying and feeling sorry for myself, I decided it was time to close this chapter of my life. This house didn't belong to me anymore. I had to make a new home for myself.

I returned to the cab, giving him directions to Blu's house. Before I left this place behind me, I wanted to see the one man I loved. I had been blowing his phone up since our fight the other day. He hadn't picked up, so I figured I'd give him a surprise visit. He was known for pop ups, so I wanted to return the favor. The taxi driver parked a few houses down, just in case Blu was up; I didn't want to ruin the surprise. When I made it in front of his house and to my surprise, there was a black Pontiac G6 outside. Blu was carless, so I knew it wasn't his shit. The car looked oddly familiar. Then it hit me! That was Tone's girlfriend car. What the hell? He took me from Tone, now he fucking her too? That was it. I was done! I took the nearest brick and sent it right through her front window. I was ready to key in the word 'BITCH' on the side of her car. Blu heard the noise and rushed outside.

"Magic, what the fuck are you doing here?"

"The better question is what the fuck is she doing here?" I said, pointing at the unknown vehicle.

"I don't even know who car that is?" He tried to lie. I had already seen the black ass girl peeking through the window.

"You must think I'm stupid, huh bitch? I'll show you better than I can tell you! This will be the last any of you wack ass people will ever see me. I hope you have a miserable life, bitch!" I was furious and filled with so much pain. I wanted him to know it too. I made my way back to the taxi and instructed him to drive. My tab was already well over two hundred bucks, and all I had left was a measly three hundred dollars. What was I going to do? I had nowhere to go.

I couldn't believe all these years were filled with so much pain. *All this shit I am going through and this ho-ass nigga still finds time and thinks it's okay to cheat on me. Fuck him! I don't even care.* I couldn't take it anymore, and I just wanted to die. Everything that I loved either was taken from me or hurt me. Then I heard a small voice speak. "It's time. Use the key!" I didn't know where the voice came from, but with that, I had a plan.

"Driver, please take me to Warren and Southfield please," I instructed him.

Once we arrived to Vicky's house, it was 9:30 a.m. My cousins should have been in school already, and I was sure the rest of the house was asleep. They didn't have jobs, so they could wake up at their leisure. I snuck in the backyard behind the detached garage and counted the five steps to find my location. I began to dig for my life. Once I touched the key, I was relieved no one had found my hiding place. Rushing back to the taxi, I took out my Bible to open the paper that was taped to it.

Chase Bank Downtown bring your ID was the only thing written on the paper. Once we made it to the bank, I headed inside with my ID and the key. When I got to the reception desk, I handed it to her and she directed me to the safe deposit vault.

Inside she searched for my box and laid it in front of me. "Knock on the door when you're ready to leave," the lady said while exiting and pulling the door behind her. It was a moment of truth. *What would be inside of this box?*

I turned the key, and once it was opened I was so confused. There was only a little amount of money in it, but I saw another key and a map. What the fuck did Queen have me on, a scavenger hunt? I gathered all of my belongings and knocked on the door. I was let out and headed to my next destination. The map said St. Louis, Missouri. I needed to fly there so I had the taxi take me to the airport. After paying him with the money Queen just gave me, I had forty-eight hundred dollars left. I booked a flight and was on my way.

Once I arrived, I flagged another taxi down and passed him the map. It was a forty-five minute ride. He parked outside of what looked to be a vacant building, but it seemed to be functioning. The note indicated that it was a storage unit and her favorite number was the unit. I made my way inside and looked for the unit number. I was so scared! What did Queen have me doing? I was all out of options, so I went with the flow. I had nothing else to lose. I had nothing! There were rows of storage places with column numbers. I looked for column nine and unit eleven since her code was always 911. I twisted the key and lifted the small gate to the storage room. To my surprise it was really empty; there were only two big duffle bags placed in the center of the floor with another note on it. Before I could read the note, I was curious to see what was inside.

I would have never expected what it was. I unzipped the first bag, and my eyes met the packages marked "Blue Magic" on each of them!

What the fuck!

To be continued . . .

NEW TITLES FROM WAHIDA CLARK PRESENTS

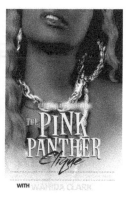

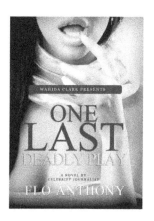

#READIT

WWW.WCLARKPUBLISHING.COM